STREET JUSTICE

Danielle felt the tension in her trigger finger. There was no question she was as fast as ever. And she had no doubt that her aim was still as deadly as the strike of a rattlesnake. "Now all three of you get off the street," she said.

Frisco Bonham shook his head. "We ain't making no noise, we ain't disturbing no peace. We'll stand where we damn well please. You run along now, before we lose our tempers."

"Yeah," Billy Boy sneered. "What do you think of that?"

"I think you've all three had your chance," said Danielle. "I'm through talking." The rifle barrel swung down from her cradling arm and exploded.

Billy Boy's pistol stopped on its upswing from his holster and flew from his hand as the impact of Danielle's slug hammered his foot to the ground, then slung him backward onto the hard dirt. . . .

Fourth in the bestselling series, including
Death Rides a Chestnut Mare,
The Shadow of a Noose,
and *Riders of Judgment*

Ralph Compton
Death Along the Cimarron

A Ralph Compton Novel
by Ralph Cotton

A SIGNET BOOK

SIGNET
Published by New American Library, a division of
Penguin Putnam Inc., 375 Hudson Street,
New York, New York 10014, U.S.A.
Penguin Books Ltd, 80 Strand,
London WC2R 0RL, England
Penguin Books Australia Ltd, 250 Camberwell Road,
Camberwell, Victoria 3124, Australia
Penguin Books Canada Ltd, 10 Alcorn Avenue,
Toronto, Ontario, Canada M4V 3B2
Penguin Books (N.Z.) Ltd, 182–190 Wairau Road,
Auckland 10, New Zealand

Penguin Books Ltd, Registered Offices:
Harmondsworth, Middlesex, England

First published by Signet, an imprint of New American Library,
a division of Penguin Putnam Inc.

First Printing, January 2003
10 9 8 7 6 5 4 3 2 1

Chapter 1

Haley Springs, Texas

When the first pistol shot rang out from the dirt street, Danielle Strange didn't flinch. As she stood at the counter of McCreary's General Mercantile Store, her hand dropped instinctively to her hip even though she knew she wasn't wearing a gun. In fact she wasn't even wearing her customary riding clothes—her doeskin skirt, her bell-sleeved women's blouse, or her long brush-scarred riding vest. But old habits died hard, she reminded herself, easing her gun hand away from where her holster would ordinarily have been. She smoothed out her gingham dress as if doing so had been her intention in the first place.

Martin McCreary didn't see her gesture. He had ducked down too quickly behind the counter to have seen much of anything. Then, just as quickly, he rose up, embarrassed and shaken, feeling he needed to explain his fearful response.

"I'm—I'm sorry, Miss Danielle," McCreary stammered. "I shouldn't have ducked down and left you standing there all alone. My nerves just ain't what they should be these days." He wiped a trembling hand across his forehead. "Ever since Sheriff Casey got himself killed, I just can't stand the sound of—"

His words cut short as another pistol shot exploded. "Lord God!" he shrieked, ducking down again.

"I'm going to see what this is all about," said Danielle, turning and walking toward the door.

"Don't go out there, Miss Danielle!" McCreary warned her. "There's a wild bunch in town. It won't make a bit of difference to them that you're a lady."

"I hope it doesn't," Danielle said, swinging the door open, then closing it soundly behind herself, leaving the bell atop the door jingling on its tin spring. Outside, a third shot exploded. Martin McCreary only flinched this time. He stood for a second, staring at the closed door, then looked around the empty store and said aloud to himself, "Well, shoot . . . I might just as well get myself a little looksee." Almost on tiptoe, he crossed the floor to the front window and peeped out guardedly from one corner.

At the far end of the dirt street, forty yards away, Danielle saw three men standing wobbly drunk, their smoking Colts in their hands. In the street a few feet from them lay the shattered glass remnants of the whiskey bottles they'd been shooting. These were young men, around the same age of her brothers, Tim and Jed, she noted to herself. Yet there was an aura of trouble surrounding these men as thick as smoke, and sensing it caused her steps to sway over to her buckboard at the hitchrail.

"Easy, Sam," Danielle said to the nervous horse hitched to her wagon. She ran a soothing hand down its white muzzle. "Nothing to get yourself spooked about," she whispered. "They're just drunk and loud."

The anxious horse settled, blowing out a tense breath. Danielle reached a hand into the buckboard and, with no wasted motion, slid the Winchester repeater rifle from its boot beneath the wooden seat. She levered a round up into the chamber and carried the rifle loosely. In the street out front of Waldrip's Saloon one of the drunken young men nudged the other two.

"Ronald, Frisco, look what's coming here," he said, directing his companions' attention toward Danielle as she approached. "It's about time this little pig-apple town sent somebody to welcome us."

"Hush up, Billy Boy," said Frisco Bonham, laughing in a lowered voice, "before you scare her away." He ran a tightly gloved finger along his thin mustache.

"She ain't looking too scared to me," said Ronald Muir, his drunken grin fading as Danielle came closer.

"Me neither," said Frisco Bonham, his leer growing more wary. From between Frisco and Ronald, Billy Boy Harper took a firm step forward, hoping this action would bring this brash young lady to a halt. It didn't.

"Excuse me, little miss," Billy Boy called out to Danielle, his pistol still dangling in his hand, curling smoke. "Can we help you some way?"

"Fun's over, boys," Danielle called out, finally stopping fifteen feet away, her rifle coming up from her side into the cradle of her left arm. All three men noticed that her right thumb lay across the hammer, her finger on the trigger. "Holster those shooters and get off the street."

"Well now, what have we here, boys?" Frisco Bonham whispered. He took a step forward and stood beside Billy Boy. Ronald Muir did the same. Not one of the three made an effort to holster their Colts. Noting it, Danielle cocked the rifle hammer and prepared herself for whatever was to come.

"You sure are a pretty little thing to be talking

so bold this hour of the day," said Frisco, his smile returning, this time appearing more sober and with no humor to it.

"Yeah," said Ronald Muir, "and we don't see no badge on your chest."

"Not that badges mean a whole lot to us one way or the other," Billy Boy piped in.

"We're without a sheriff right now," said Danielle in a resolved tone. "My name is Danielle Strange. I'm a citizen here, and I'm speaking on behalf of the town. You'd do well to holster up and get off the street. I won't tell you again."

"Oh, I see, *Miss Danielle Strange, citizen of the town,*" said Frisco Bonham with a sarcastic twist to his voice as the other two snickered drunkenly. "And what if we don't?"

"Then somebody will have to scrape you up and carry you off," Danielle replied quickly, her voice steady and low.

The snickering stopped short as silence set in for a moment before Frisco Bonham spoke. "Then I reckon we better do as we're told, hadn't we, boys? We surely don't want to get *scraped up and carried off* this dirt street."

"Sounds right to me," Ronald Muir said.

"Me too," replied Billy Boy Harper.

But Danielle wasn't buying their act. She knew what was about to happen. "Good then," she said firmly, going along with their charade. "Holster those shooters and let's all go our own way."

"Whatever you say, ma'am," said Frisco Bonham. The three men looked back and forth at one another slowly, expressionless. "You two heard the little lady," Frisco said. "Now holster up before she has to sternly raise a hand to us."

Lifting their pistols slowly and dropping them into their holsters, the three stared long and hard at Danielle. "I might enjoy a hand raised to me," said Ronald Muir, "depending on where it's raised to."

They were toying with her like three big cats teasing a helpless mouse. Danielle knew that had she been a man the fight would have already commenced. They were counting her short because she was a woman. Well, that was all right with her. She'd been treated this way before. She knew how to use her being a woman to her advantage. These men standing before her didn't realize who they were about to face off with.

For the better part of three years, Danielle Strange had passed herself off as a man in order to hunt down the outlaws who had killed her father and left his body hanging from the bough of a tree. Going under the name Danny Duggin, Danielle had acquired a reputation as a cold-blooded gunman across Indian Territory, Texas, and the Mexican hill country. But that was then and this was now, she reminded herself. A gunslinger was only as good as his or her last fight. Danielle hadn't raised a gun toward a man for over a year now. She hoped he hadn't lost her edge.

She felt the tension in her trigger finger. There was no question she was as fast as ever. And she had no doubt that her aim was still as deadly as the strike of a rattlesnake. But she knew that a year was a long time for a gun handler to go untested. But there was nobody else in Haley Springs to keep the peace. She had to do it. She hoped this could be settled without serious bloodshed.

With their pistols back in their holsters, the three men just stared at her. Frisco Bonham hooked both thumbs into his belt and rested his weight on one side, standing with belligerent bearing. "Now what?" he said flatly.

Here it came, Danielle thought to herself. "Now all three of you get off the street," she said.

"Huh-uh." Frisco Bonham shook his head. "We ain't making no noise, we ain't disturbing no peace. We'll stand where we damn well please. You run along now, before we lose our tempers."

"Yeah," Billy Boy sneered. "What do you think of that?"

"I think you've all three had your chance," said Danielle. She knew they believed they could draw their Colts whenever they felt like it. She knew they felt like they had all the time in the world. "I'm through talking," Danielle added. The rifle barrel swung down from her cradling arm and exploded.

Billy Boy's pistol stopped on its upswing from his holster and flew from his hand as the impact of Danielle's rifle slug hammered his foot to the ground, then slung him backward onto the hard dirt.

For just a split second the other two gunmen stood stunned at the suddenness of her attack. She hadn't hesitated. She hadn't offered any further warning. She'd simply said she was through talking, and then she'd shot Billy Boy down without a blink of her eye.

"Damn you, woman! Kill her, Frisco!" shouted Ronald Muir, his hand streaking up with his pistol in it. But Frisco Bonham, staring at Billy Boy as the wounded man lay wallowing in the dirt holding his foot, didn't move as quickly as Ronald Muir.

Danielle swung her rifle toward Ronald Muir, cocking it on the way. But before she got the shot off, another pistol shot resounded, this one from the boardwalk behind her. She saw Ronald Muir fall backward as a ribbon of blood streamed from his chest. She had no idea who had fired the shot, but she was grateful for the help. It gave her time to swing the rifle toward Frisco Bonham just in time to see his pistol raise halfway from his holster. Seeing that the rifle had him cold, Frisco froze for a second, considering his chances.

Behind Danielle a gravelly voice said to the stunned gunman, "Be real careful what you decide. This ground is full of bad decisions."

"You killed him," said Frisco, glancing at Ronald Muir's body. Blood spewed from the large hole in the dead man's chest.

"Deader than hell," said the gravelly voice. "And you'll be too, if you don't flip that gun over onto the ground real easylike."

Danielle only stared at Frisco Bonham. She had no idea who was standing behind her, but she'd seen whose side he was on. For now, that was good enough.

Frisco's gloved hand rose slowly, then dropped the pistol on the ground at his feet. "You both just made one bad mistake," he hissed. "That boy happens to be the brother of my boss—Cherokee Earl Muir!"

Billy Boy Harper had struggled to his feet, blood pouring from his left boot. "Earl's going to go wild-ape crazy when he hears about this!" Billy Boy said in a strained voice. "He won't abide his brother getting took down by a woman and an old bar swamper."

"He'll have to work it out the best he can," said Danielle. "Get his body across a saddle and get out of town."

"Come on, Billy Boy, give me a hand," Frisco demanded.

"Damn it, Frisco, I'm shot all to hell here," Billy Boy whined, limping over toward the hitchrail where their horses stood.

"You'll be worse than shot when Earl hears you didn't help me bring back poor Ronald's body," shouted Frisco.

Danielle stepped back and to the side as the pair struggled with the dead body and dragged it to the horses. "Hope you're all right, ma'am," said the rough voice from the boardwalk behind her.

"I'm fine," Danielle reassured her benefactor. She

looked away from the two gunmen long enough to get a look at the man who had helped her. It took a moment for her to recognize him. When she did, she smiled to herself, knowing that he wasn't going to recognize her in return. "How about yourself?" she asked.

"I'll do," said the old man. "I ain't no saloon swamper like that fool said, though."

Danielle recognized the man as an old cattle drover known only as Stick, whom she hadn't seen in over two years. The last time she'd seen Stick he was working as cook and cowhand for Tuck Carlyle, the young man who had stolen her heart back when she was on the trail of her father's killers. Danielle was eager to ask about Tuck, but she knew she had to bide her time and first explain to Stick who she was and how the last time he'd seen her she was the feared gunman Danny Duggin.

"I knew better than that, Stick," Danielle said. She turned to face the old man as, squinting warily in the direction of Frisco and Billy Boy while they rode out of town, he stepped down off the boardwalk. "I know you're a top hand and a better-than-most trail cook."

"Huh? What's that?" Stick turned to face her, taken aback by the fact that she knew his name. "Where do you know me from, young lady?" As he spoke, he eyed her closely. Danielle only smiled, cradling the rifle in her arm once again, this time taking her hand down from the trigger guard.

Stick stepped closer, looking her up and down curiously, then studying her face. "You do look familiar . . . but for the life of me, I swear I can't place you."

"It'll come to you, Stick," said Danielle. "Meanwhile, I'm much obliged to you for backing my play."

"Backing your play?" Stick chuckled and spit a

stream of tobacco juice. "You're talking like a gunman yourself, young lady." He nodded toward the bloody footprint Billy Boy had left behind. "Looked to me like you would've done all right anyways."

Danielle smiled again. "It never hurts to have an extra gun backing you up with three men like that. They struck me was as some real hardcases."

"You're a good judge of character then," said Stick. He stared off toward the disappearing figures on horseback. "I was listening to them talk in the saloon a while ago. There was eight of them here this morning. Then the other five rode out of here earlier. Lucky for us or we'd have been facing all of them. I heard one mention some cattle they sold to a rancher out near Buckston Crossing. Sounded to me like they might've rustled a herd and sold most of it to him. Of course, it ain't nothing I could swear to, just a powerfully strong hunch."

"Well, it wouldn't surprise me one bit," said Danielle.

Stick scratched his bristly beard stubble and eyed her closely again. "Now how come you to know my name?"

"I know you, Stick," said Danielle. "And I know the man you used to work for."

"Oh?" Stick looked even more curious. "Now how would you know that?"

"I just do," said Danielle. "Tell me, how is Tuck Carlyle doing these days?"

"Well, he's not doing so—" Stick caught himself and stopped in surprise. "I'll be dunked straight up!" said Stick. "You sure nailed it on the head. I worked for Tuck Carlyle for the longest time." He stepped back, staring even more closely at her, trying to place who she was, where he might know her from. "So I reckon I must know you from somewhere or other."

"You sure do," said Danielle. She looked around at the townsfolk starting to venture out now that the shooting was over. "But this isn't the best place to talk about it. Have you et anything today, Stick?"

"No," Stick replied, "but I've drunk extra whiskey to make up for it."

As he spoke, Danielle noticed a broom sitting against the front of the saloon. It looked as though the old man had come out to sweep the boardwalk before seeing the trouble between her and the three men. "Then you wouldn't turn down some beans, steak, and biscuits, I don't suppose," Danielle said.

"No, ma'am, not even with a gun to my head," Stick said. Then he hesitated. "That is if it ain't no bother to you . . . I never impose."

"No bother, Stick. After you backing me up, it would be my pleasure to fix us up some grub."

"Well then, all right, long was as you're sure I ain't putting you out any," said Stick, being polite.

"Go get your horse and ride out with me." Danielle nodded toward the west, out across the rise and fall of rocky ground to where the land reached upward into a stretch of low hills. "My place is nearby. We'll bend a couple of forks together. Then I'll tell you where I know you from."

"I'd sure love to, ma'am," said Stick. "But could you give me just a minute or two?" He jerked a thumb toward the broom on the boardwalk out front of the saloon. "I need to finish up a little job I started."

"Take your time, Stick," Danielle said. "I'm in no hurry."

Stick grinned and touched the brim of his hat as she backed away. "Much obliged," he said.

On their way out to Danielle's eighty acres of scrub grass and mesquite, Stick nodded toward a thin rise of dust far to their left and said, "That would be those two snakes we just run out of Haley Springs, if I ain't mistaken."

"I'm hoping that's the last we see of them," Danielle commented, riding in the buckboard beside Stick on his aging dun stallion.

"Oh, I sure wouldn't count on that," said Stick. "We ain't heard the last about what happened today. I can feel it in my bones." He gazed off toward the dust with a wary expression. "I don't know Cherokee Earl Muir, but I've heard plenty, and none of it's been good."

Danielle studied Stick's weathered face and, seeing the look of concern, asked, "Are you having second thoughts about what we done?"

"What?" Stick gave her a bemused look. "Why, Lord, no! I've been picking right over wrong my whole life. So far it ain't never failed me. Cherokee Earl or any of his bunch comes looking for me, they'll see I'm easier to find than stink on a polecat."

"That's how I thought you'd feel about it." Danielle smiled, then juggled the reins up and down, quickening the wagon horse's pace. "Hup, Sam," she said as the big horse seemed to snap out of a lull.

They rode quietly, sharing very little conversation for the next three miles until at length Danielle swung the wagon off the dirt trail onto a narrow wagon path leading over a rise of rocky grassland. At a wood and stone house built with its back against a bluff of protruding rock, Danielle stopped the wagon and stepped down at a sun-bleached hitchrail. "Well, here we are, such as it is," she said, putting a hand on the small of her back and stretching.

"Looks mighty fine and inviting to me," said Stick, taking a long look at the house and outstretched land surrounding it. "I always dreamed of someday having me a place of my own like this . . . somewhere a man can throw down a blanket and not have to roll it back up come morning 'less he wants to."

Danielle looked Stick up and down as he gazed

out across the land. She could tell he'd been living hand-to-mouth for a while. His boots were cracked across the tops and down in the heels. His hat looked as if it its edge had been gnawed on by barn critters. She noted to herself how thin he'd gotten since last she'd seen him. It saddened her to see a good cow-hand like Stick in such a condition.

"It's just me here running this place. I could use an extra hand if you're in no big hurry to be some-place else." Danielle said, hoping Stick wouldn't look too closely and notice that there wasn't enough going on here to keep one person busy, let alone two.

"I've no place else to be, and all the time in the world to get there," said Stick, his eyes gliding across a small corral, where six horses milled out of the heat on the shaded side of a small open-front barn. Dan-ielle was certain he saw there was no extra hand needed here. But the fact that he didn't comment on it made her realize what dire straits the old drover was in. "I'd be pleased to stay here and help you run this place, ma'am," said Stick, "long as you're sure you can use a hand."

"Oh, yes, believe me, Stick," said Danielle, direct-ing him toward the house as she spoke. "I need help. I'm not running any cattle right now, but I might, as soon as I get things fixed up around here. Right now I'm mostly dealing in horses when I can."

At the door to the house, Stick stopped and looked back again across the rough, hardscrabble land as if it were a glimpse of paradise. Off to their right, a lone buzzard swung up off its perch in a spindly cottonwood tree beside a dry creek bed. Stick smiled and took in a long, deep breath, his eyes growing a bit moist for just a second. "Ma'am, I'm glad I hap-pened onto you." The old drover's voice cracked as he spoke. "I swear, this has turned out to be my best day in a long time."

Danielle patted Stick's thin shoulder and said,

"You take your time out here, enjoy the view."
Seeing that he might need a minute or two to himself, she stepped inside and left Stick standing on the
dusty front porch in a hot passing breeze.

Chapter 2

Cherokee Earl Muir stood with a boot planted on the bottom rail of the corral, a half-empty bottle of whiskey hanging from his hand, a short black cigar stuck between his teeth. In the corral, Jorge stuck to the saddle of the bucking dapple gray as if the horse were a part of him. Along the fence, whiskey-fueled voices laughed and cursed and cheered beneath sporadic pistol shots exploding into the air. "That one-eyed Mexican can stick a horse 'bout as good as any man I ever saw," Cherokee Earl commented.

"Damn his hide," Dave Waddell growled, handing Cherokee Earl the twenty-dollar gold piece. With each rise and fall of the dapple gray, Jorge's black eyepatch flapped up and down, revealing both the clouded white eye and the deep scar running through it.

"What's wrong, Dave? Is that pretty little wife of yours going to throw a fit over you losing money to your bad ole pal Earl?" Earl chuckled to himself, then added, "I bet she's a real squalling wildcat when she's flared up. . . . Most redheads are, they say."

Waddell felt his face redden over the comment about his wife, but he acted as if he didn't hear it and nodded toward Jorge. "How do I get the show-off sumbitch off there? Shoot him?"

"You could do that," said Earl, inspecting the gold piece before shoving it down into his vest pocket. "Of course if you missed, there'd be one wild Mexican up your shirt." He grinned. "Then even I couldn't help you."

"Well, hell, Earl, I figured you could tell I was only joking," said Waddell, shying back at the thought of what he knew Jorge was capable of doing if Cherokee Earl ever sicced him on a person.

"I bet you were," said Earl, looking away from Waddell with a slight smile, dismissing the matter. The dapple gray wound down and circled the corral in a show of grudging submission. Jorge slipped down from the saddle at a trot, quickly mounted the corral fence, and grasped the first bottle of rye held out to him. He spread a broad grin, smoothed his eyepatch back into place, and tipped the bottle toward Cherokee Earl before taking a long swig.

Earl nodded his approval to Jorge, then said to Dave Waddell as he looked all around the rocky land, "This is a handy piece of ground you've got here, Dave. I could use a place like this."

"It's not for sale," said Waddell. "I'll tell you that before you go any farther."

"I never said I wanted to buy it," Earl chuckled under his breath. "I'd just like to have access to it from time to time . . . rent a piece of it, so to speak." He took the cigar from his teeth and blew a stream of smoke onto a hot passing breeze. "You could be my landlord. How does that strike you?"

"Sounds like more trouble than it'd be worth, if you don't mind my saying so," Waddell offered, making sure he didn't say something to Cherokee Earl Muir that he might regret. Earl was known for his hair-trigger temper. The slightest comment could rub him the wrong way and send him into a blind killing rage. Waddell had seen it happen more than once over the course of their dealings.

Cherokee Earl studied the wet end of his cigar for a quiet second, then said, "You mean, for instance, if I didn't pay my rent, and you had to come throw me off the place? Or if me and the boys got too rowdy of a night whilst you tried to sleep . . . something like that?"

"Well, no . . ." Waddell scratched his forehead up under his hat brim. "I just meant, the way you often get the law on your tail . . . maybe have to shoot it out with a posse or something. Being your landlord could get risky, Earl. I can't say it sounds like something I want to get involved in."

"Good then, it's all settled," said Earl as if they had just reached an understanding. "Me and the boys will hole up in that little rock canyon down along the high trail. Hell, you'll hardly ever know we're there unless we need to run down here, maybe borrow some grub or whiskey or something."

"Whoa, now wait a minute, Earl," said Waddell. "I never agreed to anything here."

Cherokee Earl shrugged. "You didn't disagree either when you had a chance."

"But I—" Waddell tried to protest, but Earl cut him off.

"Don't worry, Dave," said Earl. "You're going to make out good on this. Instead of my boys pushing leftover cattle here after offering them to half the ranchers we deal with, you'll get first pickin's. We'll bring them here, crossbrand them, fatten them up on the high grazes for a few weeks, then drive them to the railhead brokers in Kansas just like they was ours all along."

"I don't know, Earl. It sounds shaky to me." Waddell began to sweat. "I'm glad to buy a few stolen head from you now and then. I mix them in with my own, keep them till the next spring; nobody has ever questioned it. But what you're talking about is more like going into the rustling business with you as my partner!"

"Partners? Well, if you insist." Earl grinned. "I suppose we could do it that way. But it won't be a fifty-fifty split, not unless you're going down south with us, take your chances getting shot or hung like the rest of us. It wouldn't be fair to the boys."

"Hold it, Earl, *please!*" said Waddell. He held up a hand as if to stop something advancing on him. "I'm not going to go out rustling cattle, not for any-body! Now I might not mind you boys holing up temporarily in the high canyon while—"

"Then forget about riding out with us, Dave," said Earl, cutting him off. "You just keep things quiet around here so me and the boys don't have to worry about getting woke up some night to the sound of a rope slapping over a tree limb. You'll get thirty per-cent of our take, rain or shine." He grinned and drew on his cigar. "It ain't that you think your wife might not approve, is it?"

"Ellen doesn't tell me what to do," Waddell said, dismissing such a notion with a snap in his voice. The picture in his mind of a hangman's noose slung over a tree limb had turned him a little queasy. But the thought of what Earl had just said about his cut began to sink in.

"Thirty percent, huh?" said Dave.

"Yep, thirty percent," Earl repeated. "And I prom-ise the boys will be on their best behavior should they be around your missus whilst you're away on business somewhere."

"That isn't even an issue," said Waddell. "Believe me, my wife would tell me right away if someone ever acted in an untoward manner."

"Oh?" said Earl. "Well, I always admired a man who rules his own roost." He looked Dave Waddell up and down with a grin.

Dave Waddell felt uncomfortable talking about his personal life with the likes of Cherokee Earl Muir. He couldn't imagine what had taken the conversation in this direction in the first place, but he was glad when the topic changed.

"Then thirty percent it is?" Earl asked.

"Ordinarily, how much do you make on one of your trips south?" Dave Waddell asked.

Earl saw that Waddell was getting more interested. "Oh, anywhere from a few hundred on slow trip to, say, eight, nine, even ten thousand dollars for a good, fat haul along the border."

"Ten thousand dollars?" Dave Waddell looked amazed. "My God! Every steer standing on all fours in Texas ain't worth ten thousand dollars!"

Cherokee Earl cut in quickly, seeing he had overbid his hand. "We're not talking about rustling cattle, Dave. Me and the boys do other stuff besides just handle cattle. But no matter what we do, we still need a place to lay low for a while. . . . You still get the same thirty percent cut."

"What kind of other stuff?" Waddell gave him a dubious look.

"It don't matter what other stuff," said Earl. "As a partner you still get taken care of . . . for doing nothing but keeping us a hiding place ready here."

"Keep a hiding place ready?" Waddell saw this venture getting more and more involved, more and more dangerous as they talked about it. "I don't know nothing about that kind of thing. I think I better pass on it—"

"Come on, Dave, damn it," said Earl. "You're making it a bigger thing than it is. Just give it a chance. If it ain't working out in a few weeks, just say so, and we'll split up . . . no hard feelings." He offered Dave Waddell his gloved hand. "What do you say? Partners? I mean, unless you later decide otherwise?"

"Well . . ." Waddell hesitated for a moment longer, then gave in, seeing the cold steel look in Cherokee Earl's eyes. "All right, what the heck. We only live once, I reckon . . . Might as well make life a little interesting, eh?"

"That's what I always say." Earl grinned and shook his hand firmly. "Live fast, die hard . . . spit in the devil's eye, eh? *Partner*?"

Dave Waddell turned pale at Earl's words. "I don't know about that . . . I mean the *die hard* part. That ain't exactly what I—"

Earl slapped him on his broad back, cutting him off. "Just a figure of speech, Dave. Come on. Learn not to take everything I say so serious. Let's drink on it."

Earl hooked his arm around Waddell's neck and pulled him in close, almost in a headlock. Waddell grabbed the whiskey bottle as Earl shoved it hard against his chest.

"Riders coming," called a voice among the men gathered farther down the corral fence. "Looks like something's wrong, Boss. Somebody's riding upside down."

"What the—" Cherokee Earl turned from Dave Waddell and gazed out across the scorched, rocky land at the wavering figures advancing through a veil of heat. "Sherman, Jorge! Get out there and hurry them in here! Damned if that don't look like Ronald's horse."

Jorge Sentores and Sherman Fentress gave one another a look, both knowing beyond any doubt that it was Ronald Muir's horse coming toward them with a body facedown across the saddle.

"This is not so good," Jorge whispered. He made a quick sign of the cross on his chest as he jerked his broad sombrero down onto his forehead.

The other two men, Avery McRoy and Dirty Joe Turley, stared at Jorge and Sherman. "Go on out there—do like he said," whispered McRoy in a guarded tone. "If that idiot Ronald has gone and got himself shot dead, there's going to be hell to pay, sure enough."

"Why you say, 'If he has got himself shot dead'?"

asked Jorge under his breath as the pair stepped up into their saddles. "Perhaps he fell from his horse or died of a snakebite."

"Yeah, right," said Sherman. "He might've got run over whilst saving an old woman from a runaway freight wagon, but I like the odds on him getting shot dead a lot better. Either way, Earl's going to be wild-eyed loco for a month. You know how brothers are." Together Sherman and Jorge heeled their horses off toward the approaching riders. "I'm starting to wish I was anywhere but here," Sherman grumbled.

They rode out and met Frisco and Billy Boy two hundred yards from the ranch. One look at the body of Ronald Muir lying across the saddle caused Jorge to cross himself again. Sherman winced and said, "Damn, it's just like we figured." He looked at Frisco and Billy Boy. "How'd it happen? Over a poker game? A whore? What?"

"Just wait until we get to Earl," said Frisco. "I don't want to have to tell this story but once." He shook his head and let out a tense breath. "What kind of a mood is Earl in anyway?"

"Well, not bad," said Frisco, "but I expect that'll change right quick once he gets a look at ole Ronald deader than a chunk of rail iron, don't you think?"

"Yeah, I expect it will," said Frisco, lowering his head as they rode on.

When the riders entered the front yard, all four stepped down from their saddles and eased Ronald Muir's lifeless body to the dirt. Dave Waddell and the rest of the men gathered in a close group, circling Cherokee Earl, who had fallen to his knees over his brother.

"Who did this?" Earl demanded in a hoarse rasp. His gloves grew tight across his clenched fists.

"It was some old man," Frisco Bonham offered in a lowered, sympathetic tone.

"Some old man?" Earl whispered, keeping his voice even and in check.

"Yeah, Boss." Frisco went on with a slight shrug. "Who knows why these things happen? It just seems like sometimes it's the Lord's will, and all we can do is stand and wonder—"

"The Lord's will?" Earl stood up, dusting his trouser legs. His eyes had taken on dark circles of grief and rage. "Don't *Lord's will* me! I want to know what happened and what you two did about it." He pointed a long, daggerlike finger into Frisco Bonham's chest.

Frisco and Billy Boy Harper fell back a step, Billy limping on his wounded foot. His boot was missing, and a bloody bandanna was wrapped around his toes. "It's—it's just like I told you, Boss!" Frisco said quickly. "Some old man shot him dead in the street! An old bar swamper at the saloon!"

"An old bar swamper? Killed Ronald?" Earl asked, his rage building with each word. "My brother, slicker than a snake with a pistol . . . got smoked down by some old drunken bum?"

"Sorry, Boss, but yes, that's who did it," Frisco said gently.

"All right." Earl nodded his head as if forcing himself to accept the bitter news. "An old swamper killed him . . . Then you two killed the swamper? Was that it?"

Frisco and Billy Boy gave one another a worried look. "We couldn't kill him, Boss," said Billy Boy. "God knows I would have loved to! Look at my foot."

Earl looked him up and down. "This swamper shot you too?"

"Well, not exactly," said Billy. "The woman with him did this to me. She shot me. Then Ronald drew on her, and the old man shot him dead."

Earl stopped him with a raised hand. "Maybe I'm hearing this wrong," Earl said. "An old man and a *woman* did this to you and Ronald?"

As Billy Boy nodded his bowed head in shame, Earl turned a cold gaze to Frisco Bonham. "What about you, Frisco? Any holes in your foot? Any wounds you want to show us?"

Frisco's jaw twitched nervously. "Uh, Boss, you had to be there to understand how this all come about. She—the woman that is—shot poor Billy Boy. Then Ronald went crazy all at once, didn't give me a chance to back his play or nothing else! Once he was dead, there was two guns pointed at me. . . . Damn it, I was in a tight spot, had nobody siding with me."

"Yeah, I can see how that could unnerve a man all right," said Earl, "caught between a woman and an old drunken bar swamper."

"Boss, he didn't handle that Colt like a bar swamper." Frisco tried to come up with something to help himself. "Fact is, I believe he might have been some kind of gunslinger. You know, one of them hardcore killers from the old days, back before our time?"

"Shut your mouth right now, Frisco," Earl hissed, "and you might keep me from killing you." He turned his gaze to Billy Boy Harper. "You and Ronald was good friends, Billy Boy. Is there any truth at all to what Frisco's telling me?"

"Yep, it's the truth, Earl," said Billy Boy, "bad as I hate admitting it. A woman in a gingham dress and old man who was sweeping out the saloon did all this."

"A woman in a gingham dress," Earl growled to himself. "And that's all I get to go on for who killed my poor brother?"

"I heard her say her name is Strange," Billy Boy offered meekly.

"Strange how?" asked Earl. "Strange-sounding? Strange for a woman? What ?"

"No, Boss," said Frisco. "He means that *is* her name. S-t-r-a—"

"I can spell! Damn it!" Earl shouted. He swung his hard gaze toward Dave Waddell.

"Danielle Strange is who they're talking about, Earl," said Waddell. "I know her, or I should say I *know of* her. She keeps a one-hand spread over somewhere past the mesa." He nodded off toward a distant upthrust of dark rocky land. Behind it stood a long stretch of hills. "But you'd play hell finding it unless you knew where to start looking."

"She's got perfect ambush country protecting her," said Cherokee Earl. "Reckon she was smart enough to know that when she picked the place?"

"I wouldn't be surprised," Dave replied.

"Figures," Cherokee Earl grumbled. He seemed to dismiss the idea of searching the hills. "Do any of the townsfolk know the way to her place?"

"I'm sure they would," said Dave Waddell. "She deals horses. There's plenty of folks from town probably been out there."

"Then they'll tell me how to get there," said Earl with a slight shrug. "Now, who's this old man they're talking about?"

"Beats me," said Waddell. "Probably just some drifter passing through, swamping the bar for a meal and a cot in the back."

"These don't sound like hardened gunslingers to me," Earl said, narrowing his gaze back coldly in Frisco Bonham's eyes.

"Well . . . the fact is, this Danielle Strange is known to be pretty good with a gun," said Waddell.

"Yeah, I bet she is," said Earl skeptically.

Dave Waddell shrugged. "I'm just telling you what I've heard, Earl. I ain't saying it's true."

"She never hesitated a second before putting a bullet through Billy Boy's foot," said Frisco Bonham. "I reckon that's what took us all by surprise. You don't expect a woman to just up and start shooting hell out of you."

"Is she one of those women goes around wishing she was born a man?" Earl asked Dave Waddell.

"Far as I know she's not," Waddell responded, shaking his head.

Earl looked down at his dead brother. "Jesus, what a mess," he whispered in regret.

Jorge cut in. "Wants us to go kill them pretty good right now, Boss?"

"Yeah, Jorge," said Earl. "Get on your horse and go kill them both *pretty good.* They'll be standing right there in the street where these two idiots left them, just waiting for somebody to come riding in to kill them."

"*Sí*, then I go kill them right now!" Jorge sounded excited.

But when he turned, Sherman Fentress grabbed his arm and whispered close to his ear, "Jorge, he don't mean it. Just stand still here and keep your mouth shut. Give him a minute or two to let things settle."

Hearing Fentress, Earl swung around toward him, saying, "Settle? There ain't a damn thing going to settle! Not until my brother's killers are both laying dead in the dirt!"

"I know, Boss! I agree with you!" Sherman raised his hands chest high as if Earl might attack him. "I'm ready to ride into hell with you if that's what it takes. We all are! Right, boys?" He stepped away from Earl and looked to the others for support.

Earl turned to Dave Waddell. "You're going to ride into town with us . . . point out the best person to take us to this woman's spread."

"Me?" Waddell looked stunned. "Earl, I can't ride into town with you and these men."

"The hell you can't," Earl barked. "You're going

with me! Don't think you get a free ride around here, Dave! Everybody does their part!"

Waddell stared wide-eyed and speechless. They'd just gone over all this. He wasn't supposed to have to ride with this gang of rustlers. Where did Earl suddenly get that idea? "Earl, I can't go. My wife's expecting me back at the house for supper!"

"Not tonight, Dave. If you're going to be part of this bunch, you might just as well get started."

"This makes no sense, Earl," Waddell coaxed, "me riding into town with you. How are you going to lay low here after letting everybody see that we ride together? That'll ruin any chance of you using this place for a hideout."

"He's right, Boss," Dirty Joe Turley offered in a quiet tone.

Earl simmered down and took a deep breath, giving some thought to Waddell's words. "All right, Dave, you get on back to your house. Enjoy your supper," he added with a sneer. "Me and the boys will go take care of this matter and ride by your place afterward."

"Why?" Dave Waddell asked. "There's no reason for you to come by where I—"

"Just to let you know how we did," said Earl, cutting him off. "Don't worry. We won't be staying for tea." He slid a knowing glance across the faces of the gathered men and added, "Or nothing else we ain't welcome to."

Waddell felt his face tighten with embarrassment. "I was only trying to keep your being here as quiet as I can. What good's a hideout if everybody knows you're there? That's all I'm getting at." He shrugged.

"Well, thanks for looking out for us, Davey," Earl said, a sarcastic grin coming to his face. "I believe we'll be all right."

The men let out a nervous laugh, then cut it short as Earl looked at each of them in turn. "Get some

shovels and get Ronald in the ground good and
deep. I better not come by here in a day or two and
find him strung all over the ground with some varmint chewing on his innards."

"*Sí*, Boss, we take good care of him right now,"
said Jorge.

"Then get to it," said Earl. "Soon as Ronald's
planted properlike, be ready to ride into Haley
Springs. We'll snatch us up a trail guide, then head
out to those hills. We've got killing to do!"

Chapter 3

By the time Danielle and Stick had finished eating, the sun had moved over to the western sky, beginning its fiery descent toward the flat horizon. Owing to his powerful hunger, Stick had spoken very little throughout the meal. Now he finished his cup of coffee and stifled a belch. "Ma'am," he said, "I can't remember the last sit-down meal I et . . . but I swear it seems like forever."

Danielle looked down at the small portion of leftover biscuits, beans, and beef. "You're welcome to finish them up, Stick," she offered.

"Much obliged, but thank you, ma'am," Stick replied. "I'm full enough to falter as it is."

"Yet you didn't eat that much," Danielle commented.

"I always thought it an odd thing," said Stick, "that the more hungry a man goes over a period of time, the less he can eat when he sits down to big meal."

Danielle nodded her understanding. "I've got a mason jar of apricots if you'd like a helping."

"No, please," said Stick, raising a hand. "Don't tempt me. I got some wood to split 'twixt now and sundown."

"Not here you don't," said Danielle, reaching out, picking up the coffeepot, and refilling Stick's tin cup. "I've got plenty of firewood for the cookstove, enough to last the next month."

Stick looked at her firmly. "Then I've got fence to
mend or stalls to clean or something, ma'am. Where
I come from no man eats 'less he earns his keep
some way or another. I can't stay around someplace
without plenty to do. It wouldn't be right."

Danielle smiled. "Ordinarily I'd agree with you,
but by siding with me in town, let's consider this
meal as earned in advance."

"Just this once." Stick smiled brokenly and raised
a finger for emphasis. "And just because you're
twisting my arm. I'll not allow myself to be kept and
pampered in my old age."

"I wouldn't dream of it," said Danielle. "Believe
me, I'll find plenty for you to do." She stood up and
collected the empty tin plates and set them aside as
she continued to speak. "Now, I know you're too
polite to ask me again where I come from, so I'll go
ahead and tell you."

"Much obliged, ma'am. I hoped you would,"
said Stick.

Danielle stepped back from the table into the middle of the small room with both hands on her hips.
"Do you recall a couple years back, you were riding
with Tuck Carlyle and some others, pushing a small
herd of cattle across Indian Territory?"

"Well, yeah, was as best I recollect," said Stick.
"Fact is, I've left lots of hoofprints back and forth
across the Territory."

"But on this drive, a friend of Tuck's showed up
and took the evening meal with you. Remember
that?"

"Why, sure I do," said Stick. "That was Danny
Duggin who showed up. Danny was as fine a young
man as I ever met. . . . Had a little trouble with the
law if I remember correct, not that I fault him for
that. It happens to the best of us when we're young
and full of vinegar." Stick stopped and contemplated

for a second. "There was a real troublemaker with Danny though, a fella called Dunc."

"Yep, that was Duncan Grago," said Danielle.

"Yes, so it was," said Stick, eyeing her with curiosity. "Dunc picked a gunfight with one of our drovers and shot him dead." Stick took another second as if to go over the picture of the gunfight in his mind. Then he asked, "But what's all that to do with where you know me from?"

"I'm getting to it." Danielle nodded. "First, answer this one question for me. Tuck Carlyle had fallen in love with a young woman named Ilene Brennet." Danielle stepped closer, deeply interested in what his answer would be. "Did he ever go back to the Flagg Ranch and marry her?"

"Yep, he sure enough did," said Stick.

With Stick's answer, Danielle felt her heart sink. For one hopeful moment she had imagined there might still be a chance for her and Tuck Carlyle. Meeting Stick in town had brought it on. But now she knew better. "Oh, I see," she said, trying to keep her voice from sounding like her breath had just been stolen from her.

"Now then," said Stick, his curiosity having gotten the better of him, "are you gong to tell me or not?"

"They say a picture is worth a thousand words." Danielle's voice softened, the eagerness in it not as sharp as a moment before. She stepped back toward a narrow doorway and pushed aside a worn blanket. "Drink your coffee. . . . I'll be back right back."

In the small bedroom, Danielle stepped out of her dress and into her road clothes, her faded denim trousers, and her boots. Then she opened a drawer in the stand beside her bed and took out the wound-up cloth binder she had used to conceal her womanly proportions. She unrolled it and wrapped it around her chest. As she watched herself in a dusty mirror, her firm young breasts seemed to vanish before her eyes. She sighed at the memories both good and bad that posing as a man had left with her. Then she strapped her gun belt around her waist, slipped into her long riding duster, and took her battered Stetson from a peg on the wall.

At the sight of her stepping back into the room, Stick gasped and half rose from his chair, his right hand going instinctively to his pistol butt before she caught herself.

"Take it easy, Stick," Danielle said, holding her voice lower, her broad Stetson brim blacking out most of her face. "You wanted an answer, and I figured I could tell you all day . . . but it wouldn't do no good unless you saw for yourself." As she spoke, her pistol streaked up from her holster and twirled expertly on her finger, first forward, then backward. Then it slid quietly back into her holster. Stick's jaw had dropped. He shook his head as if trying to clear it.

"Miss—Miss Danielle?" The old drover couldn't hide the surprise and bewilderment in his voice. "Is that you?" But before she could answer, he added, "What am I saying? Of course it's you! But danged if you don't look and sound more like Danny Duggin than—" He stopped short, the truth sinking in. Then he dropped back into his chair with a low chuckle. "You mean to tell me, all that time, the young gunslinger Danny Duggin was really you?"

Danielle reached up, peeled her Stetson back off her head, and shook out her long hair. "If I'd had no other reason for telling you, Stick, believe me, it would have been worth it just to see the look on your face." Danielle smiled and leaned one hand on the tabletop. "That was my secret those days when I rode with Tuck, you, and the rest of the drovers. I would have given anything to tell Tuck who I really was . . . but I couldn't. I was riding the vengeance trail, and I couldn't let anything come between me and catching my pa's murderers."

"My, my," Stick murmured, shaking his head slowly, sinking back into his chair. "Tuck always said there was something peculiar about you. I reckon he was right."

"Peculiar?" Hurt flashed in Danielle's eyes. Stick saw it.

"Oh, not in any bad way," he said quickly. "Tuck said he couldn't quite put his finger on it, but that there was something odd about you, something different. He wouldn't admit it, and I know how it sounds, but I swear there were times I thought he was overly fond of you."

Danielle smiled. "Stick, you don't know how much that means to me, hearing that." Her eyes grew misty for just a second until she checked herself. "No matter how strange it might have sounded, I would given anything to know it. You see—" She stopped for a moment as if wondering whether or not to finish her words. Then she let them spill. "I love Tuck. . . . I've loved him since I first laid eyes on him. There, I've said it."

"Why, that's plumb unnatural." Stick stared wide-eyed, in shock. Then, realizing his error, he said softly, "I'm sorry, that ain't what I meant. For a minute there, I was believing that Danny Duggin actually was a man."

"I know," said Danielle. "I played my part to the hilt. There were times I came near fooling myself. Being a woman posing as a man has done things to me that'll take a lifetime for me to sort out, let alone understand." She paused in reflection, then added, "But I did what I set out to do. I've got no regrets. . . . Well, only one. I've always wished Tuck and I had met under ordinary circumstances. I believe there would have been a place for us in one another's lives."

"Oh, I see." Stick gave her a questioning look. "You loved Tuck that much, and you still do?"

"Yes, I did. . . . I mean, yes, I still do. For a while I tried to forget about my feelings for Tuck . . . even thought I'd fallen in love with another man, Federal Marshal C. F. McCord. But it didn't work out between us. He's been gone the past year. Said it was easier getting along with wanted outlaws than it was for us to get along with each other. He was right. . . . We needed to break it off clean and start over."

"C. F. McCord?" said Stick. "You mean the man the outlaws along the strip call 'The Fox?' "

"Yep, that was who I took up with," Danielle said wistfully. "And I can't fault him a bit. He tried, we both did. But in the end we both decided we was just too much for one another."

"Too much for one another, eh?" Stick repeated. "I like hearing it put that way. I reckon any man and woman who tried and failed could say the same thing."

"I suppose so," said Danielle. She shrugged. "Anyway, C. F. is gone. Tuck's gone. Now it's just me, and I don't reckon I have whatever heart it takes to ever fall in love again. I wouldn't want to if I could."

"Careful what you say, ma'am," said Stick. "I'm fixing to tell you something that might just turn your world upside down."

"What is it, Stick?" Danielle asked.

"First, tell me this, Miss Danielle. If you love a man the way you claim you love Tuck Carlyle, would you do just about anything you could to see that he never faltered or fell or got so low down that he could never get back on his feet again?"

"What are you talking about, Stick?" Danielle asked, not getting a hint of what he could be leading up to. "Of course I would. What woman wouldn't, if she truly loved a man? What makes you ask something like that?"

"Well, I just wanted to make sure that once I tell you this we'll both remember what you just said. You see, I believe Tuck Carlyle could use your help right now. Fact is, if you love the man, that might be exactly what it'll take to save his ornery life."

"What is it, Stick?" Danielle demanded. "Is Tuck in trouble? How can I help him?"

"I told you he married Ilene Brennet, but I never told you what happened." A sad expression came to Stick's weathered face as he continued. "Ilene up and died last fall."

"Oh, no, that's terrible," said Danielle. "No matter how much I love Tuck, I would never want something like that to happen to his wife."

"I know you wouldn't," said Stick. "If I thought otherwise I'd never tell you what I'm about to." He paused long enough to sip his coffee, as if it would give him the strength he needed to continue. "Losing Ilene has just about destroyed poor Tuck. He rode off plumb wild and heartbroken no sooner than she was in the ground. I'm afraid he's turned to rotgut rye and tar opium to heal himself."

"Couldn't you stop him, Stick? Wasn't there something you could have done?" Danielle sank down slowly into her chair, listening intently.

Stick shook his head. "Don't you know if there was something I could have done, I would have?"

"Yes, I'm sorry," said Danielle, reaching out and cupping her hand down over the old drover's hard, bony knuckles. "I know you would have done something if you could. Where is he, Stick? What's become of him?"

"Last we heard he was up in Greely, staying drunker than a skunk, living on black-tar opium when he can get it and swigging laudanum when he can't. He's lost everything, Danny—I mean, Miss Danielle. His cattle's all gone up in drink, along with his horses and his land. He's down to what's hanging on his back, I reckon." Stick winced, thinking about it. "God, it just tears me up inside, seeing it happen to him."

"Stick, there's got to be something I can do," said Danielle. "There just has to be."

"I swear, Miss Danielle," said Stick, "if I thought you could help him any way at all, I'd give anything to see you do it. Tuck has been just like a son to me. I'm hoping maybe there was some deeper purpose for you and me meeting in Haley. . . . Maybe it was meant to be. I'm afraid if somebody doesn't reach Tuck afore long, he'll soon be dead in some back alley or muddy street somewhere."

"Not if I can help it," Danielle said firmly. "I'll go to Greely, if that's where he is. I'll find him, and I'll—" She stopped short as if uncertain what to say next."

"You'll do what, Miss Danielle?" Stick asked quietly. He paused for a second, letting Danielle consider his words. Then he continued. "You see, it ain't easy stopping a man bent on drinking himself to death."

"I know," said Danielle. "I've seen it happen to men in every board-front town and cow camp I've been through." She stood up and paced back and forth restlessly. Finally she said, "Well, I'll figure out what to do when I get to him. Right now I'll have to take it one step at a time. Are you game for a ride up to Greely?"

"I'm always game for a ride anywhere," said Stick, "especially if it might straighten out Tuck and get him thinking right again."

"Good. We'll get ourselves a good night's sleep, be in Haley before sunup, sell off my string of horses, get us some traveling money, then strike out for Greely. Does that sound right to you?"

"Sounds right to me," Stick agreed. Then he looked at her a bit dubiously. "You won't be wearing those men's clothes will you?"

"No," said Danielle. "I'll be wearing what I usually wear these days on the trail. My doeskin skirt,
my riding blouse, and my vest."

"Not that I mind what you wear." Stick smiled.
"I'm just pleased to have something to do. I've been
wandering about like a homeless dog."

"I'll keep you busy, Stick," said Danielle. "I think
I can promise you that."

Darkness had fallen by the time Cherokee Earl Muir
and his men rode into Haley Springs. The street lay
empty except for a skinny hound who came scooting
his way from beneath the boardwalk and began barking loudly. "Shoot that loudmouth sumbitch!" Earl demanded of his men. A shot rang out, and the dog let
out a short yelp as a bullet hit the ground and dirt
kicked up against his bony legs. The mutt turned and
disappeared, barking as he fled. "I said *shoot* him," said
Earl, over his shoulder, "not shoot *at* him."

Dirty Joe slipped his pistol back into his holster
and whispered sidelong to Avery McRoy, "Ain't
nothing going please him till we catch Ronald's
killers."

"I know," Avery whispered in reply. "And like as
not, Ronald was asking for what he got."

"I wouldn't let anybody hear me say that if I was
you," said Turley, his whisper growing even softer.

"I already let you hear it," said Avery. "Do I have
to kill you now to keep you quiet?" He chuckled
under his breath.

"Don't be kidding around about this," Turley
warned.

"All right, I'll stop," said Avery McRoy, chuckling
even louder.

"What's so funny back there?" Earl asked, sounding none too friendly. Faces turned to Turley and
McRoy in the darkness.

"Nothing, Boss," said Turley. "Just laughing at the

hound." Behind dusty windows along the dark boardwalk, a small number of kerosene lamps came to life. From the saloon a half block away, three heads stuck out above the batwing doors, staring toward the sound of the gunshot. "Get ready, boys. Here comes our welcoming committee," said Earl Muir.

The three men from the saloon stepped down from the boardwalk and hurried along the dirt street. Two more men appeared out of the darkness, one from behind a door where a woman stood watching with her sleeping gown held tight at her throat.

"What's the shooting about out here?" asked one of the townsmen, sounding cross and hooking his suspenders up over his shoulders. "It's the middle of the night for God sakes!"

Stepping down from his saddle with his rifle in his hands, Earl slammed the rifle butt into the townsman's stomach. The townsman hit the ground and rolled into a ball, both arms wrapped across his middle. From the doorway the woman came screaming, her gown and robe fluttering in the darkness. "Robert! Robert!"

Earl grabbed her and threw her to the ground. "Shut up, woman, or you'll get the same thing!" She crawled sobbing to her fallen husband and tried to lift him to his feet. But with his breath still knocked out of him, all he could do was make tight gurgling sounds as he squirmed in the dirt.

Seeing what had happened, the three men from the saloon came to a sharp halt and turned around, ready to slip away into the night. But Earl saw them and called out in a threatening voice. "Get over here, you cowardly peckerwoods, before I kill the lot of you!"

As more townsfolk appeared from behind doors, Earl's men jumped down from their saddles and hurriedly rounded them up in the middle of the street.

The frightened faces looked down at Robert Blanchard lying in the dust, and at his wife, Annabelle, who knelt sobbing beside him. One townsman stepped forward to help the Blanchards, but Earl shoved him back. "You stay put. He's doing fine on his own!"

"He's hurt, and I'm the town doctor!" the man said, pointing a finger down at Robert Blanchard.

"You'll be treating yourself if you don't stand back and shut the hell up," Earl growled. He shoved the old doctor back, then called out. "Everybody listen close to what I'm saying. I ain't about to repeat myself." As he spoke, he drew his pistol and flashed it back and forth. "This morning an old man and a young woman killed my brother right here on the street in this hog-wallow of a town! I'm holding everybody here responsible! I know the woman has a spread out in the hills beyond the mesa. Who wants to be the first to tell me how to get there?"

A grizzly old teamster stepped forward and spit in the dirt at Cherokee Earl's feet. "Your brother got what he deserved. He started the whole thing. So you and him both can go straight to—"

A shot exploded from Earl's pistol barrel. The man flew backward with the blast and fell dead on the ground, a gout of blood rising from his chest. A woman screamed. The rest of the townsfolk looked on, horrified.

"Now then, who among you good folks wants to be next?" Earl called out. "I got all night and a saddlebag full of bullets. I'll kill everybody here if I have to."

Chapter 4

In the predawn light, a thick layer of smoke loomed above the smoldering remains of Haley Springs. From atop her favorite mount, a chestnut mare named Sundown, Danielle led her eight-horse string cautiously as she and Stick rode into town from the outer darkness of a sandy stretch of flatland. At the far end of the street, short flames licked at the remaining framework of the livery barn. Danielle and Stick had hurried from the moment they'd first spotted the fiery glow from a distance across the rolling land. But even pushing their horses as hard as they dared to, it had still taken them over an hour to get here. By now the raging inferno had run its course. Except for a few charred hulls, the plank buildings that had made up the main street of Haley Springs were gone.

"Lord have mercy," Stick murmured, looking around at the devastation. Embers crackled peacefully like some large animal whose hunger had been satisfied. The empty street lay as silent as stone.

Danielle brought her mare to a halt and sat studying the scene in stunned disbelief as her string of horses bunched up and stopped beside her. She shot Stick a glance, their eyes meeting for only a second, but long enough for Stick to get an idea what she was thinking.

"We don't know for sure it was Cherokee Earl and his bunch," Stick said, "and even if it was, there was no way you could have known he was coming back here." As Stick spoke, he sidestepped his horse a few feet away from Danielle as he looked around and shook his head. "But I got to say, given what happened earlier, things sure point in his direction."

"Oh, it was him all right," said Danielle. "And I should have seen it coming. When we left here after the shooting, I should have expected the unexpected."

"But all the same," said Stick, "there was no reason to—"

His words cut short beneath a blast of rifle fire coming from the direction of the fallen livery barn.

Danielle spun the lead rope around her saddle horn quickly and jumped down from the saddle. "Move 'em out, Sundown!" she shouted, slapping a gloved hand on her chestnut mare's rump, shooing the animal out of the street. The big mare knew what was expected of her. She bolted away to the right, pulling the frightened string of horses into the shadows. "Take cover, Stick!" Danielle shouted instinctively, already realizing she needn't worry about the old drover. Stick knew how to take care of himself. She saw that he had jumped down from his saddle almost in unison with her.

The rifle shot had kicked up dirt ten yards short. Danielle dropped into a crouch and hurried toward the shelter of a water trough, snatching up her Colt and firing a quick shot just to draw any incoming rifle fire away from the fleeing horses. The horses bunched up around Sundown when the mare slid to a halt twenty yards away. They nickered in fright and jerked against the lead rope. But Sundown stood firmly, keeping the animals under control.

Danielle reached the water trough as another shot whistled through the air. Stick had pulled down a well-worn Spencer rifle from its boot before his horse bolted away with Sundown and the others. Danielle heard the big rifle cock from across the street. Something didn't feel right about all this, she told herself. A third shot flashed from the dark alley. The bullet hit the ground a full five yards short and three yards to the left. A wild shot. Too wild, she thought to herself. Knowing that any second Stick would draw a bead on the muzzle flash, she called out, "Stick, hold your fire!"

Another rifle shot rang out, but then a woman's voice called out from farther away in the smoky darkness. "Is that you, Danielle Strange?"

"Yes, it's me, Mrs. Blanchard," said Danielle, recognizing the voice. "Don't shoot."

"Oh dear, Miss Danielle! I'm so sorry," Annabelle Blanchard cried in a shaky voice. "Are you all right, child?"

"I'm all right, Mrs. Blanchard," Danielle replied. "Aim your rifle at the ground and come on out where I can see you." Danielle wasn't about to be the first to step out from behind her cover. Instead, she scanned the smoky shadows and the glittering embers and saw no one else. "What's gone on here? Is there anybody else around?" she called out, wanting to make sure that anyone who might be listening would hear her voice and recognize it.

Across the street, Stick kept his Spencer rifle aimed into the darkness as Annabelle Blanchard stepped out cautiously, wearing a long sleeping gown with a long wool coat over it. Annabelle began to hurry forward when Danielle showed herself and kept her Colt down by her side in her gloved hand. "Here I am, Mrs. Blanchard," said Danielle.

"Oh, Miss Danielle!" Annabelle sobbed, letting her rifle slump down to her side. "It's been just awful here! They killed poor Klute Kinsky, the ole teamster . . . and Milton Shirley, our telegraph clerk!" She let out a tortured sigh and shuddered. "They just killed everybody." Her eyes were large and shiny with fear. Touched with madness, Danielle thought to herself, looking Annabelle up and down. "They would have killed my Robert too," Annabelle continued, "but I dragged him out of the street and hid him from them."

Danielle saw the woman was nearly delirious. She stepped beside her, giving Stick a look, and said, "Come on, Annabelle, take me to Robert. Then we'll get you something warm to drink and get you out of the morning chill."

Annabelle shivered slightly. "Yes . . . I'll take you to Robert, but I must warn you he isn't himself this morning." She looked around at the burned shamble of a town. "Not that I can blame him though, with all this going on."

With Danielle guiding her along the empty dirt street, Annabelle murmured to herself about the condition of the destroyed town. A few yards down the street, they came upon the bodies of two men who had been the first ones Earl Muir had asked for directions to Danielle's spread. When they had refused to tell him what he wanted to know, Earl and Frisco Bonham had shot them dead.

"Excuse us, gentlemen," Annabelle said to the bloody corpses as if they were still alive. Danielle continued helping her along, casting a glance over her shoulder long enough to see that Stick was gathering their horses. "I'm afraid it will take some time for this town to recover from a mess such as this," Annabelle said, stepping daintily around the bodies.

Danielle was not surprised when they approached the blank dead face of Robert Blanchard staring off toward the sky as he lay slumped against the side of a small plank shack, the only building Earl Muir and his men had overlooked in their rampage. "I was concerned about Robert at first," said Annabelle. "But now I think he's going to be all right, don't you, Miss Danielle?"

Seeing the two ragged bullet holes in Robert's chest, Danielle took a deep breath and placed a consoling arm across Annabelle's shoulders. "Listen to me, Annabelle," she said as gently as she could. "Robert is dead. . . . So are those two men in the street."

"Oh, dear," said Annabelle, raising a hand to her lips. Danielle saw the woman's eyes begin to well up with tears as reality tried to sink in.

"Yes, I'm afraid so," Danielle said, firming her arm around the trembling woman's shoulders. "And I'm going to have to ask you to be strong, Annabelle, and accept the fact that Robert and all these people are dead. Can you do that for me?"

"I-I'll try," Annabelle replied softly, but with resolve.

"Good," said Danielle. She bent down long enough to close Robert Blanchard's eyes, then stood silently with Annabelle for a moment until Stick walked up leading the horses.

"It's pretty bad over past where the saloon stood," Stick said, lowering his voice to shield Annabelle from his words.

"How bad?" Danielle asked. "You can talk in front of Annabelle. She's promised me she's going to be real strong and help us out."

"I see," said Stick. He looked Annabelle up and down, then said to Danielle, his voice still lowered, "I believe the bastards have killed everybody in town."

Danielle felt Annabelle shudder and begin to sob quietly beside her. "We're going to need your help to get these folks gathered and buried proper. Are you up to it, Annabelle?" she asked.

The heartbroken woman summoned up her courage and stepped from beneath Danielle's consoling arm. "I will be as strong as I need to be." She took a deep breath and let it out in a sigh, looking down at her dead husband's face. In the east, the first thin wreath of sunlight crept upward from the horizon, casting a ghostly silver glow over Haley Springs and its dead. "But let's get started, Miss Danielle," Annabelle added. "I can't bear to see Robert laying here this way."

"I understand, Annabelle." Danielle led the shivering woman into the small shack. Stick hitched the horses to a single hitchpole and followed. Inside the cluttered shack, Danielle took a small kerosene lantern from a wall peg, dusted it off, and lit it. Stick began to search through a line of long-handled tools leaning against the wall, quickly choosing two shovels and a pick. Danielle prepared a place for Annabelle to sit down on a nail keg near a small woodstove. With some kindling and newspaper, Danielle soon had a small fire dancing in the round belly of the stove. "I'll get some coffee from my saddlebags," she said, patting Annabelle on her shoulder. "You sit here and rest."

After a hot cup of coffee, Danielle and Stick went to work, digging graves while the sun rose higher from the eastern rim of the sky. Annabelle stayed close by them as they worked, telling them what had happened, her eyes darting around at the least little sound among the smoldering ashes of what had been the town. Yet when it came time to bury the dead, Annabelle pulled herself together. Corpse after corpse, she washed their faces and their hands, made certain their eyes were closed and that their hair was properly parted and combed. Danielle and Stick watched in silence as the woman prepared the bodies of her husband, her neighbors, and her fellow townsfolk. Then, with their hats in hand, they joined Annabelle in a short prayer over each of the dead. Once done, Danielle and Stick put their hats back on and resumed their work.

Shortly after sunup, the northbound stage arrived in a cloud of dust. Hap Smith, the driver, and his young shotgun rider, Paul Sutterhill, immediately lent a hand with the burying, using two spades they took from the small shack. It was almost noon before the tired burial group patted their shovels on the last mound of freshly turned earth. Eleven new graves now lay inside the short wall of loose stones surrounding the town cemetery. Annabelle sat quietly beside her husband's grave as the others looked on, her hands folded in her lap.

As they worked together, Danielle and Stick had filled in Smith and Sutterhill on what had happened. With each rise and fall of the pick into the hard ground, Stick had told them about Cherokee Earl and his band of rustlers, and about the shooting in town. But it was only as they finished up the last grave that Hap Smith scratched his scruffy white beard and commented on the matter. "Who in the world would have ever dreamed a band of cattle rustlers would come back and do something like this?"

"It's simple. They came back to town looking for someone to point them toward my house," Danielle said in a bitter tone. "Annabelle told me no one in this town would tell them where I live . . . so Earl and his men took turns shooting everybody."

"Lord God," Hap Smith murmured. "I reckon that only leaves you one way to go, young lady. You'll have to go find a marshal and put him onto these murders."

"That's one way," said Danielle. "But I have another idea." She turned, rolling down her shirt sleeves, and walked away.

Hap and Sutterhill both looked at Stick. "Did I say the wrong thing?" Hap asked.

"Nope," Stick replied. "But I believe she's already decided to go after them herself."

Hap Smith almost scoffed, but then he caught himself, seeing the serious look on Stick's face. "Herself?

What chance would a woman have against a bunch that would do something like this?"

"I don't know," said Stick, "but I sure plan on being there to find out."

Ellen Waddell had noticed how tense and worried her husband had been the night before. He'd barely touched his food. After supper he'd spent the remainder of the evening pacing back and forth on the front porch. She noticed that he had laced his coffee with whiskey, slipping the thin flask from inside his vest and pouring it when he thought she wasn't looking. Something was wrong, but she had no idea what it could be. Late in the evening, when gunfire resounded on the distant horizon, she had craned her neck slightly and looked off in that direction.

"Pistol shots," Ellen said attentively.

"Yes, so what?" Dave Waddell snapped, only increasing the intensity of his monotonous pacing.

"Well, nothing, I suppose," Ellen replied. But then, when the shots came again, this time in greater number, she said, "Doesn't that sound like it's coming from town?"

"Yes, damn it, it does!" Dave Waddell barked at her.

Ellen was taken aback that her simple comment had prompted such a harsh response. "Watch your language, if you please. . . . And you needn't raise your voice." She nodded toward his coffee cup sitting on the sun-bleached porch railing. "Perhaps if the coffee is too strong, I'll need to—"

"No!" Dave cut her off. "There's nothing wrong with the coffee. Can't you see I'm trying to think here? There's time when a man has more on his mind than figuring out whether or not gunfire is coming from town." He took a quick swallow of the laced coffee and muttered, "Good Lord, woman!" Then he fluttered a nervous hand in the direction of Haley Springs. "Probably just some hunter shooting at jackrabbits," he said. "Why does everything have to be such a big event to you?"

"A big event?" Ellen sat stunned for a second. "I was only making conversation."

"Then make it to yourself," Dave snapped. Then he had turned, snatched up his cup of coffee, and stomped off the porch and toward the barn.

"My goodness," Ellen had whispered to herself.

That wasn't the first time she'd seen her husband upset about something. But the next morning, when she awakened just before dawn, she noticed that his side of the bed hadn't been slept in. She arose and lit the lamp beside the bed and carried it with her through the predawn gloom. Padding barefoot out onto the front porch, wearing only her loose-fitting cotton gown, she saw Dave Waddell sitting slumped in a wooden porch rocker. She also saw the almost-empty whiskey bottle between his legs, the cork lying discarded at his feet. He stared blankly off toward Haley Springs.

Ellen shook her head and walked closer. "Dear?" she said gently, stepping up behind her husband and laying a hand on his shoulder.

Waddell stiffened, making a slight gasp of surprise. Then he turned in the rocker and looked up at her through hollow, red-rimmed eyes. "For God sakes, don't sneak up on me like that! You give a man heart failure!"

"I'm not sneaking up," said Ellen. "I was concerned about you. You didn't come to bed."

"I have other things on my mind," he snapped at her. "There are other things besides going to bed, you know. Some of us have to figure out what to do next in the world!"

"Well, pardon me," Ellen said, seeing his dark

mood and not wanting to aggravate matters further. She backed up a step.

But Dave Waddell half rose from the rocker, the whiskey bottle falling to the porch and rolling back and forth. He snatched the bottle up before the last drops could spill from it. He threw back the last drink and let out a whiskey hiss, holding onto the empty bottle as he looked Ellen up and down. In her revealing cotton gown, Dave saw clearly the outline of her breasts. He gave her a look of disgust. "Don't run around here naked like some harlot!" He shot a frantic glance at the trail, as if someone might be watching.

"A harlot, did you call me?" Ellen's voice struggled to keep her anger in check.

"I'm sorry, I didn't mean that," said Dave, relenting, but only for a second. "But have you no shame? What if somebody happened along here and saw you this way?"

"Don't be ridiculous, David." She managed to swallow her anger and keep her voice settled. "Has anybody ever come along at this time of morning? We live far from town, far from any other ranch."

Dave Waddell slung the wooden rocker aside drunkenly and raged at her. "Don't you dare make light of what I say, woman! I'm the man of this house, and when I tell you something, I don't expect it to be turned into some lighthearted joke!"

Ellen Waddell turned rigid; her words turned cold. "Oh, don't you worry, *man of the house,* there won't be anything lighthearted going on in this household for a *long* time to come." She turned in a huff and disappeared inside the house, slamming the front door behind her.

It was an hour later when Dave Waddell walked inside and looked around. The coffeepot sat cold atop the stove, which was itself cold and unfired. The table sat empty. The door to the bedroom was closed. Dave rapped on the door gently, still feeling the effects of swigging whiskey all night. "I'm—I'm sorry, Ellen," he offered. "I reckon I just lost control of myself. Will you forgive me?"

His words were met by a chilled silence. He turned and left the house and spent the next two hours in the corral beside the barn, attending horses and preparing two of them for the trail. When he returned to the house, the kitchen looked the same. The bedroom door remained closed. "Honey, I've been thinking," said Waddell, rapping again gently. "Things have been getting the best of me lately around here." He paused, then added, "Remember how you said you'd like to go up to Denver? How you said you'd like to stay a few days in one of them fine hotels, where you pull a sash and get food brought up to you?"

After a slight pause, Dave heard the latch fall on the other side of the door. He breathed a sigh of relief. "Yes, I remember," said Ellen, not giving in all at once.

"Well, I've been thinking," Dave continued. "We've got the money, and we've got the time. . . . Hell, there ain't nothing keeping us here right now. What cattle is out there is in good grazing for now. What say we just up and take off?"

"You mean, soon?" Ellen asked, opening the door a crack, enough for Dave to see that she was still wearing her cotton gown. This time he was not at all disgusted at the sight of her breasts. In fact, this time the partial sight of her through the narrowly opened door stirred desire within him.

"Soon?" Dave chuckled, putting aside any ideas he might have just had and reminding himself that there was a good reason for what he was proposing. "Honey, I'm not talking about soon! I'm talking about right now . . . this minute. I've already saddled up two riding horses. I'll open the corral and turn the rest out to graze when we leave. Denver, here we come!"

"Oh, Dave, do you really mean it?" The door squeaked open another foot. "I mean, this isn't just the whiskey talking, is it?"

"Oh, yes, I'm sure the whiskey has a hand in it." Dave smiled, putting his arms around her and pulling her against him. "But, little darling, I've never been more serious about anything in my life."

"Oh my goodness, Denver!" Ellen squealed with delight, then pushed herself away from her husband. "Don't you dare change your mind! I'll throw some things in our grip bag and be ready before you know it!"

"You do that, darling, and hurry yourself up," Dave said, cutting a quick glance across the room, out the window toward the main trail. He watched Ellen throw back a blanket that covered the dressing trunk where she kept her clothes. As she began pulling out a hat box and a pair of lady's high-topped dress shoes, Dave said, "I'll grab a couple of clean shirts and some trousers when you're done. Meanwhile, hurry up!" He clapped his hands to speed her along. "I'll make sure all the dry food is topped and stored." Another glance out along the empty trail brought a sense of relief to him. "Who knows?" he said, feeling better by the minute. "We might be gone for the next month or two."

Chapter 5

"Well, now, look here," Cherokee Earl Muir said, crossing his wrists on his saddle horn and looking down at the Waddell spread from the shelter of a pine thicket lining a cliff behind the house. Four of his six men drew their horses up quietly around him. Earl had begun to split his men up, sending Frisco Bonham and Billy Boy Harper on head, riding a different trail in case anybody followed their tracks from Haley Springs.

"Don't forget, Boss," said Sherman Fentress. "We're down to six men now."

"I ain't worried about it, Sherman," said Earl. "Dave is the only gun on the place." He dismissed the matter and sat watching Dave Waddell lead two horses hurriedly from the barn to the front of the house until the tin roof blocked him from sight. Earl spit a stream of tobacco and said, "Looks like my new partner's in a big hurry to get someplace."

"Yep, it does," said Dirty Joe. "Why don't I punch a couple holes in him for you?" He reached down, slipped his rifle from its saddle boot, and started to raise it to his shoulder.

"Put that damned rifle down, Joe," said Earl. "I don't care where Davey goes." He chuckled under his breath, turning his gaze back to the house, studying it like a hungry wolf. "I just don't want him taking that pretty little redheaded woman with him. I would call that unobliging of him."

"*Sí*, Boss," said Jorge Sentores, grinning. "I thinks maybe you gots the plan for that pretty woman, eh?"

"Watch your dirty mind, Jorge," said Earl, his voice turning tight with indignation. "I'm not some pig . . . some animal who would dishonor a man's woman, him standing by whilst I done it."

"No, Boss, of course not," said Jorge, shrugging, unable to tell if Earl was serious or not. He looked at the others for some sort of clue. The men only stared down at the house in silence.

"All right, here's the deal," said Earl without taking his eyes off the house below. "We're going down there. Any of yas says anything out of the way to that little redheaded woman, it'll take you the rest of the day to pull my boot out of your ass."

"Can't we even say howdy?" asked Sherman Fentress, tweaking his thin, well-trimmed mustache.

"No," Earl said bluntly. "You especially can't say howdy to her."

"Not even if she says howdy first?" asked Fentress.

"Keep in mind the size of my boot," Earl Muir warned. He heeled his horse forward at a walk, down onto a thin path.

"Damn," Sherman Fentress objected quietly. "I never seen a person you can't even say howdy to."

Beside him, Dirty Joe said in a whisper, "I wouldn't cross him now if I was you, Sherman. You see what he did to that town back there."

"Yeah, I saw. I also saw that nobody back there ever told him a damn thing," said Fentress. "We've got no more notion where that woman and the old man is than when we started out."

"I know Earl," said Turley. "He's got a plan. I figure instead of riding into those hills, maybe facing an ambush, Earl figures after killing all them folks, that woman and the old man has got to come looking for us." He nudged his horse forward. "Then we've got them."

"Yeah, or they've got us," Sherman retorted, looking around at Jorge and the others. "I ain't sure which."

"I think this is a bad thing we have done, killing those peoples. I always steal the cattle. I am never been a murderer," Jorge said to Avery McRoy as they stepped their horses onto the trail behind Sherman and Dirty Joe.

"Well, you are now, Jorge," McRoy said, "so tell it to yourself a few times and get used to it. You've killed once, and I expect you'll have to kill some more before this traipse is over." The five horses moved down the path silently in single file.

Out front of the house, Ellen Waddell sat atop one of the horses, a small black gelding. "Dave, I thought you were in such a hurry to leave?" she called out playfully to the open door.

"Just one second," Dave replied. He jerked open the bottom drawer of the battered oak desk sitting against the back wall and pulled out the extra pistol he kept there. He hefted the small .36 caliber Navy Whitney in his hand, made sure it was loaded, and shoved it down into his belt. Then closed and buttoned his suit coat over it. "I want to make sure we don't leave here forgetting something we might need down the road." Before shutting the desk drawer he caught sight of a dusty bottle of whiskey. "One to grow on," he said to himself. He pulled the cork, raised the bottle to his lips, and drained it. Letting out a breath, he corked the empty bottle, put it back in the drawer, and locked the desk with a small key.

"Dave . . . ?" Ellen's voice trailed off with an edge of apprehension that Dave didn't notice in his rush to get under way.

"Shhh," said Cherokee Earl, sitting on his horse beside Ellen, lifting the reins from her hands. He leaned in close to Ellen's ear and said softly in his raspy voice, "Let's surprise ole Davey, what do you say?"

"I'm coming, I'm coming," Dave replied, hurrying through the house and out onto the porch. He closed the door behind him without even looking out at the five horsemen surrounding his wife. "You know, darling," he said, looking down at the door key in his hand for a second as he spoke, "if we like Denver, we might just arrange to have this place sold and never even have to come back—"

Dave's voice stopped as he looked up, stunned at the sight of Cherokee Earl sitting on his horse, too close to Ellen, holding her horse's reins in his gloved hand.

"Never come back." Earl chuckled flatly. "My, my, this must be some outing you've got planned. *Partner.*"

Ellen looked back and forth between her husband and this stranger with a puzzled, frightened expression. "David, what does he mean calling you partner? I think you better explain."

The surrounding horsemen stifled a short laugh under Cherokee Earl's cold gaze as he looked from one to the other then back at Dave Waddell. "Yeah, Davey, I agree with the little lady. Maybe you better explain some things. I get the feeling you haven't mentioned any of us pals here to your missus."

"Earl, I haven't had the chance, and that's God's truth," Waddell said in a shaky voice. He spread his hands. "I didn't know what became of you. We heard shooting last night coming from town. I was just on the verge of clearing out of here. I was worried something had happened to you."

"No fooling?" said Earl, turning his gaze to Ellen Waddell, seeing the look of total bewilderment on her face. "And what about you, ma'am? Was you worried something might have happened to us?" He offered a sly grin, pulling on her horse's reins, drawing the animal closer to him.

"I have no idea who you people are!" Ellen said sharply. She snatched at the reins and stopped her horse, but failed to free the reins from Earl's hand.

"Yeah, but if you did know us, would you have been concerned for my safety last night with all them guns going off?"

"David . . ." said Ellen, her voice still strong but issuing a plea for help."

"Earl, turn her horse loose," Waddell said, the firmness in his voice surprising even himself.

Heavy silence set in. Cherokee Earl gave Dave Waddell an even stare and stepped his horse forward, leading Ellen and her horse beside him. He stopped a foot from where Dave stood frozen in place. With exaggerated politeness, he held the reins down to him and said, "Begging your pardon, Davey, but the little lady's horse spooked a bit when we rode in. I grabbed the reins to keep her from a bad spill. I couldn't bear to see something bad happen to such a lovely woman. . . . Could you?"

Dave's face reddened, yet there was nothing he could do but stand there, powerless. He knew that Earl Muir wasn't going to allow him much more slack after talking the way he just had to Earl in front of his own men. "Of course not, Earl," Dave said, giving Ellen a glance to see if Earl had spoken the truth. The look on her face told him that it had been a lie. But again, what could he do about it? The bemused gleam in Earl's eyes told him the same thing. Earl could do what he pleased here. . . . No one could stop him. "Thanks for stepping in when you did."

"Think nothing of it, partner," Earl said, a dark smile on his face. "You'd have done the same for me had it been the other way around. . . . If I had myself a lovely wife and something bad was about to befall her, I bet you'd be in there like a shot. I hope so anyway. Partners ought to always be prepared to look out for one another . . . become like family, so to speak." As he spoke, he stepped his horse aside and looked Ellen up and down, not even trying to hide his lewd appreciation. "I've always said partnerships should be one big happy family."

"Why does he keep saying you're partners, David?" Ellen asked, avoiding Earl's eyes, ignoring his overtures.

"Ellen, it's a long story," Dave replied promptly. "I'll tell you everything about it as soon as—"

"Come on now, Davey," Earl cut in. "We can't be having secrets in this happy family of ours, now, can we?" He gave Waddell a wink, then said to Ellen, "You see, Davey and me has had ourselves an arrangement for some time now. I bring up border cattle—what you might say is beef of questionable origins. I give Davey here part of the herd just to let me hide them out here awhile in the upper grasslands. Then I crossbrand them, take them back down, and push them to the makeup herds heading for Abilene or Dodge City. We all make a little—Davey, the rest of the boys, and me—and nobody gets hurt." He grinned and crossed his wrists on his saddle horn.

"Cattle thieves? Rustlers?" Ellen looked back and forth between her husband and Earl Muir in disbelief. Then she said to Dave Waddell, "You've been involved with a cattle-rustling operation? All those cattle that have shown up here, and you told me they were strays that wandered onto the grazing range . . . all the while they were stolen?"

Before Dave could answer, Earl stifled a laugh and said, "Oops, I sure hope I haven't spilled the beans on you, Davey. That was not my intention."

"Ellen," Dave said, fighting to keep control of his voice and to keep his wits about him, "you'll have

to let me explain everything to you. . . . And I will,
I swear I will, only not right now, not right here.
This isn't the time or place!"

Ellen Waddell saw beads of perspiration form on
her husband's forehead.

"Yeah, you best go along with your husband, Missus Ellen," Earl said, including himself in their conversation. "There ain't time for explaining things
now. We've got to get our horses changed and get
moving."

"Get moving?" Ellen stepped hurriedly down from
her saddle and stood by her husband's side. "Earl,
tell them to leave," she whispered close to his ear.

"Yep, you heard me right," said Earl. "We've got
to cut out of here fast. You heard the shooting last
night—you said so yourself. We killed everybody in
that town and left it burnt to a cinder. I reckon we'll
soon have somebody dogging our trail. I don't want
them coming out here sniffing around, maybe getting
you to tell them where we might be headed. I like
you, partner, but I've got to tell you: I'd kill a man
before I'd leave him to jackpot me to the law." Earl
gave Dave a hard stare.

"Earl, we can't go with you," said Dave, with a
sinking feeling in the pit of his stomach. "We're
heading north, going to take a few days of holiday
in Denver."

"Well, that's just fine. We'll head right along with
you," said Earl. "Never let it be said that I'd spoil a
holiday for anybody."

"Our plans are already made, Earl," said Dave,
slipping an arm around his wife's waist as if to protect her. "We prefer traveling just the two of us. You
don't have to worry about either of us telling the law
about you. I stand to lose as much as you do if I did
something like that. I don't want to get arrested for
harboring stolen cattle."

"I beg to differ with you, Davey," said Earl, "but

you don't stand to lose as much as I do." Pointing a gloved finger at him, Earl stepped his horse closer as he continued. "They'll drop the charges on you just to get to me." He turned his horse sideways to them and leaned slightly down. "I can't afford that, partner, now can I?"

Before either Dave or Ellen could say another word, Earl leaned farther down, snatched Ellen under her arm, and swung her upward. Ellen let out a short scream and batted her fists against Earl's shoulders as he held her against his chest. He stepped his horse back as Dave Waddell lunged at him.

"Let her go, Earl! Let her go!" Dave shouted. He grabbed at Earl's stirrup, but Earl cocked his boot and kicked him back a step.

"Now you've gone and done it, partner," Earl said, seeing Dave stagger backward, his hand going for his pistol. Earl drew his first, aimed it, and cocked it, keeping Ellen against him, giving Dave nothing to shoot at but his wife. "You was going to shoot me, I do believe!" Earl said in mock surprise. Dave stopped cold and spread his hands away from his gun belt.

"Earl, I'm sorry! I didn't mean it!" said Dave. "Just let her go!"

Earl shook his head. "No, no, partner. I just can't overlook something like that. I suppose I'm going to have to go on and kill you." He leveled his pistol out at arm's length.

"No, wait!" Ellen shouted, squirming against Earl's arm. "Don't kill him, please!" She spoke quickly. "It's me you want, but don't kill him! If you kill him, you'll have to kill me too—I swear it! Leave him alone, and I'll go with you. I'll do anything you say! You have my word! Just let him live."

"Well, listen to this," Earl chuckled, letting his pistol slump, not as intent now on shooting Dave Waddell. "This little honey of yours ain't no fool, Davey. She knows this ain't really about you saying anything to the law." He lowered his pistol and hugged Ellen up closer, pressing his beard-stubbled cheek to hers. "We're going to get along fine, you and me," he said, half whispering his words to Ellen as he watched the sickened expression on Dave's face.

Backing his horse without taking his eyes off Dave Waddell, Earl called out over his shoulder. "Sherman, get over here and give me a hand."

Sherman Fentress kicked his horse forward, snatching Ellen Waddell from Earl's arm as Earl held her out to him. "Keep an eye on his little filly while I step down and talk some sense to my partner here."

"Earl. Let her go, please!" said Dave Waddell. "I'm begging you." Almost sobbing, Dave stepped forward, still carefully keeping his hands away from his guns as Earl slipped down from his saddle and swaggered up to him, pulling off his right glove one finger at a time.

"Davey, get a grip on yourself." Earl threw his arm across Waddell's shoulders, drawing him close almost in a headlock, the same way he had earlier. "Listen to me, partner. We can kick this subject back and forth and call it anything we want to." He slipped Dave's Colt .45 from its holster and shoved it down behind his belt as he continued speaking. "But the fact is, I'm taking that woman with me. . . . I'm doing as I please with her, and I'm keeping her as long as it suits me. You might as well understand and get used to it." He spread Dave's suit coat open, eased the small .36 caliber pistol from his waist, and held it barrel first in his hand, hefting it, judging its weight. "When I'm through with her, you can have her back."

"No, Earl, please, for God sakes!" Dave begged, his eyes filled with tears. "Don't do this. . . . That's my wife."

"Wives, cattle, horses, what have you." Earl
shrugged. "It makes no difference to me. . . . I take
what I want. You ought to seen this coming from a
mile down the road. Hell, man, I'm a thief and a
killer. You think her being your wife means a damn
thing to me? You ought to have had better sense,
dangling something as sweet and pretty as that little
redheaded woman before my eyes. I'd be a fool not
to take a taste. What made you think you could deal
with the likes of me and ever come out ahead?"

"Earl, please—"

Dave Waddell's voice fell silent as Earl bowed him
forward at the waist and crashed the butt of the
Navy Whitney against the back of his head. Seeing
her husband fall face forward into the dirt, Ellen
screamed long and loud, scratching the outlaw and
jerking free from Sherman Fentress's grip. She hit the
ground at a run toward her husband and didn't stop
until Earl's strong hand caught her by her arm and
slung her away. She landed in the dirt and came
crawling toward Dave Waddell. Earl swooped an
arm down, caught her around the waist, and held
her hanging down his side, kicking and screaming.
"He'll be okay . . . just wake up with a headache is
all. You gave your word you'd come with me, no
trouble. You ain't backing out on it, are you?" He
flipped the Whitney around and cocked it in Dave
Waddell's direction.

Ellen caught hold of herself, seeing the gun
pointed at her unconscious husband's head. "No,
wait!" She settled down immediately. "I won't cause
any trouble, I promise. I'll keep my word."

"All right then, that's more like it." Earl eased his
grip and let her stand on her feet. He slipped an arm
around her thin waist and hugged her up close. "I
swear, woman, since the first time I laid eyes on you
from a distance, it's been all I could do to keep my
hands off you." He nuzzled his face into her long,

flowing red hair, the scent of her seeming to over-power him for a second as he closed his eyes.

"I won't be any problem from now on," Ellen said in a soft, relenting voice. "Whatever you want, I'll do it."

Earl's breath quickened at the sound of her voice. "Lord, what a waste, something like you hooked to the likes of something like him." He shook his head as if to clear it. "But that's over now." Then he turned, pulling her back to the horses. "Come on, let's get these horses swapped out and put some miles between us and Haley Springs. I've got to get an ambush set up for a couple of real tough gunslingers who're going to be on our trail." He grinned and spoke to Ellen as he dragged her along. "The more you get to know me, the more you'll come to realize that I'm a man who likes staying one step ahead of the game."

Ellen looked back once more at where her husband lay crumpled in the dirt, a trickle of blood oozing down the back of his head. Then she forced herself to swallow the bitter taste in her mouth and follow Cherokee Earl at a quicker pace, trying her best to keep up with him.

"Where we headed from here, Boss?" asked Sherman Fentress, hoping nothing would be said about the way the woman had broken free from him. But Earl was letting nothing past him.

"I reckon the first place ought to be a doctor so's you can have your face looked at. You've let this little girl scratch you like a wildcat." He walked steadily on, pulling the woman behind him. The men laughed as they stepped down and led their horses toward the corral.

Sherman turned red and touched his fingers to the stripe of blood along his cheek. "Aw, this ain't nothing. She just wiggled loose is all." He hurried to catch up with Earl.

"Yeah, wiggled loose," Earl said wryly. "Go help swap out some horses. We've been here long enough."

"But where are we headed from here, Boss?" Sherman persisted. "We told Billy and Frisco we'd meet them along the south trail."

"I lied, Sherman. . . . Those two are on their own. I used them as bait for the woman gunslinger and the old man. We're going to throw a little raid on the next town up the line, get ourselves some real money. Then we're heading north of here, where there's good ambush country. By the time Billy and Frisco tangle with the woman and the old man, we'll be higher up, able to look down at anything on our trail. This is how I'm going to play it—instead of looking all over for them, I'll keep them looking for me, right up until I'm ready to kill them."

Chapter 6

Within moments, Cherokee Earl and his men had swapped their tired horses for fresh ones from the corral. As the group gathered at the corral gate, Earl looked over at where Dave Waddell stirred slightly in the dirt. "Hold these for me, Turley," he said, handing Dirty Joe the reins to Ellen's horse. "I've got one last thing to do before I leave."

Ellen gasped as Earl turned his horse toward Dave Waddell. Hearing her, Earl looked back over his shoulder. "Don't worry. I ain't going to kill him. Bullets cost money."

As he rode his horse across the yard, Sherman Fentress said to Dirty Joe in a hurt tone, "I don't know why he didn't ask me to hold the reins. I'm the one he was always asking to do stuff like that."

"Because you messed up, you idiot." Dirty Joe laughed. "You let this woman scratch your face and make a fool of you." He jiggled the reins to Ellen's horse, grinned, and winked at her. "Ain't that right, sugar?"

Ellen looked away from Turley's leering face.

"Don't talk to her that way, Turley," Sherman warned.

Turley laughed; so did Jorge and Avery McRoy. "Boys, I believe Sherman's gone lovestricken on us."

"*Sí*," said Jorge, "and I think it is not such a wise thing, to fall for the boss's woman."

Dirty Joe's voice fell quieter, just audible to those

near him. "The boss's woman today, maybe. But who can say about tomorrow? He might decide what's good enough for himself is good enough for all of us. I don't reckon ole Sherman here would object to that, would you, pal?" He gave Sherman a sly look.

"You best watch your dirty mouth, Joe, I'm warning you!" said Sherman Fentress, his hand dropping to the pistol handle on his hip.

Ellen listened closely to every whispered word, knowing that her only chance out of this was to keep her wits and weigh every possibility. Halfway across the dirt yard, she saw Cherokee Earl turn in his saddle upon hearing Sherman's angry voice. "Can't you men be this close to a woman without it turning you into lunatics?"

The men fell silent. Earl shook his head and rode the last few steps over to Dave Waddell, who tried to struggle to his feet. "You lay right there, Davey," said Earl, bumping his horse into Waddell, sending him back face down in the dirt. "I like looking down at you."

"Don't—don't take her . . . please," Dave gasped, dirt-streaked tears streaming down his face, a string of spittle dangling from his lips.

"Oh, I'm taking her, Dave. That's already been settled." Earl grinned, drawing the Whitney from his waist. As he continued to speak, he opened the percussion gun's cylinder and dropped out all of the loads but one. "But I want it to be said that I was a good sport about this." Then he closed the gun and pitched it to the ground a few feet from Waddell's dirt-crusted hands.

"Please . . .!" Dave glanced at the pistol but made no move for it. Then he dropped his cheek back to the dirt.

"There you are, partner," said Earl, stepping his horse to the side, hoping for Ellen to get a look at what was going on. "You've got one shot in there.

Either take it at me whilst I turn and ride away with her, or else after I leave . . .'' He let his words trail, then added, "Well, I reckon you can use your imagination what to do with it then. One bullet can mean a lot to a man, depending how he uses it." He turned his horse and heeled it away, unconcerned about Dave Waddell going for the pistol. If Earl heard the sound of the pistol cock behind him, he knew he was fast enough to turn and kill Dave Waddell without batting an eye.

At the corral, Earl took the reins to Ellen's horse from Dirty Joe Turley and said to the men, "Let's ride, boys." Then, as his men heeled their horses up and rode off in a rise of dust, Earl turned to Ellen, who sat staring across the yard at her sobbing husband in the dirt. "That's it. Take one good long look at him. Did you see? I threw him a gun . . . gave him a chance to claim you or let you ride off with me. He was too scared to make a move. He'd rather wallow in the dirt to save his own hide. That ought to show you clear enough which one of us can protect a woman when it comes down to it."

Ellen summoned her courage and said with an air of defiance, "I didn't marry to have a man protect me."

Earl started at her for a second, grinned, and said, "Then maybe you should have."

Dave Waddell lost track of how long he'd lain sobbing in the dirt, his head still pounding where Cherokee Earl had knocked him cold. The sun had moved lower in the western sky by the time he collected his senses enough to drag himself to his feet and stagger to the front porch. On his way, he managed to stoop down and pick up the Navy Whitney. After collapsing onto a porch chair, he wiped his blurry eyes and checked the pistol, seeing that only one round of ammunition remained in the cylinder. For a moment he

was lost, but then the whole terrible, hopeless scene
came back to him. He gazed out and along the trail
leading up over a rocky rise to the north.

"God, what have I done?" he whispered aloud to
himself. Then he hung his head and stared long and
hard at the pistol in his trembling hands. He had no
idea how long he sat there, cocking and uncocking
the Whitney. But evening shadows had grown tall
and thin across the dusty, rocky land when he finally
left the gun cocked and raised it slowly until he felt
the hard steel tip of the barrel against the side of his
throbbing head. He took a deep, tortured breath and
held it, struggling to keep his hand from shaking
uncontrollably. He pressed back on the trigger slowly.

When the sound of a pistol shot exploded, he flung
the cocked pistol away in horror. His first thought
was that he'd done it, he'd actually shot himself
through the head. Yet, if that was the case, how was
he still here, alive and able to wonder about it? He
sat frozen, stunned, his mouth hanging open. On the
front of the house, he saw the bullet hole, right where
he had heard it thump into the plank siding. He rose
woodenly halfway from his chair, leaning toward the
fallen pistol as he looked out at the two riders coming across the front yard. "Stand real still, Mr. Waddell," said Danielle Strange. "That shot wasn't meant
to kill you. It was meant to keep you from killing
yourself."

"I—I understand," Dave managed to say, his mind
becoming clearer. He'd seen Danielle Strange in town
enough times to recognize her. He'd never seen the
old man before, but there was no doubt the two were
on Cherokee Earl's trail. He had to think up something to keep anyone from knowing he'd been a part
of Earl's stolen-cattle operation. "Thank God you've
come along!" He straightened up and wiped his
shirtsleeve across his face.

Danielle and Stick swung down from their saddles,

keeping an eye on Dave and taking a quick, steely look around the place. Danielle nodded at the Navy Whitney lying on the porch, cocked and ready to fire. "What's going on here, mister?" she asked, stepping up onto the porch, then reaching down and picking up the gun. She looked the gun over, noting the single round of ammunition in the cylinder. Then she let the hammer down gently but didn't hand the gun to Dave Waddell when he reached out for it.

Dave dropped his hand and rubbed it on his trousers. "It's not what you think, ma'am," he said.

"Oh? And what do I think?" Danielle responded.

"Well, I know it looked like I was getting ready to shoot myself. But I wasn't—that is, I wouldn't have. . . . I don't think." Dave struggled with his words while Danielle and Stick only stared at him. Finally he gave up and collapsed into the chair. "What's the difference? Maybe I should have pulled that trigger." He hung his head and continued. "I know why you're riding this way—you're hunting for Cherokee Earl and his bunch. And yes, they were here. They took my horses and my wife, Ellen. Then they rode on."

Stick and Danielle looked at one another, then back at Dave Waddell. "They took Miss Ellen?" Danielle asked.

"Yes," said Dave. Then he asked, a bit surprised, "You . . . knew my Ellen?"

"We only met once," said Danielle, "at the mercantile in Haley Springs. How long have they been gone? We'll have to catch them quick, before . . ." She cut herself off, letting her words trail, but Dave caught what she'd kept from saying.

"I'm not sure," he said, rubbing the back of his head. "Cherokee Earl knocked me out. Then they took her and rode off. It's been a while—I know that."

Stick butted in. "Damn it, man, weren't you going after them?"

"Easy, Stick," said Danielle, although she had been wondering the same thing.

"I wanted to," Dave said, a slight whine to his voice. He gestured a hand toward the empty corral. "But as you can see, they took all the fresh horses." Fifty yards away, three of the spent mounts left by Earl Muir's men grazed on scattered clumps of wild grass.

Stick said, "So instead of cooling out one of them horses and going to save your wife, you decided to blow your brains out." He shook his head.

Danielle cut Stick off with a firm gaze. She looked back at Dave, studying his eyes as she spoke. "I've got a string of horses waiting just beyond the rise in the road. Are you up to going with us to get your wife back?"

"Yes, of course!" Dave sprang to his feet. "I didn't mean to give you the notion that I wasn't interested in saving her. You just have to excuse me. . . . That lick on the head has left me addled."

"Then go throw some water on your face," said Stick. "Be ready to go when I bring the horses in here." He turned, climbed into his saddle, and looked down at Danielle as Dave Waddell staggered into the house. "Don't turn your back on that peckerwood," he cautioned her in a low, guarded tone. "Something ain't right about him."

"Don't worry about me," said Danielle, her hand resting on her pistol butt. "But let's give the man the benefit of the doubt. A hard lick on the head can take a spell to get over."

"Yeah," said Stick, backing his horse. "The question is, why'd he let a bunch like Earl Muir's boys ever get close enough to do it in the first place?"

"I wondered that myself," said Danielle under her

breath, watching Stick tug his hat brim down and ride off toward the rise in the trail.

"There, all ready to go," said Dave Waddell, coming back through the open door, drying his head on a wadded-up towel.

Danielle looked off along the trail as Stick disappeared over the rise. "He'll be a couple of minutes," she said. She looked at the empty holster on Dave's hip, much too big for the smaller, slimmer Navy Whitney, she noted to herself. Then she leveled her gaze into Dave Waddell's eyes and said, "This Cherokee Earl is known as a cattle rustler. How many head of cattle are you running now, Mr. Waddell?"

Dave Waddell made the mistake of not holding her gaze as he answered. Instead, he ducked his eyes for a second and said, "It's been a while since I pulled a head count. Must have upward of three, four hundred head maybe."

"The cattle business has gotten so good a man don't need to keep track of his holdings anymore?" Danielle asked, not even hiding her skepticism.

"Well. Miss Danielle, you know how it is," said Dave, holding the wet towel to the back of his head. "Cattle come and go on the breaks and high grasslands. But if I was held to it, I'd say I've got three hundred head, easy enough."

"You've had quite a run of luck then," said Danielle. On a bluff, she added, "Last year when I talked to Ellen in town, she said you only had about half that many."

"She did, huh?" said Dave, looking as if he couldn't understand why. He offered a weak, patient smile that Danielle saw through right away. "My Ellen's a fine wife, but she never knew beans about my cattle business. My fault, I suppose. . . . I should have told her more, I reckon. But the only gains I made this year are a couple of range strays wandering in, plus my calves, of course."

"I see," said Danielle. Noticing Stick top the rise with the string of horses in tow, Danielle decided not to pursue any more questions right then. Instead, she flipped the Whitney around in her hand and handed it to Dave Waddell, butt first. "If this is what you carry, you best load it up. If you want to borrow a big Colt .45, I've got an extra in my saddlebags."

"Much obliged. I'll take you up on the offer," said Dave, shoving the small Navy Whitney into his belt. "I normally carry a Colt, but Cherokee Earl took it after he knocked me out."

Danielle only nodded, but Dave could tell she had just asked herself how a man with two loaded guns could allow himself to be so easily caught off guard. "Look, Miss Danielle, I know how bad this looks on my part. But all I can say is that it happened so fast I never got a chance to act. There's nothing in this world I want more than to get my wife back safe and sound. After that, I don't care what anybody thinks of me."

"Take it easy, Mr. Waddell," said Danielle. "We're both on the same side here. I want Earl Muir for the killings in town, but saving your wife is all the more important." Her gaze narrowed as she added, "Anything we need to talk about can wait. Fair enough?"

"Fair enough for me, Miss Danielle," said Dave.

"All right then." Danielle stepped down and opened the saddlebags behind Sundown's saddle. She pulled out a thick cloth, unfolded it, and took out a large Colt. She checked the gun, made sure it was loaded, then passed it to Dave. "Here you go. And now that we're gong to be working together for a while, I want you to drop the Miss. . . . Just call me Danielle." She looked up at Stick and said, "That goes for you too, Stick, all right?"

Stick blushed at such an informality but nodded in agreement. "All right then, Miss—" He caught his error and quickly said, "I mean, Danielle."

*   *   *

Braden Flats, Indian Territory

Outside the New Royal Saloon, Sheriff Oscar Matheson stepped down from the boardwalk and moved out into the dirt street, getting a better look at the five men and one woman who had just ridden in from the glittering stretch of sand. It took a second for him to see that one of the men held a short lead rope to the woman's horse. What was this about? he wondered. The riders had now stopped in a low cloud of dust. They sat abreast at the edge of town, staring along the darkened shade of boardwalk over-hangs and recessed doorways. Matheson didn't like the looks of this. Keeping a wary eye on the group, he said to his part-time deputy, young Gerald Noel, "Boy, I believe you best go round up the blacksmith and some others. Tell them to bring their guns."

But Gerald didn't look up right away. He stood on the boardwalk, whittling intently with his pocketknife, shaving long, fresh-curled strips of pine from a stick.

"Did you hear me, boy?" said Matheson, raising his voice a bit, still staring at the riders fifty yards away. "We might have trouble coming."

"Huh?" Gerald raised his eyes grudgingly from his pastime, a long, curled pine sliver falling from behind his short knife blade. He managed to catch the word *trouble*. His eyes shifted in the same direction as the sheriff's. "Holy!" he exclaimed in a hushed tone. The blade of his pocketknife snapped shut. He bounded down from the boardwalk in a run, his low-topped shoes batting up dust as he cut straight across the street toward the blacksmith's shop.

At the end of the street, Cherokee Earl said, "Joe, you got him?"

"Sure do, Boss," Dirty Joe replied, raising his rifle from across his lap and cocking it on the upswing.

"Oh, Lord, it's commenced," Sheriff Matheson whispered, seeing what was about to happen. As he stepped sideways, drawing his pistol, he shouted, "Look out, Gerald!"

But instead of the sheriff's words causing the young deputy to duck behind cover somewhere, Gerald skidded to a halt on the other side of the street. He turned and looked back at Matheson, spreading his arms. "What?" he asked, having no idea that a rifle was honing in on him.

"For God sakes, Gerald, run!" Matheson screamed. He raised his pistol as he spoke and fired repeatedly toward the horsemen, hoping his shots would throw off the rifleman's aim. But it didn't work.

"Got him, Boss!" said Dirty Joe in the wake of the rifle shot resounding along the street. The shot struck Gerald Noel in the chest like the blow of a sledge-hammer. He flew backward a step, bowing at the waist, his left shoe leaving his foot, exposing his big toe through a hole in his worn-out sock. His shirt puffed out in the back. A wide spray of blood rose and fell. Gerald managed to straighten up for a second. Then he sank to his knees, his arms falling limp at his sides, and pitched face forward in the dirt.

Even as the sheriff's pistol shots whistled past them, Avery McRoy gigged his spurs to his horse's sides, drew his pistol, and shouted, "He nailed that sucker right through the heart, good as ever I've seen."

Hearing the gunfire from his shop, the blacksmith dropped his hammer. "What the hell?" he said, and hurried out the front door in time to see the horsemen descend upon the town like a pack of ravaging wolves. Three shots thumped into the front of his shop, forcing him back inside. But not for long. Grabbing a double-barreled shotgun from against the wall, he ran outside again. This time he stood his ground long enough to fire both barrels into the oncoming flurry of men, guns, and horses.

Sherman Fentress's horse took most of the double blast of buckshot in its side. Fentress felt his left leg ripped to shreds as the horse whinnied painfully and slammed into the horse beside it, the horse Ellen Waddell was riding, being led at a full run by Cherokee Earl.

All Ellen could do was hold on to the saddle horn with all her strength. Sherman Fentress's horse tried to right itself but couldn't. With Fentress himself badly wounded and barely able to stay in his saddle, the poor horse veered away blindly, still at a run, until it hit the edge of the boardwalk and rolled up onto it. Fentress left the saddle and crashed through the front plank wall of the telegraph office, landing spread-eagle on the operator's desk, sending the telegraph machine across the room.

The telegraph clerk had heard the shooting and luckily had just pushed his chair back from his desk to go see what was happening in the street. Seeing the bloody man land on his desk in a spray of broken boards, the clerk gasped and sat frozen, his hands held chest high as if he were being robbed. Fentress groaned and lay staring at the clerk, his leg chewed to the bone by buckshot, bloody face and chest filled with splinters. "God . . . I'm hurt," he managed to say.

The sound of Fentress's voice caused the telegraph clerk to snap out of his dazed state. He sprang from his chair and ran shrieking from his office out into the roaring gunfire. Six bullets pounded into him no sooner than he'd leaped out into the street. He only had time to see the bodies of the sheriff, the deputy, the blacksmith, and two other townsmen before he crumbled to the ground and joined them in death.

Cherokee Earl had stepped down from his horse and forced Ellen Waddell to step down and stand beside him, his left arm wrapped firmly around her thin waist. Inside the town's bank, Arnold Flekner, the bank president, hurriedly locked the front door. Seeing him through the glass, Cherokee Earl chuckled and said to Jorge Sentores, "Get around there, Jorge, and take care of him." Then Earl pressed his face to Ellen's hair, took a deep breath, and said to her, "Watch this. . . . He'll try running out the back door any minute now. But Jorge will smoke him."

Ellen shuddered, filled with horror by all that had just gone on around her. Yet she stood in wide-eyed silence, unable to turn her eyes from the carnage.

Jorge raced his horse alongside the brick and wood bank building, sliding the animal to a halt just in time to catch the bank president as he ran away from the back door, a ring of keys in his hand.

"No! No! Please!" the hapless banker pleaded. "Here, take the keys!" He flung them up to Jorge, but Jorge let them fall to the ground. "The money's all yours! But please don't kill me!"

Jorge shrugged. "Okay, I won't kill you. Now you go, take off, get out of here, *pronto*!"

"Oh God, thank you! Thank you!" the poor man sobbed, turning as he moved away, his legs visibly shaking through his black trousers.

"Here comes the fun part," Earl whispered into Ellen's hair, his breath hot against her skin.

Ellen managed to squeeze her eyes shut as Jorge extended his pistol down at the fleeing banker's head. Three shots resounded, followed by Earl's low laughter near her ringing ear. "See? Jorge was just funning with him. . . . I knew he'd kill him."

Ellen felt a bitter sickness well up at the back of her throat. She fought to hold it down and did, taking a deep breath and reminding herself that the only way she could survive this lot that had been cast upon her was to refuse to let this or anything else get to her. She knew this was only the beginning. There were worse things ahead of her, and if she wanted to live through this, she had to prepare herself mentally. *You can do it! You can do it!* she repeated to herself. By sheer determination, she forced herself to block out Earl's words as his raspy voice whispered to her. She forced herself to no longer smell his hot breath or feel his smothering, hot arm around her.

"Hey! Hey! Wake up now! You're missing everything!" Earl chuckled, shaking her back and forth against him. Her eyes had closed slightly. But now she stared silently up at the grinning, beard-stubbled face held so close to hers. "You're riding with a rough bunch, darling. It ain't going to get no better, so you might as well learn to take it."

As he shook her, she felt the edge of a pistol butt dig into her side. It was the pistol that he'd taken from her husband and shoved down into his belt. She had a sudden urge to grab the pistol and use it on herself before he could stop her. But something kept her from doing it. *You don't deserve this,* she told herself. *You're not the one who should die.* She put the notion of grabbing the pistol out of her mind for now and said in a meek voice, "I'll be all right." Then, biting her tongue to keep from shouting it aloud, she said to herself as she imagined her hand closing around the pistol butt the first chance she had when he wasn't looking, *I'll take anything a worthless pig like you can dish out.*

Chapter 7

For more than two hours Cherokee Earl's men pillaged and terrorized the helpless town. With a bullet through his right shoulder and another through his left hip, Sheriff Oscar Matheson could do no more than get out of the gunmen's way and stay out of their sight. Avery McRoy and Dirty Joe forced the town doctor, Latimar Callaway, to clean and dress Sherman Fentress's leg wound and the many cuts, scraps, and broken ribs Fentress had received when he'd blasted headlong through the front wall of the telegraph office. Once the doctor had finished, he left Fentress lying on the billiard table and nursing a bottle of red rye in the New Royal Saloon. Making sure no one was watching, the old doctor hurried from the saloon to the livery barn, where he'd left Sheriff Matheson resting on a pile of fresh straw.

"Who goes there?" Sheriff Matheson asked, hearing the barn door creak open as a sliver of sunlight striped across the dirt floor.

Dr. Callaway whispered as he closed the door and heard the sound of a pistol cock in the grainy darkness, "It's me, Oscar, dang it! Don't cock that hammer at me. The shape you're in, that thing could go off. Then who'd be left here to look after you?"

"Sorry, Doc," Sheriff Matheson said in a weak voice. Lying with his back propped against a stall post, he let the cocked pistol drop across his lap. The doctor stepped into the stall and frowned, seeing the

pistol in the faint striped sunlight through the cracks
in the barn wall. "Give me that," Dr. Callaway said,
stooping and taking the gun from Matheson's hand.
He let the hammer down and shoved the pistol into
the holster lying by Matheson's side. "Confounded
guns!" he growled. "They're the cause of all the trouble in this world."

"Don't start on guns, Doc," Sheriff Matheson said
in a voice labored with pain. "If I hadn't had this
with me a while ago, I reckon I'd be dead right
now."

"I suppose," the doctor grumbled, already opening
the dressing on the sheriff's upper right chest. "Of
course, if those jackasses didn't have guns, they
couldn't have shot you in the first place. That's how
a more civilized man would reason with it."

"I'm all for civilization, Doc," Matheson said, offering a tired, painful smile. He nodded toward the
street beyond the dark, quiet shelter of the barn. Distant laughter rose above the sound of breaking glass.
"How bad is it out there?" Two pistol shots roared
from the direction of the saloon.

"It's bad enough," the doctor said, shaking his
head as he examined the sheriff's wounds. "The
blacksmith buckshot one of them, sending him sail-
ing. The ringleader laid up at the Crown Hotel with
some woman under his arm before the smoke
cleared. Poor Gerald's dead, so's our telegraph
clerk . . . our banker, the blacksmith too. We didn't
have many folks here to begin with. This will just
about do us in."

"The Crown Hotel, huh?" said Matheson.

"I saw him go there," the doctor replied. "Can't
say the woman looked real happy. They might've
just had a lovers' spat or something."

Thinking about it for a moment, Sheriff Matheson
said, "I sure did let this town down, didn't I?"

"Hush, Sheriff," said the doctor, "you know better

than that. You did the best you could. Nobody will ever fault you for what's happened here."

"I fault myself," said Matheson.

"Then I reckon that's your own stubborn lawman's prerogative," said the doctor, looking closely at the wound before closing the sheriff's shirt over the bloodstained bandage, "so I won't waste my breath arguing with you. I won't change this dressing until it clots up some more." He turned his attention to the dressing beneath the sheriff's split trouser leg. "Lucky this one didn't hit the bone. A feller your age gets a shattered hip bone, he's ready for the pasture, if he can even walk out to it."

"Yeah, a feller *my age* . . ." Matheson let his words trail in contemplation.

"No offense, Sheriff," said Doc Callaway. "But like myself, you've grown long in the tooth."

"I reckon I have, Doc." A silence passed as the doctor spread the split on the sheriff's trouser leg, pulled back the corner of the bloody bandage, and looked at the wound. Sheriff Matheson let out a long breath. "I was getting ready to retire, hand in my badge, you know."

The doctor turned his eyes upward, looking at the sheriff above his spectacle rims. "I had no idea."

"Well, it's true," said Matheson. "I've got a daughter I ain't seen since she was nine . . . when her ma up and left me in Abilene. She's married to a rancher out in California. They've got two freckle-faced kids. She wrote me, said, 'Pa, come on out, meet your grandchildren.' " He nodded and gazed off across the darkened barn. "That's where I was retiring to."

"Well . . . you still can, can't you?" the old doctor inquired, closing the bandage, then the split trousers.

Sheriff Matheson continued staring off as he spoke. "She said they've got a room off to the side of the house where I could stay—close the door and be left alone days I didn't want to talk to nobody." He grinned. "I reckon folks with grandchildren never get lonesome for talk or for getting their stories listened to."

"I reckon not," said the doctor. "You could go there, say, a week from now, maybe two. Lay low for now. Let this bunch of trash clear out of here. Give these wounds time to heal, and then head for California. Nothing's stopping you."

"I know it," said Matheson. His fingertips brushed the tin star on his chest. "My daughter said you can ride less than three miles from her front door and stand on a cliff that looks out over the ocean. Can you imagine that, Doctor?"

"Sounds real fine, Sheriff," said Dr. Callaway. "I envy you."

Another silence passed, and the doctor saw the trace of a tear in the sheriff's tired, distant eyes. "Well, hell, Sheriff," he said with resolve. "I suppose you'll want me to bring you a shotgun?"

"Yep. The biggest 10-gauge double-barrel you can find, Doc," said Sheriff Matheson. "I'd hate going out with whimper instead of a bang."

"But can you get on your feet and walk by yourself?" the doctor inquired.

"I'll walk on my own when the time comes. I might need you to help me to my feet." The sheriff managed a thin, tight smile. "I reckon you'll do that much for the only man in town who ever kept his bill paid."

Dr. Callaway returned the thin smile. "Well, I can see you're feeling much better." He patted a hand on the sheriff's good shoulder as he closed his black bag and stood up. "I want you to know I'm not the kind of man who can shoot a person, Sheriff, no matter how justifiable the situation."

"I understand, Doc," said Matheson. "I'd never ask you to. Just get me a shotgun and get me on my feet. Wearing this badge has always meant I'd be the one to take the bullet . . . or give it, however way the chips fall."

The old doctor nodded as he backed away toward the door. "I'll be back as quick as I can."

Sheriff Matheson watched the door open a crack then close. Outside, Dr. Callaway slipped unnoticed along the backs of the buildings toward the New Royal Saloon, where he knew the owner kept a spare loaded shotgun stuck beneath a whiskey pallet in the stockroom. On his way to the back door of the saloon, the doctor saw the first steam of smoke rise atop the buildings from the direction of the telegraph office. "Sonsabitches," he whispered to himself, hearing hoots of drunken laughter from the street.

Finding the rear door to the saloon unlocked, the old doctor slipped inside and held his breath as he passed the open stockroom door and saw Sherman Fentress lying atop the billiard table, drunk and waving a cocked pistol back and forth aimlessly. Dr. Callaway kept an eye on the wounded gunman as he slipped over to a darkened corner where a wooden pallet lay supporting a half dozen whiskey crates. Before his eyes grew accustomed to the darkness, the doctor reached a hand out to the crates. But instead of feeling the rough wood, he felt the familiar round hardness of a knee bone and jerked his hand back, startled, as a deep voice said, "Doc, what're you looking for, slipping around back here?"

"Damn it, Leonard! Scare the bejesus out of a man!" the doctor cursed in a whisper. "Sitting here in the dark like some lunatic!" He collected himself and took a deep breath, looking at the darkened face of Leonard Whirley, the saloon owner, sitting slumped atop a whiskey crate. Atop Whirley's head, a ruffled-up toupee sat crooked and slanted too far to one side. "Fix your hair, Leonard. It looks like a rat's got his head stuck in your ear."

The saloon owner reached up, adjusted the toupee,

and smoothed it down. "Sorry, Doc. Had I expected company, I would've been better groomed."

The doctor shot a glance out to the billiard table, seeing the bartender carry a fresh bottle of rye from behind the bar and hold it out to Sherman Fentress's grasping hands. Then he said, looking back at Whirley, "Sheriff Matheson is still alive and kicking. I reckon you know why I'm here?"

Whirley nodded and moved his right foot to one side. The doctor stooped down, pulled out the shotgun, blew dust from it, and broke it open, taking pains to keep his actions quiet. "There's a couple extra loads down there if you want them," said Whirley.

"Why not?" said the doctor, reaching back under the pallet and bringing out two shotgun loads. He dropped them into his pocket.

Watching the old doctor check the loaded shotgun, the despondent saloon owner said, "Believe it or not, I was just thinking about pulling that out myself. There's only five of them, one already wounded all to hell. I figured I could walk out and blast that bloody buzzard off my pool table, then go to the street and take my chances with the rest of them."

"Only five, huh?" The doctor stared at him for a second, then said, "Five is no small number when there's guns pointed at you."

"I said I was just thinking about it, Doc," said Whirley. "I never said for sure that I was going to do it."

"That's what I figured," the doctor said. "While you've been *thinking* about it," he said, clicking the shotgun shut, having seen that both barrels were loaded, "our sheriff is getting ready to do it." He looked the saloon owner up and down. "Of course, I don't suspect he'd be opposed to some help, if you'd like to join him."

Whirley swallowed a dry lump in his throat. "Who was I kidding, Doc? I ain't going to do nothing but sit here thinking how bad I want to. I ain't no hero. . . . I never was." His hand went nervously to his hairpiece. "I can always think things out, how to go about doing something like that. I can picture it in my mind clear as day. But I ain't got the sand to kill a person." His shoulders drooped even more. "I reckon all I can do is roll onto my back and show my belly like a beat dog."

"Don't be hard on yourself, Whirley," the doctor relented in a low tone. "I can't shoot a person either." He ran a hand along the glistening black gun barrel. "Oh, I say it's because I'm in the healing arts. Truth is, I'm as big a coward as you. I just plain ain't got the guts."

At the Crown Hotel, Cherokee Earl stepped into his trousers and pulled them up, turning back to face the bed where Ellen Waddell had just sat up and pulled a blanket around herself, clasping it under her arms, holding it closed in front. "What did you expect?" she said flatly, keeping her eyes from looking directly at him. "I've been dragged here against my will . . . by a total stranger. I've seen my husband left for dead."

"Well, I reckon I just expected a little more fire and thunder, darling," said Earl mockingly as he leaned forward, took her by the chin, and tilted her face up, forcing her to look into his eyes. "I might've thought that *just maybe* you'd be a little obliging, seeing as how I didn't leave you dead in the dirt. You know I could have had my way with you back there on that three-cow spread, then left . . . no witness, no nothing."

"Then why didn't you?" Ellen said, carefully weighing how much snap to put into her words.

"What kind of an animal did you think I was? Did you really think that I would just throw in with you after what you did to my husband?

Earl found himself stuck for words, looking into her eyes, not fully understanding what he was looking at. There was something puzzling about this woman. She hadn't fought him, hadn't resisted him. She in fact had done everything demanded of her. Yet he felt now as he'd felt before they'd arrived. He felt as if he hadn't touched her. Her eyes seemed to look straight through him. They made him think that, whatever he might say, she had already heard. "Don't play with me, woman!" he hissed, holding her chin roughly between his finger and thumb and leaning close to her face. She didn't so much as flinch or brace herself. She sat limp, spineless, he thought, but still untouchable. "Do you hear me?"

"I hear you," she said calmly, not trying to avert her eyes now but rather staring into his so steadily that he himself had to look away for a second.

"See . . . I believe there's more than meets the eye with you, little lady. I think maybe ole Dave Waddell didn't know the whole story on you when he hitched you to his wagon."

"I don't know what you're talking about," said Ellen, her eyes still steady, still cool and fixed.

"Yeah, I bet you don't," said Earl. "I get the feeling that you were an old hand at this sort of thing long before you crawled under Dave Waddell's blanket."

"Then you are badly mistaken, sir," said Ellen. "Mr. Waddell is the only man I have ever known."

"Until now, you mean," said Earl, a trace of a triumphant smile coming to his face.

"No . . . including now," she said distantly. "This doesn't count. This is just something that happened that never should have. It is best forgotten."

Earl stood frozen for a moment. Then he said with

an almost hurt sound to his voice, "Well, I ain't going to forget. And I still ain't had my fill of you."

"Very well," Ellen said softly. She started to unwrap the blanket from around herself in submission.

"Wait, damn it, not now." Earl stopped her, tucking the blanket back up under her arms. "That ain't what I meant." He ran his fingers back through his hair in frustration and chuckled. "See? See what I mean about you? You're as cold, spiteful, and deliberate as any whore I ever laid hands on. You don't fool me any longer."

"You think I'm a sporting woman?" Ellen asked flatly.

"I think you have been at some time or other," Earl offered.

"And if I was?" said Ellen. "Would that make any difference?"

Earl shrugged. "I wouldn't waste any more time on you if I was convinced you were. I have no respect for a sporting woman. I never did. I want a woman who is *my* woman—*mine alone*." He thumbed his bare chest.

"So you kidnap me? You force me to go to bed with you?" said Ellen. "That's the kind of woman you want? A slave?"

Earl looked confused. "Don't put words in my mouth. If I thought you was ever that kind of woman, I reckon I'd just turn you over to the rest of the boys, then ride on."

Ellen looked away now and took a breath, running a hand across her damp forehead. Then she sat quietly until Earl said, "So? Are you? I mean, was you ever?"

"No, of course not," said Ellen. "I was a schoolteacher, a professional woman, before I met my husband."

Earl reached out and suddenly grasped a handful

of her red hair, forcing her eyes back to his. "You're lying, ain't you?"

"If you think I'm lying, do what you just said." She stared back at him unflinchingly. "I'm powerless to stop you, whatever you've got in mind."

"Awww, damn it!" Earl turned loose her hair roughly, shoving her head sideways. "It doesn't have to be this way, woman! All you got to do is get used to being with me instead of Dave. Why is that so hard to do?"

Ellen stared at him. "Not hard at all if I were a bitch dog, or if I were the kind of woman you accused me of being. But you just said if I were that kind of woman, you would have no more use for me." She paused and shook her head. "I think you need to do some thinking about—"

Her words were cut short by a knock on the door and the sound of Dirty Joe's voice in the hallway.

"Yeah, Dirty, what is it?" said Earl. Before Joe Turley answered, Earl said to Ellen, "We'll finish this some other time."

Ellen didn't even bother to answer.

"Boss," said Turley from outside the door. "You said to come wake you up, tell you when we've done all we set out to do here."

A silence passed; then just as Dirty Joe started to knock again, Cherokee Earl growled in a sleepy voice, "All right, damn it to hell! I heard you! Hold your horses."

Dirty Joe looked back and forth quickly in the hallway as if to find some horses and do as he was told. But as the door opened a bit, Dirty Joe snatched his hat from his head and stood rapidly smoothing down his hair as Cherokee Earl stood, before him wearing only his trousers, his belt and fly both hanging open. "You sure are getting a case of the *propers,* ain't you, Dirty?" Earl opened his eyes wider and added, "Did you bring me any flowers?"

Dirty Joe looked embarrassed and wrung his hat brim between his hands, saying quickly in his own defense, "Boss, I just thought it might be the lady opening the door is all. . . . I didn't figure it would look right, me standing here with my hat on. That's all I meant by it, honest."

"I believe you, Dirty Joe," said Earl in a tired voice, stepping back and flagging him into the room. "If I'd thought otherwise, I'd have cracked your skull."

Inside the room, Joe started to speak, then fell silent when his eyes fixed on Ellen Waddell. She sat on the edge of the bed, shivering in spite of the heat, a blanket wrapped around her. She stared at the wall as if it were a thousand yards away. Her red hair lay damp and curled against her forehead and her bare shoulders.

"Well, Dirty," said Earl, seeing what affect a half-naked woman was having on this dumbstruck cattle rustler, "are you going to tell me what's gone on out there, or did you just stop by for tea?"

"Well, uh—" Dirty Joe stammered. "We, uh, looted all the, uh, cash from the, uh, bank—"

"Hold it, Dirty," said Earl, cutting him off. He reached out with both hands, took Dirty Joe by the shoulders, and turned him away from the woman. "Now try again."

Dirty Joe wiped a trembling hand across his brow and took a deep breath. "Sorry, Boss. What I meant was, the bank money came to a little over three thousand dollars." He settled himself and went on. "We got Sherman Fentress patched up and liquored up, and it looks like he might be all right. Jorge set fire to the telegraph office, so ain't nobody going to be telling on us . . . not for a while, anyway." His eyes drifted back around toward the woman as he spoke. "We, uh . . ."

"Joe, damn it!" said Earl, a threat rising in his voice. "Look at me when you talk!"

"Yes, Boss!" Joe snapped his eyes back to Earl. "We swapped out what fresh horses we could find, loaded a few bottles of rye for the trail . . . and I reckon we're ready to cut out of here most any time now." He felt his eyes draw toward the woman, but this time he caught himself and pulled them back to Earl. "When you're ready, that is."

"Good work, Dirty," said Earl. He started to say something else, but a shotgun blast coming from the street below caused both men to duck instinctively. "What the . . . ?" They both hurried to the window and looked down.

"Over there, Boss!" shouted Dirty Joe Turley, pointing down at the dirt street out front of the New Royal Saloon. In the open door of the saloon, Sherman Fentress lay flat on his back, his bandaged wounds ripped to shreds by the blast of the 10-gauge shotgun. His bloody right hand grasped the bottom edge of one of the batwing doors as if it were the only thing keeping him from sliding downward to hell.

"That damned old sheriff!" Earl growled. On the street below, Sheriff Matheson came limping toward the hotel, dragging one foot behind him and using a born pole as a walking stick. The double-barreled shotgun was propped against his good hip, a curl of smoke still rising from its tip. "I reckon I'll have to kill that old bastard again—this time it better take!"

"Boss, let me go down and—"

"Huh-uh," said Cherokee Earl, turning and snatching his holster from a peg on the wall beside the bed. "I'll take care of this myself, *personally*." He quickly buttoned his fly, buckled his belt, and slung his gun belt around his waist. As he buckled the gun belt, his eyes went to Ellen Waddell. "Get dressed!" he commanded, snatching up his boots and throwing them under his arm. But as she rose slowly from the edge of the bed, he glanced impatiently toward the window, then said to Dirty Joe Turley, "Stay here and make sure she gets dressed. . . . Make sure she doesn't try to sneak away. Don't take your eyes off her for a minute." Earl slung his shirt over his shoulder. He grabbed his hat.

Joe's eyes widened. "But what if she does try to make a run for it? What do I do about it?"

Cherokee Earl had already made it to the door and swung it open. Stopping for only a second, he said to Dirty Joe as he gazed coldly at Ellen, "What the hell do you think I would want you to do, Dirty Joe? I'd want you to *kill* her!"

Chapter 8

No sooner had Cherokee Earl left the room than Dirty Joe Turley turned red-faced to Ellen Waddell and said, "Ma'am, you heard him. Now get yourself dressed, with no funny stuff."

"Funny stuff?" said Ellen quietly. She seemed to consider his words for a moment. "All right, excuse me." Picking up her dress from the bottom bedpost, she walked halfway across the room toward the door to an adjoining room.

"Wait up now!" said Dirty Joe. "You heard the boss." He took a step forward, stopping less than three feet from her. "He said not to take my eyes off you . . . and I'm not about to."

"I understand." Ellen seemed to once again ponder what he said. Then she turned loose of the front of the blanket and let it fall to the floor around her feet. At the sight of her standing naked before him, Joe Turley actually jumped back and gasped.

"My God almighty!" He looked at her, then jerked his head away; his hat fell from his hands. He quickly looked back at her, then ducked his eyes with a hand raised as if to hold the world in place while he gained his bearings. "Ma'am, cover yourself, please! You're going to get me into big trouble!" He shot a frightened glance at the door as if Cherokee Earl might return at any second.

"What's it going to be then?" Ellen said, her voice taking on a slight authority. "Do I go in there and dress? Or do I dress here while you stand and watch me?"

"Ma'am, please, just stand still and put that dress on! I won't look—only hurry though!" said Dirty Joe.

"Joe," she said, her voice low and silky, "just between you and me, I don't mind if you look . . . a little, that is."

Dirty Joe felt the hair on his neck tingle. He turned his eyes back to her, the sight of her pearly-white skin causing him to have difficulty breathing.

Ellen stood with her dress clasped in one hand and held between her naked breasts. She held her feet shoulder width apart, the dress hanging down the middle of her, leaving little to the imagination. "I always say it costs nothing to look."

"Yes, ma'am. . . . I mean, no, ma'am! I mean, God almighty, you are the most beautiful woman I ever saw!" He rocked back and forth on his boot heels, opening and closing his hands. It seemed to take all his self-control to keep from lunging upon her.

She smiled coyly, half turning from him as she gathered the dress and raised it over her head. He caught a glimpse of fiery red hair and pale white thighs. "Tell me, Joe, why does he call you Dirty? You look as clean as the rest of this bunch."

She waited on dropping the dress down past her head, taking her time, knowing how much she was torturing him.

"Yes, ma'am, I am. Clean, that is. It's just a moniker, you know? Like some men they call *Lefty*?"

"Oh, I see," she said. She dropped the dress down and smoothed it, the open buttons up the midriff still exposing her breasts. "But isn't that a case where the person is left-handed?" she said softly.

"I—I don't know," Dirty Joe stammered. "Nobody ever called me Lefty."

Dumber than a cellar rat, Ellen thought. *Perfect*. She

closed the dress in front and buttoned the lower buttons one at a time, slowly. "Does it bother you that he leaves you here alone with me?"

"God, no," Dirty Joe grinned. "This is the best thing happened to me in a long time!"

"Will you get my shoes for me, Joe?" She nodded at the dust-covered shoes beside the bed. As he scurried past her to get them, she almost felt her hand brush the handle of the pistol on his hip. She fought to keep herself from snatching it up and shooting him, then making a run for it. But run to where? What would that get her—a few minutes of freedom before they caught up to her? She was in this game to stay alive. She had to play it on out. She would know when the time was right.

"Why would it bother me?" Joe asked, coming back and dropping the shoes before her. His breathing was labored. Sweat had beaded on his brow. He stood close to her. She could feel the heat of him.

"Just that maybe he thinks you're not man enough to try anything," she said tauntingly, "the way some of the others would, the two of us alone like this."

"Ha! He knows I'm as much man as the next." Joe looked her up and down. "He just knows he can trust me, is all. I've been with Earl for a long time." He extended a hand slowly toward where her dress remained open in the front.

But she artfully stepped away from his probing hand and said, nodding down at her shoes, "You'll have to help me, Joe."

"Huh?" Dirty Joe seemed to have gone blank for a second.

"My shoes," she said, almost in a whisper. "Will you bend down there, put my shoes on me?"

"Well . . ." He glanced at the door but had already begun to sink down onto his knees. "Sure, I reckon I can do that." He picked up her left shoe.

She placed a hand on his bare head for support

and entwined her fingers into his thick, damp hair. "There now," she said, almost moaning, raising her foot and propping it onto his knee. "Do it for me."

He fumbled, her foot in one hand, her shoe in the other. She raised her dress above her knee. "Ma'am, I hope this is going to be our little secret, me and you getting this close," he said.

"I'll never tell a soul, Joe," she said, guiding her foot, helping him slip it into the trembling shoe. "You can count on it."

"Lord, I hope so, ma'am," he said, his voice turning thick with passion. "I hope I can count on you. He'd kill us both if he was to ever think—"

"Shhh, hush, Joe." She cut him off, reaching down, taking his hand, and placing it inside her thigh, just above her knee. "Now, if I told him, whose fault would it be? It would be mine, wouldn't it, Joe, getting you to do this?" She pressed his hand there, slicing a breath as if in ecstasy.

"Oh, yes, ma'am, it would be," Joe said, giving in, letting go of his fear of death for the moment. "It would be indeed." He tried to raise his hand farther up, but she stopped him.

"No, Joe, not now," she whispered. "Not now, but soon. I promise, *soon*."

"Ma'am, now I'm this far, I just don't think I can hold off," he said, panting, his hand fevered and trembling.

"But we've got to wait, Joe. Please!" She struggled halfheartedly. "Right now I need a friend, Joe." She entwined her fingers in his hair again and pulled his head up, pressing his chin into her flat lower belly. "Will you be my friend for now, Joe?"

"Oh, yes, ma'am," he gasped, clinging helplessly to her. "I *am* your friend . . . your *best* friend. . . . You can *believe* that!" Outside the open window, the sound of a shotgun roared, followed by repeated blasts of pistol fire. But Dirty Joe only heard them from a distance, through the pounding of his pulse and the rush of hot blood through his veins and his senses.

On the dirt street, Cherokee Earl stopped long enough to pull his socks from inside his boots. He put them on, then stepped into his dusty boots and stamped them onto his feet. He pulled on his shirt as he walked toward the spot where the old sheriff lay crumpled in the street. Blood spilled from the sheriff's lips as he struggled to speak. From the middle of the street, Avery McRoy and Jorge Sentores closed the open space between them and came forward also, each of them flipping out the spent cartridges from their pistols and replacing them as they walked.

Cherokee Earl looked up at the open hotel window as he reloaded and said, "What the hell's taking Dirty Joe so long?"

"Where is he anyway?" asked Avery McRoy.

"He's getting the woman dressed," said Cherokee Earl.

"Oh?" Avery McRoy and Jorge looked at each other. McRoy raised an eyebrow and said, "I wish I'd heard you ask for volunteers. I'm a good hand at getting women dressed . . . or undressed, either one."

"Shut up, McRoy," said Earl. "I couldn't leave her alone. I left him to watch her, make sure she didn't take off."

"Again," said McRoy, "had I only known you was looking for someone to—"

"Do you think I won't open your belly, McRoy?" Earl spat at him. Having reloaded his Colt, Earl slapped the cylinder shut and cocked it with a snap of his thumb. "Huh? You think I have a sense of humor when it comes to my woman? Do you?"

His woman! "Easy, Boss!" said McRoy. "No, I reckon you don't! I was just making man talk, is all! Hell, I take it back."

Cherokee Earl eased the pistol down and turned

slowly to the sheriff in the dirt. "Look at this old buzzard. Still trying to set things right for himself." He leveled the pistol down at arm's length. Seeing the sheriff struggle to speak, Earl said, "What's that, old-timer? What're you saying?"

The sheriff summoned all his strength and rasped, "You son of a low, white-livered—"

"Whoa, now!" said Earl with a dark chuckle. "You can't talk about my mama that way!" The pistol jumped once in his hand, and the old sheriff fell silent. "The hell's the matter with you anyway?" he said to the still form. As he looked down, he saw the faintest flicker of the sheriff's wrinkled eyelid. "I'll be switched if this old turd ain't still alive."

"You're kidding," said McRoy, leaning in for a better look. He reached his hand out and cocked his Colt toward the sheriff's head. "I'll fix that."

But Earl stopped him. "Forget it. Hardheaded as he is, it'll just ricochet, hit one of us." He looked up toward the hotel window as he holstered his Colt. Beside him, McRoy and Jorge did the same. "What the hell is taking him so long?"

McRoy and Jorge gave one another a look, but neither offered any comments. "We got a good take from the bank, Boss," said McRoy, changing the subject.

Earl ignored him. "Jorge, get up there and see what's keeping them," he said, growing irritated. "I'd like to set fire to a few buildings before we leave . . . if that doesn't interfere with anybody's plans." There was a sarcastic snap to Earl's voice.

"*Sí*, Boss, I'll tell them to hurry up," said Jorge, hurrying off across the street toward the hotel.

Earl and McRoy turned back and looked down at the sheriff, seeing that the man was still alive and had even managed to claw his hand toward the shotgun lying two feet away in the dirt. McRoy chuckled and kicked the shotgun closer to the sheriff's hand.

"There you go, old slick. Grab it and give us hell."
He grinned at Earl. "It ain't loaded, of course."

Earl said to the sheriff, "You sure know how to
try a man's patience, you old bastard." He drew back
his boot and kicked the sheriff in the face. The sheriff
fell limp.

McRoy's grin broadened. "If you ain't careful,
you're gong to hurt him, Boss."

Inside the door of the Crown Hotel, Jorge met
Dirty Joe and Ellen Waddell coming down the stairs.
He gave Dirty Joe a questioning look and said, "Ev-
erything is mostly all right, Dirty?"

"Yeah, why?" asked Joe, a defensive look coming
to his eyes.

Jorge shrugged, looking the woman up and down.
"Boss, he say why it take you so long. He send me
to get you so we can burn some buildings. Now you
hurry up, eh?" As Jorge spoke, he reached out and
took Ellen by the forearm to hasten her along.

"Take your hands off her, Jorge!" Dirty Joe bellowed, shoving the Mexican back a step. Both men's
hands went instinctively to their pistol butts. Then
Dirty Joe caught himself and said, letting his hand
fall, "He told me to keep an eye on her, not you. I
don't like nobody horning in when it's me supposed
to be in charge of something, all right? *Comprende?*"

Jorge raised both hands in a show of peace. "*Sí,
comprende, mi amigo!* I mean nothing by it."

"All right then, let's forget it," said Dirty Joe, getting himself fully collected.

Ellen watched closely, taking in every action, examining every response between the two men.

"I reckon it just took her longer than it should to
get dressed," Dirty Joe said.

"*Sí,*" said Jorge. He looked Dirty Joe up and down.
When Joe reached for the doorknob, Jorge stopped
him. "*Uno momento,*" he said.

Joe stopped with his hand still on the knob. "What

do you want, Jorge?" His tone of voice turned a bit testy.

"Do like this before you go out there," said Jorge, rubbing his own chin vigorously.

"What the hell?" Dirty Joe gave him a strange look.

"You have lint on your chin," Ellen cut in, lowering her eyes modestly. She idly smoothed down the wrinkled front of her gingham dress.

Dirty Joe picked at his beard stubble with nervous fingers, his face red and frightened. "Damn . . . I don't know how I got that," he muttered, seeing—and knowing that Jorge saw as well—the small fleck of lint and a short scrap of thread that had undeniably come from Ellen's dress. "Much obliged, Jorge."

Jorge shook his head slowly, giving Joe a warning gaze. "Don't tell me *much obliged*. I want to know nothing about what is going on. This is not my business. When Earl hears about this, you are on your own."

Opening the door, Dirty Joe allowed Ellen Waddell to step outside. Then he stopped and said to Jorge, "What do you mean by that? You going to tell him?"

Jorge said, "I am not loco. It is a bad thing that I want no part of."

"It ain't what you think it is, Jorge," said Dirty Joe. "Nothing happened between us, I swear."

"It is no business of mine," Jorge said, stepping through the open door after the woman.

"Answer me, Jorge," said Dirty Joe. "Are you going to tell Earl?"

Jorge only shook his head and walked on.

From across the street, Cherokee Earl called out, "It's about damn time! We need to get a move on." He turned from the limp body of Sheriff Matheson and walked toward the hitchrail, where fresh horses stood ready to go.

Matheson opened his eyes thinly and let his hand

crawl once again to the stock of the shotgun. With all his waning strength, he forced his free hand inside his coat pocket, found the shotgun load, and brought it out. He saw the woman and the two men coming across the dirt street. *God*, he whispered to himself, *just give me one more round.*

Jorge gave Avery McRoy a telling glance as they all met up near the horses.

"What's going on, Jorge?" McRoy asked, looking at Dirty Joe and the woman.

"He is playing with dynamite, that one," Jorge whispered, nodding toward Dirty Joe.

"You mean, him . . . and her?" McRoy looked stunned. "Dirty Joe and a woman?" The prospect of it seemed ridiculous to him.

"*Sí*," said Jorge. "It is so. And now that I know about it, I must be a part of their secret. So it is I who is in the big trouble."

Dirty Joe caught a trace of Jorge's words and snapped his head toward him. "What the hell are you saying, Jorge?"

"I said nothing," Jorge responded. "But I am not such a fool that I will put myself on the spot for you."

Five horses away at the other end of the hitchrail, Cherokee Earl busily riffled through the bank bag, taking a loose count, too occupied to pay attention to what was being said.

"Yeah?" Dirty Joe stepped toward Jorge. "You best keep your mouth shut about me, *Mex!*"

"Or what?" said Jorge defiantly. He dropped his hand to the pistol on his hip. Then he called out to Cherokee Earl as he kept his eyes on Dirty Joe. "Hey, Boss, I got something to tell you."

"You son of a—" Dirty Joe's words were cut short by the blast of the shotgun from where the sheriff lay dying on the ground. The shot lifted Jorge a foot off the ground and hurled him sidelong up onto the boardwalk. Ellen jumped back a step but stayed calm, seeing Earl, Dirty Joe, and Avery McRoy turn as one, their pistols coming up cocked from their holsters.

They fired with accuracy, but their shots were powerless against the old sheriff. He lay dead, a slight smile of satisfaction on his weathered face, his eyes staring blankly upward at the wide, clear sky.

Cherokee Earl turned slowly to Avery McRoy, his pistol cocked and still smoking. "You stupid sumbitch! You kicked that shotgun right back into his hands! I ought to blow your empty head off!"

"Boss, it was empty! I never meant for something like this to happen! I swear to God I never. Who the hell would have thought that old man was going to be able to do anything but go on and die?"

"Yeah, he went on and died, but not before he killed Jorge," said Earl, his temper easing down to a simmer as he lowered his pistol and stepped up onto the boardwalk where the Mexican lay dead. "One more mistake out of you, McRoy, I'll drive a barrel spike through your ears and leave you nailed to a tree somewhere." He stooped down beside Jorge Sentores. "This man was not only one hell of a thief and gunman, but he could stick on a horse better than any man I ever saw, white or colored. Now some flea-bitten lawdog has gone and sent him straight to hell." He looked around at the pillaged town, a sadness in his eyes. "I don't even feel like burning nothing else right now." Down the street, flames licked out and upward from the telegraph office. Farther down the street, the livery barn boiled in a cloud of black smoke.

McRoy and Dirty Joe looked at one another. "That ain't like you, Boss," Joe offered.

Cherokee Earl didn't answer.

Ellen Waddell stood back by the horses, a cold gaze in her eyes as she stared from one face to the next. When Dirty Joe looked at her, she softened her expression enough to offer a trace of a guarded smile just between the two of them. Then, as he turned his eyes back to Jorge's bloody body, Ellen's eyes stabbed at his back like sabers. She knew she had gained some ground for herself by the way that she had resisted Cherokee Earl without putting up a struggle. No matter what she had done, Cherokee Earl would have overpowered her and taken what he wanted anyway. All a struggle would have gotten her was a beating, and that might have been exactly what an animal like Earl would enjoy. She had no time to nurse a broken nose, battered ribs, or worse.

No, thanks, she thought. She could force herself to play this game. She just had to keep her head and bide her time. She had to keep control of her faculties at all times. She had to keep from showing any emotion, no matter what the situation. The main thing was to stay alive. But if that wasn't possible, she promised herself that, like the old sheriff lying dead in the street, she would not go down without a fight.

When Cherokee Earl turned a gaze toward her and saw the way she was staring at them as they gathered around Jorge's body, his face grew tight with anger. "What the hell are you looking at? This man was a good friend of mine! I reckon you think the more of us that dies, the better your chances of getting away—is that it?"

Ellen didn't answer. Instead, she stared down at the ground, letting her helplessness show.

Cherokee Earl took a step toward her, noting her meek demeanor, and noting as well the way that Dirty Joe and Avery McRoy were watching him. "You ain't fooling me, woman!" Earl growled. "I see through your way of acting pitiful . . . thinking somebody is going to speak up and come to your rescue!" He stalked closer, tightening a fist at his side. "But it ain't going to happen, do you hear me? It ain't

about to happen!" He stopped short at the sound of
Dirty Joe behind him.

"Boss, leave her alone," Dirty Joe said.

A deathlike silence fell around them. Earl turned
slowly, his eyes fiery with rage. "What did you say
to me, Dirty?"

Avery McRoy cut in before Dirty Joe could speak.
"Boss, he means we ain't got time to fool around
with that woman. We're down to three of us now
till Frisco and Billy meet up with us. We got folks
on our trail . . . and more coming once word gets
out across the Territory. Let's get moving. You can
smack her around anytime."

Earl looked at the body of Jorge Sentores lying on
the bloody boardwalk. McRoy was right, and Cherokee Earl knew it. This was no time to go shooting
one of his own men, no matter what the situation.
He looked the woman up and down. All right, he'd
had her, and so far all she'd been was a disappointment. Whatever he decided to do with her would
have to wait. "You're right, McRoy, we got to get
moving." His eyes went to Dirty Joe, but only for a
second, and only long enough to give him an admon-
ishing look. Then he said to McRoy, "Avery, you
take the lead rope for a while. . . . I got to do some
thinking." He rubbed his sore shoulder, the one he'd
used leading Ellen's horse by its reins before he'd
taken the time to stop along the trail and tie the short
lead rope to the horse's bridle. He'd never seen a
woman have so much trouble keeping a horse
moving.

Ellen saw Dirty Joe stiffen a bit at Earl's words.
But she knew this was no time for Joe to say anything. She saw jealousy in Joe Turley's eyes as he
watched Avery McRoy step forward and say, "Sure
thing, Boss." Then Avery stood before her and jerked
his thumb toward her horse and said, "Okay, ma'am,
up you go. Let's get you into the saddle."

Ellen shot a quick glance to Dirty Joe as if to say there was nothing she could do about it. Then she stepped over to the horse, hiked her dress slightly, and said to Avery McRoy in a modest tone of voice, "I can't reach it on my own. . . . You'll have to give me a hand." As she swung up into the saddle, she saw the seething expression on Dirty Joe's face. Looking down at Avery McRoy, she took a second longer than she needed to turn loose of his shoulder. "Thank you," she said softly, giving him a slight squeeze before letting go.

When the rest of them had mounted and headed north along the street out of town, Dirty sat rigid in his saddle, staring straight ahead at Cherokee Earl's back. He said to Avery McRoy out the side of his mouth in a harsh whisper, "I saw how you was making up to her."

Leading Ellen's horse by the short length of rope, McRoy replied in the same tone of voice. "Making up to her? Jesus, Dirty, Boss asked me to help her up and lead her horse. What was I supposed to do?"

"Huh-uh," said Joe. "He asked you to lead her horse. He never said nothing about lifting her up that way, taking your time, putting your hands all over her!" His words grew stronger as he spoke. He actually leaned closer to McRoy, so close that McRoy stepped his horse away from him.

"Take it easy, Joe!" said McRoy. "This ain't nothing to get worked up over."

"I ain't worked up, damn you!" Dirty Joe said, his voice getting loud now.

Five yards ahead of them, Cherokee Earl turned in his saddle and looked back. "What the hell's going on back there? Are you two scuffling about something?"

"Uh—no, Boss," McRoy offered, collecting himself and leveling his hat brim. "Just a dispute over which one of us was the best friend to poor Jorge is all."

"Arguing over the dead," Earl said flatly. He shook his head as he looked forward. "Let the dead bury the dead—that's what the good book says."

"The hell does he know about the good book," Dirty Joe whispered.

"The hell does any of us?" McRoy chuckled. The two looked at one anther and laughed quietly, the storm between them having passed for now.

Close behind Avery McRoy, Ellen Waddell sat with her eyes lowered, looking down, not missing a word they said. She kept a slight tension on the reins in her hands, causing her horse to drag a bit, just enough to keep McRoy's arm having to constantly stay in a strain, keeping the horse from lagging.

McRoy gave a jerk on the rope and caused Ellen to have to let the horse come forward, almost beside him. "Lady, you can't ride worth a damn!" McRoy said to her.

"I'm—I'm sorry," Ellen replied meekly, "I'm not used to—"

"Leave her alone, Avery," said Dirty Joe. "She's just a woman. You can't expect her to ride like a man, can you?"

McRoy took a deep breath, not wanting to start arguing with Dirty Joe all over again. "No, I reckon not," he said. They rode on, Ellen once again letting the horse lag back on the lead rope.

Chapter 9

Danielle drew Sundown to a halt and looked forward along a saddle of rock above the winding trail. On the other side of the trail stood a short stretch of jagged rock, not as tall, perhaps no more than thirty feet, but just as impenetrable. *A perfect ambush spot*, she told herself. She drew the chestnut mare sidelong and sat waiting for Stick and Dave Waddell to catch up to her from thirty feet back. She looked down at the two sets of horse tracks they had been following. The tracks belonged to Frisco Bonham and Billy Boy Harper.

"What's the matter?" asked Dave Waddell, seeming eager to keep moving. He nodded down at the hoofprints. "They're leading straight ahead."

"I know," said Danielle. "Nothing's the matter. But we're going to swing wide here and take shade beneath the mesa until the sun drops behind us. It'll only be for three or four hours."

"Three or four hours? What for?" asked Dave, looking back and forth between Danielle and Stick as he halted his horse.

"Because she said so," Stick cut in gruffly, having little tolerance for Dave Waddell.

Danielle was more patient. "Because that's a bad stretch of trail." She nodded ahead. "One rifle along that ridgeline can drop one or two of us or our horses pretty easily, and that would just about put this manhunt out of business."

"But what good is waiting going to do us?" Dave asked, still not seeing the point in wasting precious time. "This sounds like you're both afraid to catch up to these people!"

Danielle reminded herself not to let him upset her. She tipped her hat brim back and wiped her gloved hand across her wet forehead. "Because, Mr. Waddell . . . right now, with the sun high, we make a clear target going along that trail from the west. But once the sun drops behind us, anybody looking down along a gun barrel is going to go about half-blind from sun glare."

Dave Waddell considered what she'd said, his face growing red because he hadn't realized it in the first place. He saw Stick give a smug grin and spit a stream of tobacco. "Well," Dave said, still unable to give up his position, "I don't see how that's going to help. If somebody's up there, they can still shoot us, sun glare or not."

Danielle nodded slowly. "That's true, Mr. Waddell. But it's all about who gets the best advantage, them or us. Stick and I are going to take shade, rest the horses, and ride in with the sun to our backs. If you feel like you've got to do it a different way, I understand. . . . We'll pick your body up when we come through."

Turning Sundown, Danielle stepped the mare off the trail, Stick following close behind her. "Wait, please," said Dave. "I didn't mean to be testy with you. I'm going along with you on this. Hey, I never claimed to know a lot about this sort of thing."

"Leave him behind," Stick said to Danielle. "I don't trust that peckerwood."

Danielle grinned but slowed her mare enough to

let Dave Waddell catch up. "Neither do I, Stick. But it is his wife they've taken. I reckon that alone can cause a man to act a little crazy."

Stick slowed a bit beside her. "All right, whatever you say." He looked back as Dave Waddell hurried his horse forward. "I just can't get a good picture of how he says things happened. Maybe I just slept too many nights with my head on a cold saddle."

Danielle grinned. "Maybe you have at that," she said and heeled her mare forward.

They rode around the base of the tall mesa and into a shaded area. Even though the air was still dry and hot, the heat was not nearly as violent as it was on the open, sun-beaten flatlands. While they rested themselves and their horses, they ate jerked beef and hardtack and chased it down with tepid canteen water. The horses stood picketed, grazing among clumps of wild grass less than twenty feet away. Stick took this rest period as an opportunity to clean and inspect his shooting gear. His pistol lay broken apart on a blanket he'd spread before him on the dirt. Danielle sat watching the animals as she chewed on a long blade of grass.

"I just can't stand waiting here doing nothing," said Dave Waddell. He'd turned even more restless after he'd eaten. While Danielle and Stick had rested for an hour and a half, he'd spent much of the time pacing back and forth, raising a small cloud of dust around his feet.

Stick looked through the barrel of his pistol, blew through it, and wiped it with a worn bandanna. "You were given a choice, Waddell, remember?" he said calmly.

"I know, I know," said Dave. "I'm just nervous by nature, I suppose. I just can't stand the thought of my poor wife being with a rotten piece of work like Cherokee Earl!"

"Thought you didn't know the man," said Stick, paying Waddell little interest.

"I don't *personally*," said Waddell. "But I don't have to personally know a skunk to know how bad it smells."

Stick nodded. "I agreed with that." He picked up the cylinder to his pistol and rolled it back and forth slowly between his palms, inspecting it.

Dave Waddell stopped and let out a breath, then said, "Look, I know that neither one of you has much use for me. You don't trust me, and I don't know why. But that doesn't really matter. All I'm after is getting my wife back alive."

"That's what we're interested in also, Mr. Waddell," said Danielle. "So what's eating you?"

"I think you could tell me more about what's going on," said Waddell, "instead of leaving me in the dark until the time comes to decide things." He jerked a thumb back toward the trail they'd been riding. "Like back there a while ago. I had a right to know why you wanted us to pull off out of the sun. Once I knew it, I went along with it, didn't I?"

Stick and Danielle looked him up and down. "Okay," said Danielle, "what is it you want to know?"

It took Dave Waddell a moment to realize she meant it. Then he said, "All right, for starters, when these men's trail split up before you followed the five horses to my place, how did you know which set of tracks to follow? What made you think Cherokee Earl was still with the five horses you followed to my front yard instead of the two horses that went up into the hills?"

Danielle took the length of grass from her mouth and tossed it away. "It's an old Apache trick they're doing, Mr. Waddell," she said. "They'll drop off one and two at a time until you're left looking at an empty trail if you're not careful. In this case, there was only seven of them to begin with. The two that split off had to either draw us off the others' trail or ambush us. They pulled up above us. Then they watched our move. Once they saw we weren't going to split off after them . . . they began to look for a good spot to hit us from." She nodded at the jagged hill line along the trail ahead. "My bet is, that's it."

Dave Waddell swallowed a dry knot in his throat. "And all we can do is ride into it?"

"Any better ideas?" asked Danielle.

"What about one of us riding up, getting around the hills behind them?" Waddell asked.

"No good," said Stick, fitting his cleaned pistol back together and wiping it with the bandanna. "On flatland like this, they'll see us split up long before we get into their trap. All they'll do is light out, make us chase them. While we chase these two, the rest get farther away."

"And so does my wife," Waddell said, sounding helpless.

"Yep, that would be the case," said Stick.

"So all we can do is get the sun to our backs and ride in there like tin ducks at a shooting gallery?" Dave asked.

"Well, maybe not," said Danielle. She looked back and forth between the two men, then said, "I've been giving that some thought while I was sitting here. They'd see us if one of us split off now. But once we get inside the narrow trail between the rocks, it'll be a different story." She considered something, then said, "I'd sure like to take them alive, hear what they've got to say about your wife."

Dave Waddell didn't answer, realizing that these two were most likely Billy Boy Harper and Frisco Bonham, and that they had already split off from the rest of the gang before Cherokee Earl came to his spread and took Ellen.

"There's no way a horse can climb off the trail up into that hill line," said Stick, neither he nor Danielle noticing Waddell's silence.

"No, but a person can on foot," said Danielle. "If I can find a blind spot along the trail, I can slip up out of the saddle with a rifle and get up along the high ridges before anybody knows what hits them."

Stick shook his head. "No, Danielle, that's too dangerous. Anybody climbs up there it'll have to be me, or Waddell here."

"Me?" Dave Waddell looked sick all of a sudden.

"No, I'll do it," said Stick.

"It's my idea. I'm the one who's going to do it," Danielle insisted.

Dave Waddell looked relieved.

"No, it's a bad idea," said Stick. "Too risky. Besides, if you climb all the way up and they're not up there, all you've done is worn yourself out for nothing."

"If that's how it turns out, so be it," said Danielle. "But I'm going, and that settles it." She looked back at the sun, gauging it. "It's a half-hour ride to the hill line. By the time we get there, the sun ought to be dropped about right." She stood up, dusting her trouser seat, and walked away toward the horses.

Waddell and Stick stood looking at one another for a moment. Then Stick said, "Well, you heard her. What are we waiting for?"

Within minutes the three of them had gathered their horses, bridled and saddled them, and readied them for travel. On their way along the flat, dusty trail, Danielle kept a close eye on the level of the sun lowering behind them. "Keep it slow and easy," she said to the two men. "We've got to time it just right to the foot of the rocks. And remember: if we can, let's take them alive." They slowed the pace of their horses and rode loosely abreast until the trail tipped slightly up and narrowed into a jagged, rock-lined path barely three horses wide.

"Get ready, Stick, here I go," Danielle said, easing her mare's reins to him as she rose and posted in her stirrups. As the mare stepped past a crevice snaking upward into clinging mesquite brush and creosote bushes, Danielle slipped her rifle from its boot and moved sleekly from her saddle into the rocky upthrust.

"Be careful," Stick whispered, watching her disappear into the steep hillside as the horse continued without breaking its slow, steady stride. Hearing Stick whisper, Dave Waddell looked around to see what was going on. But in the blink of an eye, it seemed, Danielle's saddle was empty and Stick was staring straight ahead. Looking up along the crevice ledge, Waddell saw a creosote bush tremble as if stirred by a gust of wind. Then Stick said to him in a gruff whisper, "Don't look up! Look ahead!"

"Sorry, I—" Waddell stammered. "I just didn't realize when she would make her move."

"All the better," Stick said, his waxen expression giving in a little to a faint smile of pride. "This is one young woman who knows her way around the rough country." He heeled his horse on, keeping the chestnut mare close beside him.

In the narrow crevice, Danielle climbed until she perched for a moment twenty feet up and looked down along the trail at Stick and Waddell riding forward. Knowing that any moment they could draw fire from the ridge above them, she caught her breath and hurriedly climbed upward, moving as quietly as possible. At the crest of the ridge, thirty feet above the trail, she hurried along across loose rock and buried boulders, looking down as she caught up with Stick and Waddell. Seeing their shadows and the shadows of the horses stretched in front of them on the rocky path, she squinted at the sunlight glaring on their backs.

"That's good, Stick," Danielle whispered to herself.

"Keep it just like that." Then she slipped along the ridge in a crouch, rifle in hand, scanning back and forth along both high ridges atop the thin trail.

She moved along the ridge, getting ahead of Stick and Waddell on the trail below as the ridgeline sloped upward. At the peak of a higher cliff, she looked just in time to see two riflemen stretched out on a flat rock and looking down their rifle barrels toward the trail. Their appearance came to her so suddenly it caused her to duck down for a second. She leaned against the side of a half-buried boulder and silently eased the lever of her rifle back and forth, chambering a round. Then she leaned slightly and looked down at Stick and Waddell. There was no question the riflemen had seen them. They were only waiting now for the two hapless riders to get beneath them before they opened fire.

Even in an ambush situation, Danielle could not abide shooting the two men without first having them face her. Rising from behind the sunken boulder, she cocked the rifle and called out as she took aim. "Up here, you dry gulches!"

Frisco and Billy Boy Harper knew what was coming as they rolled onto their backs, already taking aim at her. Danielle's first shot nailed Billy Boy in the shoulder and slammed him back down onto the flat rock. He yelped like a kicked dog. His rifle went off as it flew from his hands and out over the edge of the cliff. But Frisco Bonham proved to be quicker than his companion. As Billy Boy rolled back and forth, writhing in pain, Frisco Bonham rolled sidelong over the edge of the cliff onto a dangerously thin ledge. He managed to fire a shot that ricocheted off the boulder in front of Danielle and whined away into the sky. "You're not taking me back alive!" Frisco shouted.

"That thought never crossed my mind," Danielle called out, ready for her shot when Frisco raised up to take aim at her. On the trail below, Stick and Waddell had both dropped from their saddles as Frisco Bonham's discarded rifle thudded to the trail in front of them. Stick was also ready for Frisco's move. He raised his rifle and took aim.

"It's that damned woman again!" Frisco raged aloud, as if he couldn't believe his eyes. He started to squeeze off a shot, but seeing him level his rifle, both Danielle and Stick fired at once, catching the outlaw in a cross fire from above and below. Dave Waddell squatted behind the cover of a rock, holding the reins to the horses. He winced, seeing the two shots hit Frisco Bonham and twirl the outlaw like a top.

"*Ayiiii—!*" Frisco screamed. He spun off the slim ledge and pummeled and bounced and slid and rolled until he spilled onto the path beside the rock where Dave Waddell sat holding the horses. Not knowing if the outlaw was dead or alive and not wanting to take a chance, Stick stepped over and planted a boot firmly on Frisco's back, pinning him to the dirt. Blood flowed from a wound in Frisco's right shoulder and another in his left side.

"Lay still now," said Stick, "or I'll put the next one in the worst place you can think of."

"You've . . . got . . . the wrong . . . man," Frisco managed to gasp into the dirt.

Stick grinned wryly. "You've said them words so often they've become second nature to you." He jostled his boot against the wounded outlaw. "Now shut up and lay still till we get your partner."

Atop the ridgeline, Danielle worked her way down to Billy Boy Harper. He sat squeezing his bleeding shoulder, his wounded foot swollen to twice its size beneath a dirty bandage. "Damned if you ain't gone and shot me again," he seethed, staring at Danielle with hate-filled eyes. "If I could draw this pistol, I swear I'd blow you to kingdom come!"

"You already would have if you and that snake

you ride with could have gotten the drop on us," said Danielle, stepping down onto the flat rock, lowering her rifle, and drawing her pistol from her holster.

"What?" Billy Boy looked incensed by her suggestion. "Woman, you don't know what you're talking about! We had no idea you was even on this trail. We was just watching, making sure some road agents weren't trailing us. That's the God's honest truth."

Danielle laid the rifle flat as he spoke, keeping him covered with her Colt. Then she reached over and lifted his pistol from his holster and shoved it down behind her gun belt. "Now listen close, because I'm only going to ask one time. Where is Cherokee Earl headed with Dave Waddell's wife?"

Billy looked genuinely bewildered. "Hunh? His *wife?*"

"You heard me," said Danielle. "Earl has Waddell's wife. Where would he be headed with her?"

"Dang . . . !" Billy Boy turned loose of his wounded shoulder long enough to scratch his head with his bloody hand. "I knowed Cherokee had a powerful hankering for that little redheaded woman, but I never thought he'd go so far as to snatch her up." He spread a bemused half-smile. "I was wondering what ole Dave was doing fanning our trail that way."

"Keep your voice down," said Danielle. "I don't want Waddell hearing you." She craned her neck enough to look down over the edge to where Stick stood with his boot on Frisco's back thirty feet below. Stick stared up toward her, his pistol cocked at arm's length and pointed down at the wounded outlaw.

"Now what's the story?" she asked. "How do two birds like Waddell and Cherokee Earl come to light on the same limb?"

"What kind of break do I get if I tell you?" Billy Boy cocked his head to one side, looking smug.

Danielle swung her pistol barrel across his fore-head, not hard, but hard enough to raise a welt. "You better worry about the *break* you'll get if you don't tell me," she said, drawing the pistol back for another swipe.

"All right! Take it easy!" Billy Boy pleaded. "I'll tell you whatever I can." He ducked his head slightly. "I never seen a woman so prone to acts of violence!"

"And we've only just started." Danielle gave him a cold stare.

"Dave Waddell started out buying stolen cattle from us a year ago," Billy Boy said quickly. "Nowadays most of the cattle we rustle goes through him. He's gotten chicken-rich off of us. Earl took a liking to his wife the first time he ever laid eyes on her. Can't say as I blame him." Billy shrugged with his good shoulder. "She's a looker, that one."

"I see," said Danielle. "So Cherokee Earl and Dave Waddell were business partners?"

"Well, yes, you might as well say," said Billy. "Only for some reason, Waddell never seemed to be able to admit it to himself. Used to really tighten Earl's jaw . . . Waddell thinking he was so much better than the likes of us. I'd say that had something to do with Earl wanting to take his wife, wouldn't you?"

"I have no idea," said Danielle.

"Well, I think it must've." Billy noted that the bleeding from his shoulder wound had grown worse. He loosened his bandanna from around his neck and tried to tie it around his shoulder, failing miserably.

"Here, give it to me," said Danielle, stepping over and taking the bandanna. As she tied it around his shoulder, up under his arm, she continued. "But as far as you know, Waddell never stole any cattle himself, just provided a place and bought the ones rest of you rustled?"

"That was the way of it," said Billy Boy. He looked

closely at Danielle as she tended his wound. "Any chance of you letting me go, after me telling you and all? That, I mean, and promising never to do anything wrong again in my life?"

"No, there's not a way in the world I'll let you go," said Danielle, "so save your breath. We'll turn you over to the law first chance we get. I'll tell them you was helpful with information. That's all I'll do for you."

"I was afraid of that," said Billy Boy, raising a small hideaway derringer he'd snuck from inside his shirt as she took care of his wound. "You've shot me for the last time, woman!" he shouted.

From below, Stick and the other two only heard the sound of Danielle's Colt, the big pistol drowning out the sound of Billy Boy's derringer. "Danielle?" said Stick. "Are you all right up there?"

A silence passed, and Stick took on a concerned look. "Danielle. Answer me. . . . Are you all right?"

"I'm shot, stick," Danielle replied in a strained voice. "I'm all right . . . but this little sidewinder shot me."

"I'm coming!" Stick shouted.

"No, Stick!" Danielle shouted. "Stay there!"

"Why?" said Stick. "You're shot—you need help!"

She wasn't going to risk saying any more about what Billy Boy had just told her. Instead, she just said, "Stick, stay down there. I'm all right."

But Stick wouldn't hear of it. He reached down, snatched Frisco's pistol from his holster, and said to Dave Waddell, "Keep an eye on this one! I'm going up to get her!"

"Sure thing," said Dave Waddell, pointing his pistol at Frisco Bonham. Recognizing Waddell's voice, Frisco turned a surprised look at him as Stick hurried away up the steep, rocky hillside.

"Well, well," Frisco whispered. "Look who we've got here."

"Hello, Frisco," said Waddell, keeping his voice low. "Where's my wife, you rotten bastard?"

"Your wife? How in the hell would I know where your wife is, Waddell?" Frisco said.

The two stared at one another for a second. Then the picture of what was going on began to form inside Frisco's head. "You mean to tell me Earl has taken off with your little redheaded wife?" He shook his head. "I always figured he would someday, but damn, you mean right after me and Billy split up with him and the others on the way to your spread? Is that when?"

Waddell sat tight-lipped. His knuckles turned white around his pistol butt. "If you've got nothing for me, than I've got only one thing for you!" he hissed.

"Hold on, Waddell," said Frisco, seeing the serious intent in the man's red-rimmed eyes. He flashed a quick glance at Stick climbing hand over hand, getting closer to the top. "I can't tell you where he'd take her, but I might be able to take you there." He looked up again, then back at Waddell.

"You're not taking me anywhere," said Waddell.

"Oh? Well, then, that's a shame . . . because you see, I know Cherokee Earl a lot better than you do." He lifted an eyebrow as if asking whether Dave was interested in hearing more. When Dave made no response, Frisco continued. "I believe you can get your wife back if you show up and ask real polite. She might be a little worse for the wear, but we can't always have everything our way, can we?"

Dave Waddell fought the urge to put a bullet through his forehead. Frisco seemed to be able to read it in his eyes. "I know you're all stoked up right now," he said, "but give it time to sink in. See where your best chance lies. As soon as I get these wounds patched up and we can see our way clear, you be ready to help me make a move. Then we'll go get your wife back. Fair enough?"

Dave considered it for a moment. Frisco saw the color begin to come back into his face as his knuckles slacked off around the pistol butt. "I'll think about it," Dave finally said.

Frisco took a short breath of relief. His eyes gestured upward to where Stick was still climbing the hillside. "You don't want to spend too long thinking about it, Dave," Frisco cautioned. "Seems to me like you made your decision last year which side of the law you stood on. Nobody twisted your arm, getting you to buy our stolen cattle. I don't suppose you happened to mention all that to the old man and woman, did you?"

Dave Waddell's expression answered for him.

"That's what I thought," said Frisco. "It must've slipped your mind."

"I told them no more than I had to." He looked more troubled as he spoke.

"It's a hell of a spot you're in, ain't it?" A trace of a sinister smile came to Frisco's lips. "The devil's knocking at your door, Dave. You've got to figure out real quick whether or not you're going to answer." Again he nodded upward toward Stick's back. "You quit those kind of folks the day you crossed over to us. You ever want to see your woman again, you better prepare yourself to do whatever it takes. I can promise you those two will never make it to where Cherokee Earl's trail will take them."

"I told you I'd think about it," said Dave Waddell. His hand slackened around the pistol.

Chapter 10

With a hand pressed against the bullet wound low in her left side, it took much effort for Danielle to make it over to the edge of the cliff. When she did, she looked down at Stick, who was no more than a few feet below her. "Stick, I told you not to come up here! I'm all right!"

"Hunh?" Stick looked baffled, staring up at her as he reached to pull himself over the edge. Looking down to the trail below, Danielle saw the rifle barrel reach up above the top of a rock. She couldn't see who was behind it, but whether it was Dave Waddell or Frisco Bonham made no difference. The intent was the same. As she saw the rifle barrel, she also saw Stick falter and almost lose his footing. As he rocked back, she was torn between going for her pistol to give him some covering fire or grabbing his hand to keep him from falling.

"Hurry, Stick!" she shouted, hoping to get him up over the edge in time. She threw her right hand down to him, ignoring the pain in her side. But Stick had no understanding of what was going on below him. He only knew he had lost his balance. He grasped wildly for her hand.

But the rifle shot caused him to stiffen just at the second their fingertips touched. Danielle saw the stunned look come upon his weathered face at the same time the bullet exited his chest. She made an extra lunge forward, but his hand had already fallen farther away from hers. She could only watch as his face registered a look of regret. "I'm . . . sorry," he gasped. Then he fell backward and tumbled down until he came to a halt in a swirling cloud of dust and rock on the trail below.

Another shot exploded. This one kicked up flecks of rock only inches from Danielle. There was nothing she could do for Stick. She ducked down only slightly, long enough to draw her Colt. Then she came up quickly, her eyes scanning for a target. But all she saw was a brief glimpse of the two men and a rise of dust from the horses' hooves. She heard the long neigh of her chestnut mare and saw the animal rear above the rocks and come down running while the sounds of the horse string and the two riders disappeared in the other direction.

Danielle held her pistol at arm's length with both hands, taking careful aim, preparing for the moment when Frisco Bonham and Dave Waddell would ride into view farther down the trail, where the rocky cover parted for a few yards. But when they did streak along that short stretch of open trail, she lowered her pistol, knowing the shot was too far out of range. Her eyes went down to Stick. Although badly wounded and injured from the fall, he was trying to raise his pistol from his holster. "Lay still, Stick!" Danielle shouted. "I'm coming!"

Even with pain gripping her side, Danielle hurried down the steep hillside. Reaching Stick on the dirt trail, she sank onto her knees and turned him over, resting his head in her lap. "Stick, lay still! You're going to be all right!"

Stick coughed and struggled with his words. "Save that talk . . . for some tinhorn. I'm done here."

Danielle knew he was right, it just took her a second to accept it. "Oh, Stick," she said with deep regret. "I told you to stay put. Why wouldn't you listen to me?" Her voice was shaken by grief. She hugged

his head against her, seeing the scrapes, cuts, and
bruises he'd acquired from the fall. On her leg she
felt warm blood oozing from the wound in his back.
The exit wound in his chest looked fierce and
hopeless.

"I—I tried, Danielle," Stick gasped. His glazed
eyes stared up into hers. "It's hard . . . for a man—"

His words stopped short, but she knew what he
meant. "To take orders from a woman," she whispered, finishing his words for him.

He offered a faint smile. "Don't hate us . . . for
how we are."

"I don't, Stick," she said, trying hard to keep tears
from spilling from her eyes.

"You . . . get out of here," Stick said in a faltering
voice. "Go find Tuck Carlyle. . . . Promise me?"

"I will, Stick, I promise," said Danielle. "As soon
as I settle up with these rats, I'll go find him."

"No," said Stick, taking all his waning strength to
shake his head. He gripped her forearm with his
bloody hand. "Go now! Forget . . . these people.
This . . . ain't felt right . . . from the start."

"Stick, you know I can't let this go," Danielle said,
unable to keep the tears back any longer at the sight
of this good old man dying in her arms. "Don't ask
me to promise something like that."

Stick patted her arm. "I know, I know." A short
silence passed. Then he said, "You and Tuck . . .
remember me kindly."

"Of course, Stick. How else could we possibly remember you?" She wept openly now.

"Quit that," Stick said. He offered a weak smile.
"I've had the best . . . of lives. Look at me . . . leaving
a beautiful woman crying over me." He swallowed,
a knot in his throat. "If I'd . . . been a younger
man . . ." His words trailed; then he added, "Well,
I reckon you . . . know how I feel about you." His

eyes closed softly, with no promise of ever opening again. Danielle felt him turn limp in her lap.

"I know, Stick," she whispered. "I know." She lowered her cheek to his for a second and sat quietly cradling him in her arms. At length Danielle felt the chestnut mare press her warm muzzle against her neck. She turned her face up to the animal. "Good girl, Sundown," she said, raising one gloved hand and stroking the mare's face. "You did fine, just fine."

She lifted Stick's head from her lap and stood, gazing down the thin path where the dust of the fleeing riders had begun to settle. She thought about Stick's words: *This . . . ain't felt right . . . from the start*, he'd said. He was right, and she knew it. From the beginning, the day she'd met the three drunken rustlers in the street at Haley Springs, no one had taken her seriously. Even after putting a bullet through Billy Boy Harper's foot, they hadn't learned any respect for her.

She was a woman doing a man's job. Nothing more, she thought, than some novelty act in a traveling show. Through her grief at Stick's death and the dark anger she felt for his killers, Danielle also felt a weariness that ran so deep it made her ache inside. Some things never changed. She should have realized that coming into this mess. She began to chastise herself. Who did she think she was, that just because she could ride and shoot and handle herself like a man . . . ? *Stop it*, she told herself, forcing the train of thought from her mind. What was done was done, and she couldn't go back and change the past. All she could do was try to influence the future.

With the pain in her side throbbing and sharp, she took down her lariat from her saddle, looped it around Stick's feet, and walked the mare slowly, dragging Stick's body to a wider spot along the trail.

With the help of the mare and the rope, she spent the next hour raising rocks from the ground until she'd uncovered a spot the proper size for a shallow grave. Then she rolled Stick over into the grave and as carefully as she could rolled the rocks back over him. "It ain't the best, Stick," she said quietly, standing bowed slightly at the waist, her hand pressing a bandanna to her side, "but it's the best I can do." With her hat between her hands, she stood with her head slightly bowed and said, "Lord, I'm too hurt to know what to say over this good man right now. I never knew him that long, but he sure fit what I would call an angel . . . if I was you. Amen." She stepped back and wiped an eye and put her hat on.

In moments she had dragged herself up in her saddle and heeled the mare into a slow walk. Pain radiated in her side and stabbed her with each step. Danielle didn't look back toward Stick's rocky grave, nor did she look back along the trail in the direction his killers had taken. Pursuing them would have to wait. She was shot deep. It was a small wound, but the bullet was lodged inside her, and that gave it the potential to turn bad. She'd have to get somewhere and have it removed before infection set in. Once that was done, she'd need a couple days' rest. *Time to make new plans,* she thought to herself, heeling the mare's pace up a bit. Then she'd be back on the trail. She would track down Stick's killers and settle all accounts.

The horses were winded by the time Dave Waddell and Frisco Bonham hit the low stretch of flatlands. They had moved at a fast pace down the narrow trail until finally Frisco sat back on his reins and brought both his horse and the string of horses to a halt. As the string bunched up beside him and Dave Waddell slid to a stop almost in their midst, Frisco said,

"That's about enough running for one day, Davey Boy. You heard her say she'd been shot." He let the horses circle amongst themselves and settle. "I figure Billy Boy must've got to that derringer he carried while she wasn't looking and put a bullet in her."

Dave Waddell sounded worried when he replied. "I don't know. She was sure able to shoot at us."

"Yeah, but she's hit," said Frisco. "No matter how tough she thinks she is, unless she's a complete mumbling fool, she'll have to take care of that wound. She ain't coming after us."

"I hope you're right," said Dave, looking back, already regretting what he'd gotten himself involved in but realizing there was nothing he could do now but see things through.

Frisco studied the frightened look on his face and chuckled under his breath. "Looks like I've got a born worrier on my hands, Davey Boy."

"I don't like that name," Dave Waddell snapped. His horse spun beneath him in a rise of dust. He still held the Colt Danielle had lent him in his hand. The smaller Navy Whitney pistol was stuck down behind his belt.

"Don't get so riled," said Frisco. "It's only a name."

Dave Waddell glared at him. "I just don't like it," he said.

Frisco shrugged. "There's no harm intended. We all called Billy Harper Billy Boy."

"It ain't the same," said Waddell. "So don't do it."

Taking note of Waddell's firearms, Frisco said, "All right, take it easy. I'll remember that from now on! No cause to get cross about it." Frisco had Stick's rifle, but it was stuck down in the rifle boot. Ever since they'd made their getaway, Dave Waddell had managed to stay behind him, keeping a close eye on him. Too close for him to make a move, Frisco thought. But that was okay. He needed Dave Waddell for now. Once he got out of this tight spot, he could either kill him or let him live. It meant nothing to him.

"Which way?" Waddell asked in a no-nonsense tone of voice.

"Settle down, Waddell," said Frisco. "I told you I'd take you to Earl and your wife . . . and I will."

"The woman was following their trail north," said Waddell, "but now you and I are headed back the other way."

"Yep, that's right," said Frisco. "That's because I know where they're going, and I know the round-about way Cherokee Earl will take to get there."

His answer satisfied Dave Waddell. "Okay, then, take me to them."

"I will." Frisco raised a finger for emphasis. "But first things first."

"First things first? What are you talking about?" Dave demanded.

"I'm talking about we need some grub and some traveling money before we can get anywhere. It's a long ways to where Cherokee Earl and the boys go to play," said Frisco.

Dave Waddell didn't like the nasty grin on Frisco's face, knowing what his words were implying. "We'll be all right," said Dave. "Let's get going."

"Be all right?" Frisco cocked his head, giving Dave a sarcastic look. "Waddell, have you got any food in your saddlebags? Any coffee even?"

"No," said Dave. "We had jerked beef, some beans, and coffee with us. But it was in the woman's saddlebags."

"Well . . . it ain't decent," said Frisco, "traveling without coffee, far as I'm concerned. Or money either," he added.

"I'm not robbing anything or anybody, Frisco," Waddell said firmly, "so don't even bring it up."

"I wasn't about to," said Frisco. "All I was going to

say is, we can take these horses over to the old north wagon trail and maybe sell them to one of the relay stations. They always have an eye out for fresh horses."

Dave thought about it for a second. "Is that on the way to catching up to Cherokee Earl?"

"Well, yes," said Frisco, sounding put out. "Why the hell else would I bring it up?" He shook his head as if in disgust. "You're going to have to start trusting me, Waddell."

"Yeah, I'll do that," snapped Waddell. "Now let's get going." He dropped his horse a step back behind Frisco and gestured with his pistol barrel. Frisco heeled his horse forward, leading the string. He grinned to himself, staring straight ahead.

They rode hard the rest of the day, barely stopping long enough to rest the winded horses. It was late dusk before they stepped down and made a dark camp beside a thin trickle of water running down the middle of an otherwise dry creekbed. Frisco Bonham slept flat on the ground, snoring loud and deep, wrapped in a blanket from behind Stick's saddle. Dave Waddell also wrapped himself in a blanket, but he slept light. He spent the night with his back propped against the dirt bank, his big Colt still in his hand, resting across his lap.

At daylight, Frisco stood up and coughed loudly just to see how soundly Waddell was sleeping. When Waddell didn't stir, Frisco said in an urgent tone, "Waddell! Wake up! Time to get moving!"

But Waddell showed no startled response. Instead, he tipped his hat up calmly and looked at Frisco standing fifteen feet away in the gray morning light. "I'm not asleep, Frisco," he said. "I've just been waiting on you." He flipped his blanket open, revealing the big Colt. After letting Frisco get an eyeful of the pistol and the way it had been lying there ready for him, Dave Waddell stood up, shook out the blanket, and walked to the horses.

Frisco grinned. "I always admired a man who looks out for himself."

They prepared the horses for travel, filled a canteen from the trickle of creek water, and once on the trail, didn't stop until the sun stood high overhead. They had stepped down from their saddles and led the horses for almost a mile when Dave Waddell asked, "How much farther to a relay station?" He felt light-headed from not having eaten since early the day before. His empty stomach growled.

"It's still ten miles or so," said Frisco. Looking all around the barren sand, cactus, and creosote, he added, "Hell, I ain't waiting any longer. I'm going to eat something even if I have to put down one of these horses." He looked Dave Waddell up and down and asked, "Have you ever et a horse?"

"No," said Dave, "and I'm not going to start today. Ten miles is not that far. We can hold off that long."

"Maybe you can," said Frisco, "but I'm a man who must fill his needs as quick as they arise." He stepped around beside the horse and reached for the rifle in the saddle boot.

But before he could draw it, he heard Dave say, "Hold it. Look at this!"

Turning, Frisco gazed out through the glittering sunlight. Three hundred yards away, a streaming rise of dust boiled up behind a rollicking stagecoach pulled by six galloping horses. "Well, don't this just beat all? Ask and ye shall receive!" Frisco shouted laughingly, outstretching his arms as if embracing salvation.

"Thank God," Dave Waddell whispered. He let out a tired sigh of relief. Stepping forward, for the first time allowing Frisco behind him unwatched, Waddell raised both arms and waved them back and forth slowly. "He sees us," he said over his shoulder, still waving as the driver slowed the rig.

"Look at him," said Frisco as the stagecoach drew closer. "Not a care in the world . . . nobody even riding shotgun for him. That's dangerous as hell in this country."

At thirty yards, Dave Waddell saw the white beard of the lone driver as the man began slowing the coach horses down to a walk. At thirty feet, Dave called out gratefully with a hand raised toward the coach. "Much obliged, mister. We were just wondering if we were ever going to—"

The sound of the rifle blast so close behind him almost knocked Dave Waddell off his feet. "Jesus!" he bellowed, throwing a hand to his assaulted left ear. At the sudden explosion, Waddell had squinted and ducked his head to the side. Now, looking at the coach driver, he saw the red splotch on the man's chest, saw he'd slammed backward and fallen sidelong, the coach reins dropping from his hands, giving the coach horses free run.

"You son of a bitch!" Waddell yelled, turning toward Frisco and reaching for the big Colt in his belt. But Frisco had already jumped into his saddle. The horse came streaking past Waddell, Frisco beating its sides with the rifle barrel as he nailed his spurs to it.

Sidling his horse up to the coach, Frisco dropped the rifle into its boot and leaped from his saddle. Catching the climbing rung, he swung up onto the driver's seat. He shoved the driver's body aside, snatched up the fallen reins, and reared back on them, bringing the spooked horses under control before they had time to get into a run.

"Whoa!" said Frisco, letting the horses circle out off the trail and back, settling them.

Dave Waddell watched the circling coach with fire in his eyes, his hand tight around the raised Colt, the rifle blast still ringing in his ears. "Get down from there, Frisco! You rotten, murdering—"

Again his words went unfinished. The coach came around onto the trail facing him, and from Frisco's right hand a cocked, sawed-off shotgun pointed down at him. "If you keep calling me names, Davey Boy, you're going to hurt my feelings." He grinned.

Dave Waddell took on a sickly look. The pistol lowered to his side. "Don't shoot me, Frisco, please," he said. "All I want is my wife back. . . . I never asked for none of this."

"Shoot you, hell!" said Frisco. "Quit talking crazy. Put that pistol away and give me a hand here." He set the brake handle on the coach, rocking it to a halt as the horses stopped. "There's most always a dollar or two in these strongboxes."

"My God, we're robbing a stage?" said Dave as if he couldn't believe what was happening or how suddenly he'd become a party to it.

"I don't know how you can say we're *robbing* it," said Frisco. "This old buzzard's dead. He can't object."

"But—but he's dead because you killed him!" Dave exclaimed as if he could point out to the man the terrible thing he'd just done.

"Davey Boy, you just keep going on about the same thing, don't you? Of course I killed him! How else was I supposed to get what he's got without him putting up a fight for it?" Somehow, the way Frisco said it, it all made sense in this twisted, vile way of thinking.

Dave shook his head as if to clear it. But he let the hammer down on the Colt and shoved it down into his belt. The shotgun in Frisco's hand made all the difference in the world. Now they were back on equal ground. He didn't want to get on Frisco's bad side, not after seeing how easily this man could take a life. He noted how, now that Frisco had the shotgun and had taken the edge from him, he'd gone right back to calling him Davey Boy. That meant something, Waddell was sure.

"Go back there and check under the luggage flap," said Frisco. "See if he didn't bring along some grub of some sort. I swear I could eat the hind end out of a running bobcat." He raised the heavy strongbox and pitched it out to the ground. "Here, shoot this lock off first."

Frisco watched closely and kept his hand ready on the shotgun until Dave reached down with the Colt and took careful aim. The Colt jumped in his hand, and Frisco laughed to see the lock disappear from the strongbox. "Good shot, Davey Boy! Damn, I'll make a highwayman of you before it's over!" He leaped down from the driver's seat and landed beside Waddell. Then he dropped to his knees, opened the lid to the strongbox, and riffled through the contents, keeping the shotgun in his right hand, the butt propped on his thigh. As if having just become aware of Dave Waddell's presence, he looked back over his shoulder and said, "Are you going to check back there like I told you? See if there's any grub?"

Without a word, Dave Waddell turned and walked to the rear of the stagecoach.

"You're going to have to quit being so bashful, Davey Boy," Frisco called out as he began tearing open letters and checking for any cash in them. "We've got a long trail before us getting to Cherokee Earl and your pretty little wife. I'm counting on you to pull your own weight."

Dave Waddell stopped midstep at Frisco's words. He stood for a second, letting them sink in. A sickness almost overwhelmed him, but he fought it down, his fists clenched at his sides. His first thought was to make a break for the horses, jump into the saddle, and ride. Ride as far and as fast as he could. But then he pictured his wife with Cherokee Earl.

His knees went weak for a second; then he forced
the picture from his mind, swallowed the bitter taste
in his mouth, and walked to the rear of the dusty
stagecoach. God help him, he'd become one of them.
He was no different in the eyes of the law from the
man who had actually pulled the trigger and killed
the stage driver. No court would listen to his flimsy
excuse. He was an outlaw, plain and simple, whether
he'd meant to be or not.

"How in the world did you end up here?" he
asked himself, untying the dusty canvas flap and
throwing it open. His eyes moved across the small
wooden crates all neatly stacked and tied down,
some of them stating their contents in black letters,
others leaving it to his imagination.

"Anything to eat back there?" Frisco called out.

"Don't see anything," Dave replied. "But I'll
search around some." He reached in, untied the rope
from the wooden crates, and pulled them down
around his feet. Eagerly, he picked up the first one
and began loosening its top. Since he was here, he
might as well see what this life had to offer.

Chapter 11

By the time Danielle had reached the flatlands she sat bowed in her saddle. The pain in her side had grown worse. The bleeding had slowed almost to a stop, but the flesh surrounding the wound had turned puffy and flaming red. The intense heat made matters worse, draining what strength the bullet in her side had not already taken away. It had been up to Sundown to lead them the last few miles to the beginning of the dirt street into town. Danielle sat slumped, suspended on a narrow edge of semi-consciousness and losing ground.

From an alleyway where he'd taken up a regular guard position ever since Cherokee Earl and his gang had raided the town, Leonard Whirley crouched with the 10-gauge shotgun—the same shotgun that had fallen from the dead sheriff's hand. Leonard could tell that this wasn't one of those who had sacked the town, but he remained cautious and slipped back through the alley and down behind the buildings until he reached the rear door of the doctor's office. He knocked sharply and whispered to the wooden door, "Doc, it's Whirley! Open up! A woman's riding in. Looks like she's shot!"

"Shot?" Dr. Callaway slipped the bolt back on the door and stepped out into the alley, hooking his wire-rimmed spectacles behind his ears. "Another woman? This one's shot? What the hell's gotten into women around here?"

"I don't know, Doc," said Whirley. "I just thought you better know about it."

"Good thinking, Whirley," the doctor replied, buttoning his vest as the two hurried along the back alley. On their way, they spotted a buckboard wagon loaded high with furniture and household items headed out of town along a back road. "There goes Orville Jones and his family," the old doctor said, shaking his head. "They're all leaving here like rats from a sinking ship. This town will be a dusty spot on the trail in another week."

"I know," said Whirley. "I'm already thinking of boarding up the New Royal and heading for New Mexico Territory. I'm giving up on Braden Flats."

"I hate saying it, but me too," the doctor replied. They rushed along until they reached the spot where Whirley had stood a moment ago. They saw the chestnut mare standing in the middle of the street. On the ground Danielle lay where she had fallen. The mare nudged her gently but got no response. Danielle appeared lifeless in the dirt. Dr. Callaway studied the situation for a moment, rubbing his chin.

"Come on, Leonard, this one looks like she's done in," said the doctor at length.

"Wait, Doc, this might be a trick," Whirley replied, his right hand going nervously to his toupee.

"Dang it, Leonard! Why would it be a trick?" He flagged Whirley forward with his hand. "Come on, help me get this poor woman off the street. Worry about your hair later."

After they rushed to the middle of the street, it took a few tries for Dr. Callaway to shoo the chestnut mare away from Danielle long enough for him and Whirley to scoop her up off the street and carry her back to his office. Sundown loped along behind them, her reins dragging in the dirt. As the men stepped up onto the boardwalk, the mare paced back and forth, shaking her mane and blowing out a restless breath. "Don't you worry ole gal," Doc Callaway said over his shoulder to Sundown from the open doorway. "We'll take good care of her."

When they laid Danielle onto a gurney in the room next to the doctor's office, Doc Callaway said to the bar owner, "I'm going to have to undress her, Whirley. You go hitch the mare to the rail and see she gets some water and grain. I'll put her up at my barn tonight, since we've got no town livery barn left." Thinking about what had happened to the barn, Callaway grumbled under his breath as he unbuckled Danielle's trousers. "The dirty sonsabitches."

Whirley turned and slipped out the door. The old doctor eased Danielle's trousers down as carefully as he could. But still she moaned in unconscious pain. "Whoo-ie," said the doctor, seeing the inflamed, swollen flesh surrounding the small bullet hole. "Nothing worse than shooting a body with a dirty little derringer, I always say."

Danielle's eyes opened for a moment. "Who—who are you? Where am I?" she asked, reaching to grasp the doctor's wrist as he pressed his fingertip gently against the tortured flesh.

"Nobody you need fear," the doctor replied. He pushed her weak hand aside. "I'm Dr. Callaway. This is Braden Flats . . . what's left of it, anyway. That's as much as you need to know for now. You got a nasty little bullet lodged in ya." He probed gently with his fingers. "We need to get it out of there before it festers up any worse. I'll have to do some cutting."

Danielle looked around the room with bleary eyes. "Is my mare all right?" she asked.

"Yeah, I'd say she's right enough. She gave us a hard time when we went to move you here."

Danielle gave a weak smile. "That's my mare for

sure," she whispered. Then she lowered her head back to the pillow on the gurney and said with resolve, "Cut away, Doctor. I'm all yours."

Seeing she had slipped back into unconsciousness, Dr. Callaway rubbed her hair back off her damp forehead. "I'll make it as painless as I can, young lady," he whispered to her. "You look like you've been through plenty enough already."

For the next half hour, Whirley waited in the doctor's office, pacing to the window every few minutes and keeping an eye on the road leading out of town. While he stood at the window, he shook his head as he saw another heavily loaded wagon amble into the distance across the rolling flatlands.

"She's all stitched up now," said the doctor's voice from the door to the next room.

"Did she ever wake up, Doc?" Whirley asked, straightening his crooked toupee.

"Yep," said Dr. Callaway. "She woke up before I started, then again when I was closing the incision."

"Well, what did she tell you?" Whirley asked. "Had she run into the same bunch that raided us? Did they do that to her?"

"She said it was different men, but from the same bunch," said the doctor. "She's on their trail for doing the same in Haley Springs that they did here. They killed an old drover who rode with her. . . . They kidnapped that woman who was with Cherokee Earl." Considering the situation, he added, "I thought right off that there was something wrong there. I hate thinking that man took advantage of that woman right here in Braden Flats, and we never lifted a finger to stop him."

"Hell, Doc, we didn't know," said Whirley. "Besides, what good would we have done anyway? Our sheriff is dead from trying to stop them. What chance would we have had?"

"I don't know," said the doctor. "None, I suppose. I ain't got it in me to kill. Some men are born with a killing trait, but some of us ain't. Sometimes I wish it was otherwise, but I can't deny how I am."

"Then we did all we could," said Whirley. "So put it out of your mind and think no more about it."

"I reckon you're right," said the doctor. He looked off across the barren land to the slight rise of dust still stirred up from the wagon, which was long gone from sight. "This is a hateful, cussed place, Whirley. I wish to God I'd never laid eyes on it."

A silence passed. Then Whirley straightened his toupee and smoothed it down again with both palms of his hands. "Me too, Doc," he said as if in defeat.

For the next week, Danielle, following the doctor's orders, was forced to rest and keep the wound treated in order to arrest any further infection. She did so grudgingly. She took her meals and lodging in the same small room where Dr. Callaway had treated her. She began moving around slowly with the help of a cane on the third day. Leonard Whirley managed to be close by her side every waking hour. Danielle could see the saloon owner was taken with her, and she tried to treat him as a casual friend, hoping that was as far as it would go. But Whirley grew more smitten as each day passed.

On the fourth day, having loosened the stiffness in her side, Danielle moved about the room and the doctor's office without the cane, limping slightly. The swelling had begun to dissipate from her wound. On the fifth day, when Whirley went to the doctor's barn to feed and water Sundown, Danielle was in her boots and went with him. She wore her gun belt to get used to the weight of it again, her Colt tied down to her right thigh.

"You sure heal quick," said Whirley, noting that

she no longer limped as they crossed the empty street and walked toward the doctor's house on the outskirts of town.

"I have to heal quick," Danielle replied. "The longer I wait here, the colder the trail." She had filled in both Whirley and Doc Callaway on everything that had happened. "I owe it to the Waddell woman to find her and free her from Cherokee Earl. It makes no difference what her husband has done. I've got to help her. I'll deal with him when the time comes."

Whirley nodded as they walked along. Lifting a hand to his toupee out of habit, he said, "Miss Danielle, if I might be so bold, I think you are about the prettiest woman I ever laid eyes on."

"Well, thank you, Mr. Whirley," said Danielle, seeing where this might be headed and wishing she could stop it before it got there. But it was no use.

"The thing is," he continued, "I'll soon be leaving this shi—I mean, mud-hole . . . and I'm going somewhere clean and sophisticated. Maybe Santa Fe. Maybe Tombstone. I ain't sure." He stopped and turned to her, touching her arm gently and stopping her also. "But wherever I go . . . I'd be honored to have you by my side." He swallowed and ventured, "That is to say, as my lawful wife, Miss Danielle. . . . Everything would be on the up and up, of course."

"That certainly is a gentleman's proposal, Mr. Whirley," said Danielle, "and I appreciate it. But I'm afraid I must turn you down. I'm on the trail of these murderers, and I don't plan on stopping until I've finished what I started." She gestured toward the doctor's barn, and together they continued walking.

Whirley looked let down but at the same time relieved. "Well, at least I got a chance to ask," he said in all earnestness. "Some fellows never get this close to a respectable woman."

"I'm flattered you feel that way, Mr. Whirley." They walked on.

"Can I ask you, Miss Danielle, is it me, or are you just not interested in marrying at this time?" Whirley's eyes turned soft, almost pleading for the right answer.

"It's nothing against you, Mr. Whirley, although you have to admit we hardly know each other. It's just that I'm not interested in marrying anybody right now. Someday maybe, but not now. If I was, there's a man in Colorado . . ."

"Well, I'm glad to hear that," said Whirley good-naturedly. "For a minute I wondered if maybe there was something wrong with you."

"You mean if I'm not interested in marriage, there must be something wrong with me?" Danielle felt the tightness in her voice and tried to shake it off.

"I didn't mean that the way it sounded," said Whirley. "Of course there's nothing wrong with you."

Danielle offered a smile of reconciliation. "That's good to hear," she said.

Whirley shrugged. "But if you don't mind me saying so, Miss Danielle, I believe it's awful foolish of you . . . going out there after Cherokee Earl and his bunch."

"Oh, really? Foolish, you say?" Danielle cocked an eye.

"Well, yes, foolish," Whirley said with finality. "Doggone it, Miss Danielle, it don't make sense, a little woman like yourself trying to do a man's job. Heck, most men wouldn't attempt to go after Cherokee Earl even with a posse backing them up! You're talking about going after him alone."

"And because I am, it's foolish of me," Danielle said flatly, staring straight ahead.

"Please don't take offense," said Whirley, "but let's face it. That Colt is almost bigger than you are. If you ever had to draw and shoot at somebody, how do you expect to ever get it—"

The Colt streaked upward too fast for Leonard Whirley to see it clearly. All his eyes caught was a flash of sunlight on polished steel. Then four shots exploded as quickly as she could cock and fire. With each shot, a short length of chain holding a long wooden sign above the New Royal Saloon disappeared form one corner after the other until the sign collapsed to the street in a large puff of dust. Leonard watched, hunkering farther down with each shot, his arms rising and wrapping across his head as if to protect his toupee, his mouth agape.

"One thing's for sure—you know what to say to turn a girl's head." Danielle opened her Colt, dropped out the spent cartridges, and replaced them while smoke still curled from the barrel.

"Wait, Miss Danielle!" Leonard called out, staring at his downed wooden sign for a moment in disbelief as he hurried to catch up to her. "I didn't mean nothing by it, honest! I wouldn't say something to offend you for nothing in this world."

"I believe you, Mr. Whirley. I really, truly do," said Danielle. "It's just the way things are in this world. The only time I feel foolish is when I start making myself believe things might have changed." She walked on, still without facing him.

For the next two days she avoided Leonard Whirley, but on the morning she left Braden Flats, Danielle made it a point to stop by the New Royal Saloon and thank him for having looked after Sundown for her.

"I wish you would stay another few days," said Dr. Callaway when she stepped into her stirrups out front of his office. "You've been the first paying customer I've had for the longest time. I hate to loose you."

Danielle smiled down at him. "I wish you and Mr. Whirley weren't leaving here," said Danielle. "I expect there will be no town here in a few weeks."

The old doctor scratched his head as if considering it, then he said, "Well, I suppose we'll just have to wait and see."

With dried food in her saddlebags, and grain for Sundown, Danielle turned the chestnut mare in the street and rode away at an easy pace, eyeing the burnt remains of the telegraph office on her way. There was no way she would give up on hunting Cherokee Earl and his gang. The more she saw of their handiwork, the more she was convinced that she had to put a stop to them. She thought it a bit peculiar that neither the doctor nor Leonard Whirley had been able to tell from Ellen Waddell's actions that she was being held against her will. But she realized that in a life-or-death situation a woman might very well go along with her captors until she saw a chance to break away. At least Danielle hoped that was the case, having lost so much precious time here.

At the edge of town, Danielle brought the mare up into a trot, testing the tenderness of her healed wound, feeling no pain there. She studied the hoof-prints in the dirt, knowing that the trail had grown cold. Cherokee Earl and his gang could be any number of places by now. Once again she was on her own, the same as when she'd hunted her father's killers. She was used to being alone, yet she missed having Stick beside her. From now on she had to watch her own back, not always an easy task for a woman unescorted in a man's world.

Danielle knew her best bet was to stay on the north trail, follow it toward the highlands and see what, if anything, had happened along the string of towns that lay ahead of her. She was certain that a man like Cherokee Earl couldn't go along without causing more trouble. His gang had tasted blood at the past two towns in a row. She was betting they would be wanting more.

Chapter 12

Following a narrow stream running down from a stretch of rocky hills, for two nights in a row Danielle made her camp alongside the water's edge. The first night had been uneventful, sheltered as she was beneath a deep cliff overhang. But on the second night, in the hours before dawn, Danielle was awakened by Sundown nickering low and warily from where Danielle had grazed her in sweet grass less than twenty yards away. Hearing the mare, Danielle rolled quietly from her blanket, her rifle in hand. She crouched back out of the circling glow of firelight, listening for any sound out of the ordinary. For the rest of the night she stayed back away from the fire, blanket wrapped around her, barely seeing the silhouette of the mare in the moon's glow.

At first light, Danielle picked up Sundown's bridle and walked down to where the big mare stood waiting. Sundown turned her head to face Danielle, and Danielle reached out a hand and rubbed the velvety muzzle. "Easy, girl," Danielle whispered.

As she stroked the mare, her eyes searched along the stream, up along the rock ledges and into the darkened shadows and crevices. "What was up there?" Danielle asked quietly, as if at any moment the mare might answer. "Don't you worry," she added. "Whatever it is, if it's still there, we'll find it soon enough."

She lifted the bridle onto the mare's muzzle, adjusted it, and led the animal back to the campsite only a few yards away. Yes, there was someone watching her, she felt it plain as day. Unseen eyes followed her until she passed out of sight back into the rocks bordering the stream. Instinctively, she checked her Colt, then placed it back loosely into her holster. "Yep," she repeated quietly to herself and the mare. "We'll soon find out."

Without preparing coffee or food, Danielle saddled the mare. Then she cleared the camp and rode off along the north trail alongside the stream before sunlight had crested the eastern skyline. Just past sunup she reached a place where the land flattened for the next few hundred yards before swooping upward again. Still following the stream, Danielle purposefully skylined herself to the hill trail below. She didn't let herself be seen for long, just enough for whoever might be watching to know that she was not using good caution. Something a foolish woman would do, she reminded herself with a wry smile.

Had someone well-skilled with a rifle wanted her dead, right then would have been a good time to make their play. But they would have had to strike quickly, and even then risk everything they had on one shot. With a fast break for cover, she could easily duck into the rocks before they set their sights on her again.

As she rode, she watched both right and left, barely turning her head in either direction but rather shifting only her eyes beneath her lowered hat brim. Along the way she caught a glimpse of a wisp of trail dust stirring from the rocks and scrub juniper running parallel below. Whoever was down there was hurrying now, wanting to get past her and climb up onto the trail inside the rocks. That made sense, she thought. They weren't out to ambush her. They wanted her to come upon them all at once, in surprise, face to face. All right, she would give them

that. At a point where the trail climbed back up into
the rocky hills, she prepared herself, letting her right
hand rest on her thigh only inches from the butt of
her Colt.

With the craggy hillside rising on her left and the
winding stream on her right, she eased the mare
along at a slow walk until suddenly, as if out of
nowhere, two men appeared on the trail before her.
One man held a cocked rifle pointed at her from less
than thirty feet away. The other stood confidently,
with a pistol hanging loosely in his hand. "Well,
well, look here, Brother Daryl," said the one with the
pistol. "What a pleasant surprise."

"I was just thinking that very same thing myself,
Brother Lon!" said the one with the rifle. "You never
know who you're going to come upon up here in
these rocks. Could be a snake or a scorpion," he said,
widening his eyes in mock fright.

"So true," said the other. "But then again it just
might be some tender young dove."

Danielle stopped the chestnut mare with the slightest tap of her knees. The mare turned slightly, quar-
terwise to the men, then stood as still as stone. "Your
best hope is for the snakes and scorpions," Danielle
said. "This dove ain't as tender as you'd like."

Both men had spread wolfish smiles, but the smiles
melted away at her words. The one with the pistol
said to the other without taking his eyes off Danielle,
"Well, Brother Daryl, there's our answer. It's her, all
right. Cherokee Earl said she was a rash, rude,
wished-she-was-a-man kind of woman."

Danielle felt her senses perk. Immediately, she
picked up on the man's words and replied, "Didn't
you wonder why Cherokee Earl didn't come looking
for me himself? Why's he so busy he can't handle
his own gun work?"

"He's busy sparking his new bride, up in Drake,"
the man replied.

"Shut up, Lon," said the rifleman, stepping forward. "Can't you see she's just trying to milk you for information?"

"She can milk all day. It suits me," the other replied. His face turned stonelike, his eyes dark and caged. His voice went flat and iron-hard. "She ain't going nowhere after today."

Danielle felt a cold, calm resolve wash over her. "I take it you two are brothers?"

"That's right," said the one with the pistol. "Daryl and Lon Trabough, at your service." His death-mask expression remained the same. "I'm Lon," he added, "the handsomest one."

"What's it to you?" said the one with the rifle.

Danielle allowed a slight shrug. "Well, Daryl, I'm always curious about those I'm fixin' to kill."

"By God, let's go on and kill her and be done with it, Lon," said Daryl, working his fingers restlessly on the rifle stock. "I've no tolerance for a sharp-tongued woman!"

"Easy, Brother Daryl," said Lon, still keeping his eyes on Danielle. "How often is a man blessed with this kind of situation? Earl wants us to kill her. He never said we couldn't have a little fun first."

"I don't like it," said Daryl.

"Oh, but you will, Brother Daryl, by the time it gets around to you," said Lon.

Danielle sat silently, waiting, watching, knowing. Beneath her, the mare hadn't much more than breathed. Together, horse and rider could have been a statue except for the flutter of a hot breeze as it licked at Danielle's hat brim.

"Now lift that pistol, pitch it away, and climb down here," said Lon. "We're going to start by getting a good look at you without all them clothes hiding your better nature."

Danielle raised her knee and lifted her leg over the saddle slowly. She paused, suspended for a second, looking both men up and down. "You're about my size, aren't you, Lon?" She let herself slide down from the saddle and stood with her feet shoulder-width apart.

Lon Trabough had a hard time containing himself. His lips quivered a bit at her words. "Oh, don't you worry, you sweet little morsel. I'm just exactly your size!"

"That's what I thought," Danielle said coolly.

"Now lift that pistol, and let's get started!" Lon demanded eagerly.

"Whatever you say, Lon." Her first shot hit Lon in the dead center of his sweaty forehead, the impact of it flipping his hat backward off his head. The shot came so fast, her pistol only a streak of shiny metal coming up from her holster, that Lon stood staring blankly for a second, a stunned grimace on his face as blood spewed from the back of his head. Then he sank to his knees as if ready for prayer and collapsed forward onto his face.

"Lon, Jesus!" Daryl Trabough saw the gout of blood and brain matter spray past him. It rattled him long enough for Danielle to almost take her time putting two bullets through his heart. He dropped limply in the dirt. Only then did Sundown seem to ease down and shake out her mane.

Danielle walked forward, reloading her Colt. When she reached out a boot toe and rolled Lon Trabough's head to the side, she saw only a minimal amount of blood on the back of his shirt collar and none down the back of the shirt itself. "Yep, you're just about my size," she said quietly to herself. She holstered her pistol, stooped down, and began undressing him.

Stripping Lon Trabough down to his long johns, Danielle carried his clothes out into the shallow stream and scrubbed them with a small bar of lye soap she carried in her saddlebags. She rinsed them, soaped them again, rinsed them again, and hung them to dry over the rounded tops of scrub juniper and mesquite bushes. While she waited on the wet clothes to dry, she took down the lariat from Sundown's saddle, looped it around the corpses' feet, and dragged them both downstream amid jumbled piles of rocks and spilled boulders that years of wind and rain had washed down from the hillside.

She loosened the rope, looked down at the two bodies, and dusted her hands together. She stood silent for a moment and took off her hat in reflection. The mare stood close by her side. "Lord," Danielle said, bowing her head slightly, "I know it's not right taking another person's life, and I wish I hadn't had to do it. But you saw how it played out. They couldn't have made their intentions any plainer and it still be fit for Christian ears." She paused for a moment with her hat in her hand. "I doubt these two snakes ever did anybody any good in this life. So whatever you do with them is fine by me and better than they deserve. Amen."

Danielle placed her hat back down on her head, tightened it, and turned and walked away, leading the mare back across the rocky ground to the trail. Having missed a lot of sleep the night before and breakfast early that morning, Danielle ate some jerked beef and dried biscuits, then napped for the next couple of hours. When she awakened she gathered the clothes, feeling where the trousers were still a bit damp, and walked off into the cover of rocks and brush. While Sundown waited, Danielle unwound the binder she'd carried for the past year in her saddlebags. She took off her women's clothes and wrapped the binder firmly around her, flattening the curve of her breasts.

Once she had changed into the men's clothing, she took her time folding her doeskin skirt, her bell-sleeved blouse, and her long soft leather riding vest.

Back at Sundown's side, Danielle placed her women's clothing carefully down into her saddlebags, strapped the saddlebags shut, and patted them with her hands. "I hope this is not for long," she said absently to the chestnut mare. "Looks like the only way to get respect in a man's world is to *be* a man."

Danielle unstrapped the rolled-up riding duster from behind her saddle, shook it out, and put it on. Then she stuffed her hair up under her hat, stepped up into her saddle, and patted the mare on the neck. "Let's go, Sundown," she said. "We've been down this trail before."

Drake, New Mexico Territory

Cherokee Earl sat atop his horse and spoke down to Buck Hite, an outlaw gangleader he'd met upon arriving in town. Earl had decided that Buck Hite and his gang would fit nicely into his plans. Buck stood holding the reins to Ellen Waddell's horse. Ellen sat stone-faced, staring straight ahead. "Don't wait around too long for Daryl and Lon Trabough, Buck," Earl said. "I need you and your gang in Cimarron as soon as you can get there."

"What day do you need us there, Earl? We'll make sure we get there on time."

Cherokee Earl gave him a blank stare. "If you knew what day the main silver load comes in, you wouldn't need me at all, now would you, Buck?"

"I meant nothing by it, Earl," said Buck. He tried to hand Earl the reins to Ellen's horse, but Earl refused to take them. Instead, he flagged Avery McRoy forward and gestured for him to take them. McRoy looked put out at the task.

"Just make sure you get there soon," Earl said gruffly to Buck Hite. "I only need men I can count on."

As Earl spoke to Buck Hite, Dirty Joe slipped his horse forward ahead of McRoy, saying to him in a guarded voice, "I've got her reins, Avery."

"Much obliged," McRoy whispered in reply. "Leading her has made my arm sore as a boil."

Earl leaned slightly down to Buck Hite and said, "Buck, I'll tell you this much. . . . Your boys Daryl and Lon killing that woman and old man for me has gotten you a top spot in my operation. Once we pull this bank job you'll wonder why we didn't get together years before now." He gave a thin, quick smile, then straightened in his saddle and leveled his hat. Looking back and forth along the street, he shook his head. "This whole damned town is made of mud. I'm glad you talked us out of burning it."

Buck Hite only nodded, tipping his hat as Earl, McRoy, and Dirty Joe backed their horses and rode away, Joe leading Ellen's horse, which stayed right up beside his. "There goes trouble in the making," Buck Hite murmured to himself, seeing the flushed and aroused look on Dirty Joe's face and the guarded smile the woman passed to him. Buck shook his head and walked back to the Ace High Saloon, where his men awaited him.

At the edge of town, Ellen Waddell slowed her horse back a step, deliberately making Dirty Joe fall behind with her while McRoy and Cherokee Earl rode on ahead. "Come on, Miss Ellen!" Joe whispered warily. "He's going to suspect something." He jerked her horse forward.

"All right," Ellen replied in a hushed tone, "but can't you see he's already tiring of me? He'll soon pass me off to McRoy or one of those men back there, or anyone he feels like—"

"Shhh, don't say that, Ellen! I'm not going to let that happen to you. . . . I swear I won't."

"Then you better do something quick," Ellen said, letting her horse ride sidled against his, "or it's going

to be too late, and you and I will never be together."
She gazed deep into his eyes and said, "I can't stand
the thought of us never being together, can you?"

"God, no!" he said, a slight tremor in his voice.
"But what can I do about it right now?"

She moved her eyes from Dirty Joe's slowly, making sure that his eyes followed hers to McRoy and
Cherokee Earl's backs. "You know what to do, Joe,"
she whispered with finality.

Dirty Joe stared at the two men for a moment, the
tendons in his neck drawn tight at the thought running through his mind. "Soon, Ellen. . . . Soon, I
promise."

Back in Drake at the Ace High Saloon, Eddie Ray
Moon, Clifford Reed, and Fat Cyrus Kerr stood huddled at the bar and listened to Buck Hite talk about
their newly formed alliance with Cherokee Earl and
the plans for meeting him and his men for the up-
coming bank robbery up in Cimarron. "I'd feel better
about everything if Daryl and Lon was already back
here with us," said Fat Cyrus. As he spoke, he hiked
his baggy trousers up under his belly, the weight of
his gun belt constantly working them downward.

"Me too," Clifford Reed agreed. "I'm a little
spooked about it, to tell the truth."

"*Spooked?*" said Buck Hite, showing an amount of
contempt for Reed's words.

Reed wasn't a bit embarrassed. "Damn right,
spooked," he said with conviction. "It ain't natural,
what Earl told us about this woman, and it was a
mistake sending two of our men back to ambush her.
How long should it take two men like the Trabough
brothers to gun down her and one old man?"

"When you start running things, Clifford, you can
ask them kind of questions," Buck Hite said, jutting
his chin, not liking the way Reed questioned his
judgment in front of the other men. "But right now

I'm still the top bull of this herd." He tapped a thumb on his broad chest. "I sent them because I told Cherokee Earl I would. You don't throw in with a man like Cherokee Earl Muir unless you've got something to offer."

Fat Cyrus tossed back a shot of whiskey and wiped his thick hand across his mouth. "Earl was down to only two men and himself," he said, "not counting the fact that he's riding around with a woman draped across his lap. Looks to me like we're holding the most cards in this game."

"Yeah," said Buck Hite, "we might be holding the most . . . but the most ain't always the best. I don't care if he's got a woman and her house cat on his lap. We've thrown in with him." He looked at each of the three men's faces in turn. "Boys, Cherokee Earl is an old hand at this business. He knows the upper country and every hiding place up there. He knows ranchers who'll hide him out and crooked sheriffs who'll tip him off when the law's gotten too close." He leaned in closer and said almost in a whisper, "He's even got inside information on the bank in Cimarron . . . knows when there's a big shipment of money coming in to pay for silver from the silver mines all across the Territory."

"When is it?" Fat Cyrus asked.

Buck looked at him in disbelief. "Well, now, Cyrus," he said wryly, "if I knew when it was coming, I reckon I wouldn't need Cherokee Earl at all, would I?"

"Oh," said Cyrus, nodding. "I see what you mean."

Buck Hite shook his head, then said to everybody, "Don't ever think I enjoy giving my gang over to somebody else. But for now, if we ever plan on getting ahead, Cherokee Earl is the best way to do it. Sure, he's short of men right now . . . got somebody

dogging his trail. But why else would he be taking
us in?" He looked at each of them again, his eyes
asking if they were with him.

Clifford Reed nodded. "I had complaints, Buck. I
just needed some filling in."

"All right." Buck stared at him, his hand resting
on his pistol butt. "Are you properly filled in?"

"Sure." Clifford shrugged, reaching for the whiskey bottle that stood on the bar. "I'm good."

"What about you, Cyrus?" Buck asked. "Anything
else I need to fill you in on? I had eggs and potatoes
for breakfast . . . went to the jake about an hour
ago . . . been going pretty regularly the past few
weeks."

Fat Cyrus looked away from Buck's cold stare.

"What about you, Eddie Ray?" Buck asked the
thin, hollow-eyed gunfighter with a pointed chin.

Eddie Ray Moon had been rolling himself a smoke
while Buck spoke to the other two men. Now he ran
the cigarette in and out of his mouth, wetting it, and
let it hang from his lips as he spoke, taking a long
match from his shirt pocket. "Do I look like I give a
rattling bag full of dry horse shit?"

Fat Cyrus and Clifford Reed chuckled as Eddie
Ray struck the match and lit the cigarette. Turning
his eyes to Buck Hite, he let go of a long stream of
smoke and shook out the match. "Makes no difference to me who we ride with, long as the money's
right." He shot Clifford Reed a look of contempt. "I'll
try not to get too spooked by this woman and her
grandfather or whoever the hell the old man is." He
made a show of flipping the burnt match away, then
leaned back against the bar as if getting comfortable.
"You figure out what you want done, then just let
me know. I'll kill them so quick they'll forget they
was ever born."

Chapter 13

Cherokee Earl and his party had been gone from Drake for three days when Danielle rode in on the chestnut mare. Dressed in the clothes she'd taken off of Lon Trabough, she looked exactly as she'd intended, a young gunman on the move: lean, wily, and sizing up everyone who passed before him. To Buck Hite and the others, the young gunman looked no different from any other saddle tramp coming in off the high range. Yet, watching the mare pass by the Ace High Saloon, seeing the young gunman with his duster opened in front, revealing the big tied-down Colt perched on his hip, something strikingly familiar caught Fat Cyrus's attention. He just couldn't put his finger on it.

"What have we got here?" Cyrus said to Clifford Reed, the two of them standing on the boardwalk of the Ace High.

"Beats me," said Clifford. "But he sure carries himself like he's cock of the walk." Both men watched in silence for a moment as the young gunman rode by. "Nice mare though," Clifford offered under his breath.

"Think I ought to go get Buck?" Fat Cyrus asked, hiking up his trousers.

"Why?" said Clifford Reed. "Alls he'll do is what we're doing—staring and asking questions."

From behind the batwing doors of the Ace High, Eddie Ray said, "Don't you suppose it would be a

good idea if somebody went and asked this new-
comer what he's doing here in Drake? Don't know
about you boys, but I always like to have an idea
who might or might not be carrying a badge."

"That's no lawman," said Cyrus. "I'll wager you
on it."

"No, I don't think so either," said Clifford.
"There's something about a lawman you can always
spot . . . too well fed or something. This boy is a
straight-up gunman, an outlaw just like us, far as
I'm concerned."

Eddie Ray stepped out onto the boardwalk and let
the doors flap behind him. "One thing's for sure:
neither one of yas would ever know what he is if it
meant walking your lazy behinds over and asking
him."

"I'll go if Buck asks me to," said Fat Cyrus, both
him and Clifford Reed watching the rider ease the
mare up to a hitchrail out front of a low adobe and
stone hotel.

Clifford Reed said, "You're right, Eddie Ray, we
ain't going over and asking him a damn thing. . . .
But you know what? I figure that's something you'd
be wanting to do by yourself, tough guy that you
are and all."

Eddie Ray took a deep draw on his cigarette and
said through a stream of smoke, "Tough guy that I
am . . . I think I'll do just that." He flipped the stub
of the cigarette away and stepped down off the
boardwalk. "Get us a beer, Fat Cyrus," he said over
his shoulder. "This shouldn't take over a minute or
two."

The two men watched Eddie Ray Moon saunter
across the street and run his hand along the chestnut
mare's damp side as he walked past the hitchrail to
the door of the hotel. "That damned fool," said Clifford Reed, staring alongside Fat Cyrus. "Whoever

that gunman is, I almost wish he'd send Eddie Ray
back out with a tin can tied to his tail."

"Yeah, me too," said Fat Cyrus, easing forward
down off the boardwalk. "Come on, let's get over
there close to the window. I want to listen to this."

In the small lobby of La Rosa Negra Hotel, Danielle stood signing the leather-bound guest register,
her saddlebags over her shoulder, her rifle under her
arm. She used the name she'd used in the past when
she'd traveled as a man, Danny Duggin. Finishing,
she slid the register across the ornate countertop into
the waiting hands of the Mexican woman across
the counter.

The woman started to close the register, but the
voice of Eddie Ray Moon said firmly from the front
door, "Not so fast, Falina." He slipped over quickly
beside Danielle and placed his hand down flat on the
register. Danielle only stared at him from within the
dark shadow of her lowered hat brim. "I'd like to
see who we have visiting us."

Falina drew her hands away from the register,
shooting a worried look back and forth between the
two faces at the counter. "*Por favor!* I do not want
the trouble," she said in stiff English.

"And you won't have any trouble, at least not from
me," said Eddie Ray, spreading a harsh grin at the
stranger with the lowered hat brim. "What about
you, Mister . . . ?" He consulted the register, then
finished his words. "Mr. Danny Duggin. Any trouble
coming from your direction?"

Danielle lowered her tone of voice a bit and added
some gravel to it. "If there was, you'd be past knowing about it by now," she said.

The words stung Eddie Ray. His grin disappeared.
He took a step back from the counter, letting his right
hand poise near his pistol butt. "Did I just hear a
threat in there?"

Danielle stared at him from the darkness beneath the broad hat brim. "You figure it out," she said, swiping her free hand across the countertop and picking up the key to her room.

Seeing her gun hand busy holding the key, Eddie Ray grew bolder. As Danielle turned to walk away toward the stairs, Eddie Ray stepped around in front of her, blocking her way. "I already have figured it out," he said, his fingers opening and closing near the pistol butt. "I say you and me are going have to do some settling up before you go a step farth—"

Danielle cut his words with her rifle butt, jerking it forward from under her arm to nail Eddie Ray's nose flat to his face.

Falina gasped and threw both hands to her face. Eddie Ray staggered backward, blood flying from his crushed nose, his arms flailing out at his sides. His bootheel caught the edge of a brass spittoon and caused him to lose balance for a split second. But that split second was all Danielle needed. She stepped quickly forward, sidled close to Eddie Ray, stuck the rifle barrel between his legs, and tangled his legs with a hard twist of the rifle. Eddie Ray went to the floor face first, a muffled scream resounding as his smashed nose met the hard clay tiles. With the toe of her boot, Danielle reached out and kicked his pistol from its holster, then kicked it across the tile floor, under a long divan.

Outside the open window of the hotel lobby, Fat Cyrus and Clifford Reed both winced at the sound of the rifle butt slamming into Eddie Ray's nose. They winced even more when they'd slipped a peep over the window ledge in time to see his face smack the hard floor. Seeing the young gunman walk away from where Eddie Ray lay writhing on the clay tiles, Clifford and Cyrus ducked away from the window and stared at one another. "Suppose we best go help him," said Clifford.

"Why? Looks like it's over now," said Fat Cyrus.
"Besides, that peckerwood has had that coming for
the longest time. I'd have busted his head myself
long before this except I know it would come down
to gunplay. . . . Ain't no way I'm as fast as he is."

"Me neither," said Clifford. "Come on, we can at
least drag him up off the floor."

"Yeah," said Cyrus, grinning. "I want to hear him
explain how this all went wrong for him."

In her small hotel room, Danielle heard men's muffled voices as Clifford Reed and Fat Cyrus helped
Eddie Ray Moon to his feet and half carried him out
the door. Falina, feeling bolder now that she'd seen
one of the gunmen brought down a notch, ran over
to the divan and pulled Eddie Ray's pistol from beneath it. She quickly unloaded the pistol and
dropped the bullets into her dress pocket. Then she
ran to the door, holding the empty gun with two
fingers. "Here . . . take your stinking pistol with
you!" she shouted, heaving the gun out into the dirt.
"And don't come back to this place with your rude-
ness!" The pistol hit the ground with a thud. Clifford
and Fat Cyrus managed to keep from laughing aloud
at the hapless Eddie Ray hanging between them, his
boot toes still dragging the dirt a bit as they walked.
They looked down at Eddie Ray's gun.

"Damn, Eddie Ray," said Fat Cyrus with a grin as
he stooped to pick up the pistol. "That fellow caused
you to get your pistol all dirty." He shoved it down
in Eddie Ray's holster. "Now you'll have to clean it."

"I'll kill him," Eddie Ray gasped, his swollen broken nose giving his voice a deep nasal twang.

"Kill him?" Clifford chimed in. "My God, man!
You ought to thank him for not eating you alive. The
shape you're in, he could have set your boots on fire
and you couldn't have stopped him!"

"The hell did you say to him anyway?" Fat Cyrus
asked, tormenting Eddie Ray.

"I forget," Eddie Ray mumbled as they dragged him on toward the saloon.

"If I was you I'd sure try to remember," said Cyrus. "So you never make the mistake of saying it again!"

Danielle watched the men through a drawn window curtain she held slightly parted. When they went inside the Ace High Saloon, she took her hat off, poured tepid water from a pitcher into a wash pan, and washed her face. Then she placed her hat on her head, carefully stuffed her hair up under it, and picked up her rifle from where she'd laid it across the bed. A soft knock at the door drew her attention.

When she eased it open a crack, Falina held out her hand and said, "Here—I take the bullets from his gun so he cannot shoot anyone." She dropped the six bullets into Danielle's outstretched hand and smiled. "*Por favor*, do with them as you will."

"*Gracias*," said Danielle. She returned the woman's smile and closed the door softly.

Pocketing the bullets, Danielle left her saddlebags in the room, walked outside to the hitchrail, and led Sundown around behind the hotel to a long row of stalls. There she grained the chestnut mare, watered her, and wiped her down with a handful of clean straw. Almost an hour had passed by the time Danielle left the row of stalls and walked back along the alley alongside the hotel.

Nearing the end of the alley, she saw two men step in slowly, blocking her way to the street. One held a pair of saddlebags in his hand. *Hers* . . . ? she wondered. Glancing behind her, she saw two more blocking her way back toward the stalls. One of these she recognized as the man from the lobby of the hotel. Good, she thought. They were coming to her no sooner than she'd arrived in town. She smiled to herself and slowed her pace, still walking forward.

"Hold it right there," said one of the men in front of her, seeing that she seemed to have no hesitancy about walking right through them. He held up a hand toward her. "Danny Duggin," the man said, "we don't like saddle tramps soiling up our town." He gestured a hand, and the other man stepped forward. "Clifford, give him his bags."

Clifford Reed pitched the saddlebags to Danielle's feet. She glanced down at them, then slowly looked back at Clifford and Buck Hite. Behind her, Danielle heard footsteps hurrying, trying to sneak up on her. She spun, her Colt snapping up from her holster, cocked and ready, stopping Fat Cyrus and Eddie Ray Moon in their tracks. "You're back for more?" Danielle said in her best man's voice, low and gravelly. Her pistol pointed straight at Eddie Ray's broken nose. A thin trickle of blood still ran down his upper lip.

Seeing how quickly Danny Duggin had gotten the drop on two of his men, Buck Hite said under his breath, "Jesus, boys, he could have killed you both." He stared at Eddie Ray Moon. "I thought you said he hit you while you weren't looking."

"That's the truth, Buck," said Eddie Ray. "We was just talking, then all of sudden, *bam!* He hit me with his rifle butt."

Danielle watched in silence, her pistol still cocked, still pointed. Fat Cyrus and Clifford Reed passed one another a knowing glance. Buck Hite saw it and said, "Is there something you boys ain't told me? If there is, you best say so now, before somebody gets killed here."

"We might have seen the whole thing through the hotel window," Fat Cyrus said hesitantly.

"You might have?" Buck Hite shouted. "By God, either you saw something or you didn't!"

"All right," said Clifford Reed, coming clean. "We saw this man bust Eddie Ray in the nose. . . . But he didn't do it on the sly. Eddie Ray had his bark on and was fixin' to draw on him." His finger pointed at Danielle. "This Duggin was just faster. He smacked the cold yellow piss out of him."

"That's a damn lie, Buck," said Eddie Ray. "This man ain't nothing!" He also pointed at Danielle. "I'm faster than he'll ever hope to be with a gun! I wasn't prepared is all."

Danielle listened. If this was a chance for her to work her way into the confidence of some of Cherokee Earl's men, she needed to defuse the situation. She lowered her Colt and looked at Buck Hite. "Maybe you and your pals better go somewhere and work all this out . . . figure who did what." She reached down and scooped up her saddlebags. "Meanwhile, I'll be at the saloon. . . . It's been a long ride up here."

"Not so fast, Duggin," said Buck. "You came up from the south range?"

"Yep," said Danielle. As she spoke, she noted Buck Hite looking her up and down. Did he recognize the shirt she was wearing as once having belonged to Lon Trabough?

"I sent a couple of good men down along the trail—the Trabough brothers. They should have been back before now. Maybe you saw them."

"Yep, I saw them," said Danielle, draping the dusty saddlebags over her shoulder and raising her rifle up under her arm, the way she'd carried it earlier. Seeing the rifle butt up under her arm, Eddie Ray took a cautious step back from her. "They said they'd just finished up some messy business with somebody along the trail. Said they were on their way back to Drake."

"Oh . . ." Buck Hite eyed Danielle's shirt again. "Then I expect I should be seeing them here most any time?"

"I wouldn't count on it," Danielle said flatly.

"Why not?" Buck asked.

"Because I killed them both deader than hell," Danielle said.

The men seemed to snap to attention. "You what?" Buck stared in disbelief.

"They got belligerent and out of hand." Her eyes beneath the hat brim went to Eddie Ray. "They started asking too many questions, just like this one did before I rifle-butted him."

"You'll play hell ever getting the drop on me again, Danny Duggin!" Eddie Ray raged. "I can damn sure promise you that!"

Danielle looked down at the pistol in his holster, saw the dust still on the handle and the hammer, and took a chance on him not having checked or dusted it off since their earlier encounter. "Mister, I've got the drop on you right now. . . . You're just not smart enough to know it."

Shaking with anger, Eddie Ray touched a wadded-up bandanna to the trickle of blood on his upper lip. "Buck," he said. "Let me shoot this smart-mouthed turd, please! Right here, right now! I've got to kill him. . . . I've *got* to!"

Danielle spread a tight smile beneath her hat brim. "Give him the go-ahead, Buck," she said. "It ain't like he's apt to hurt anybody."

"That does it, Buck! Everybody stand back!" Eddie Ray screamed, his face red, his purple nose appearing to almost throb with boiling rage. "I'm going to kill him!"

"All right, Mr. Danny Duggin," said Buck Hite, stepping back and making room. "Looks like you've gone and dug your own grave. Eddie Ray is not a man to fool with when it comes to a gunfight."

Danielle turned to face Eddie Ray. "Let's get to it then, Eddie Ray," she said in a hissing voice.

"Damn right, let's get to it," said Eddie Ray. Then he said to the others, "Cyrus, Clifford, stay out of this. . . . He's all mine!"

Eddie Ray's hand streaked down to his pistol butt, but before he could lift the pistol, Danielle's Colt was out, cocked and pointed at his swollen nose. Eddie Ray's face turned sickly green; his hand was frozen on the holstered pistol.

Danielle had him, and she knew it. But instead of firing, she let down the hammer on the Colt and spun it on her finger. Eddie Ray had another chance. He almost snatched his pistol up, but then stopped again when Danielle's Colt pointed at him, again cocked and ready. She moved closer to him. "You just can't seem to get that gun out of the holster, can you, Eddie Ray?" she said, taunting him in a quiet voice. She spun the pistol again, saw the thought cross Eddie Ray's mind again, then stopped the Colt and pointed it again just as he was on the verge of drawing. Again he froze. Again she came closer.

"Damn it to hell!" Eddie Ray shrieked, almost sobbing in his frustration and fear. "Either shoot me or back off! I can't stand this!"

"Then you've had enough?" Danielle asked, her Colt still menacing him. Before he could speak, she spun the Colt again and stopped it, cocking it in his face only a few inches from his broken nose.

"I've had enough! Yes, I've had enough," said Eddie Ray in defeat, wincing, holding his free hand up as if to protect his swollen nose.

Danielle pulled the trigger on the Colt but caught it with her thumb just before it struck the bullet. Eddie Ray, Clifford Reed, and Fat Cyrus gasped. Buck Hite just watched, liking the way this young gunman handled himself.

"You wasn't going to shoot nobody anyway, Eddie Ray," Danielle said in a low gravelly voice. She lowered her Colt, reached into her pocket with her free hand, took out the six bullets, and pitched them to the ground at Eddie Ray's feet. "Your gun ain't even loaded. Think I'd trust you with a loaded gun . . . the way you was acting earlier?"

"You've got to be kidding!" said Buck Hite. He stepped over, yanked Eddie Ray's pistol up from his holster, slung it open, and checked it. His eyes widened, then narrowed as he turned them to Eddie Ray. "You stupid peckerwood! This man unloaded your pistol? You didn't even check it before coming back here looking for a gunfight? I ought to bend this barrel across your chin!" He drew the pistol back, then stopped himself, with Eddie Ray standing dumbfounded.

Danielle holstered her pistol and stepped away through an opening Buck Hite had left for her. "Are you looking for work?" Buck asked before she had gone two steps.

"No, thank you," Danielle said over her shoulder. "Work is the last thing I'm looking for."

"Well, what the hell are you looking for?" Buck asked.

"Easy money," Danielle said, a flat smile coming to her lips.

There was silence for a second as her words sank in. Then Buck Hite chuckled, Clifford and Fat Cyrus slowly joining in. "I figured it went without saying that you're looking for easy money," said Buck. "We wouldn't know how to spend any other kind."

"Now you're making more sense," said Danielle.

"Wait a damn minute," Eddie Ray demanded. He tuned to Buck Hite. "What about him killing two of our men?"

Buck Hite cocked his head at Danielle. "Yeah, what about that, Danny Duggin? Bad as I need men, you went and killed two of them."

"Yeah," said Danielle, "but I figure it's an even trade. I didn't kill Eddie Ray. That's *one*. . . . And I'm throwing in with you. That's *two*."

The men laughed, except for Eddie Ray. "He's got a point there, Eddie Ray," said Buck. Buck looked at Danielle. "Do you have any qualms about what you have to do to make this easy money?"

"Not in the least," said Danielle.

"Come on then," said Buck, "I want to buy you a drink." He looked back at the others. "Boys, get your drinking done—we leave first thing in the morning."

"Where are we headed, Buck?" Danielle asked.

"We're headed north to meet up with a pal of mine named Cherokee Earl Muir." He beamed proudly. "Ever heard of him?"

"Sure have," said Danielle.

"Then I reckon you know that riding with him is about as big as you get in the business of outlawry."

"That's my thought exactly," Danielle said as they walked on.

Buck Hite hooked a thumb in his belt. "Stick with me, Danny Duggin. . . . You'll be glad you did."

"I'm glad already, Buck," Danielle replied.

Chapter 14

Sheriff Clarence Wright walked from the St. James Hotel back to his office two blocks away. He had a lot on his mind, most of it involving an already-large amount of money lying in the Cimarron bank at that very moment, and more money coming anyday. These unusually large amounts of money were sent to Cimarron to pay for the shipments of silver coming in from mining operations all across the Territory. Why the large mining company's home offices back East had chosen his town for this transaction was beyond him. But there was no use in him fretting over it. The money was here, the silver was arriving. All he could do was keep a tight rein on things. In his hand Sheriff Wright held a federal court summons he had just received. On top of everything else, he had now been called to appear in court. That would put his town in a dangerous position for at least a week. He sighed, folded the summons, and stuffed it inside his coat pocket.

Out front of his office he stopped for a moment and watched the scruffy young man on the boardwalk sweep road dust off into the street. Sheriff Wright needed help bad. This man had shown up in town two weeks earlier, down and out and looking like the only thing that could save him would be the next drink of whiskey he poured between his lips.

He'd drifted into Cimarron looking for work, and Wright had taken a chance on him. So far the man had stayed sober enough to sweep up and do some minor roof repairs on the jail building. But that was a long way from being trusted as a deputy, Sheriff Wright reminded himself, watching the broom swish back and forth.

"What the hell?" Wright murmured to himself. "I'm desperate." He called out as he walked up onto the boardwalk and opened his office door. "Carlyle, come in here for a minute. . . . We need to talk."

Tuck Carlyle followed the sheriff through the open door, a gnawing feeling already welling up in his stomach. His first thought was that he'd done something wrong. Why else would the sheriff want to talk to him? Inside the office, before the sheriff got a chance to speak, Carlyle said, "Sheriff, I would have had the sweeping done a lot sooner, except the hitch-rail out front had gotten wobbly. . . I tightened it up some."

"Close the door, Carlyle," said the sheriff. "This ain't got nothing to do with the sweeping. You've done a fine job ever since you been here."

"Then—then what's wrong?" Tuck asked.

"Wrong?" The sheriff frowned beneath his bushy eyebrows. "Hell, there's nothing wrong. In fact, I want to see how you feel about taking on a better job here, maybe becoming a temporary deputy. If it works out, maybe even doing it full-time. You interested?"

"You know I was a drunk for a long time, Sheriff. Do you think it might be too soon yet to go trusting me with that kind of responsibility?"

"If I thought it was too soon, I wouldn't have asked you," said the sheriff, a patient smile forming behind his drooping gray mustache. "Now back to my question. . . . Are you interested?"

"Well, yes," Tuck said hesitantly. "I suppose I am."

"You suppose you are," said the sheriff, repeating his words. "You'll have to do better than that, Carlyle."

Tuck raised his head, squared his shoulders, and looked the sheriff in the eyes. "I *know* I'm interested, Sheriff. Thanks for having this kind of faith in me. I realize you don't know me, Sheriff, so you don't know how far I've sunk since my wife's death. But the fact is, I wasn't always a down-and-out drunkard. At one time I had my own spread. Before that I was a trail boss, drove cattle for some of the biggest ranches in the country."

"No man was born a drunk, Carlyle, so I figured you must've been something else along the way. I might not know you real well, but I've watched you enough to see that you've just gotten pretty far down, and now you're trying to get back up. When a man does that," the sheriff said, stepping around behind his battered oak desk, opening a drawer, and taking out a tin badge, "I believe it's only right that the rest of us give him a chance. Someday you might again own your own spread. Who knows, I might come to *you* looking for work. Meanwhile, welcome to being my deputy."

"I don't know what to say, Sheriff," said Tuck, taking the badge and looking at it for a second before pinning it on his shirt.

"Just say, 'I do.' " The sheriff grinned. He held up his thick right hand and said, "Do you solemnly swear to uphold the laws of this town to the best of your ability, so help you God?"

"I do," said Tuck Carlyle, quickly raising his right hand as Sheriff Wright spoke.

"There, it's done," said Wright. "You are now officially an officer of the law. Conduct yourself accordingly."

"I do . . . I mean—I will," said Tuck. He lowered his right hand.

Sheriff Wright reached down and opened a larger, deeper desk drawer. "I don't suppose you own a gun, do you?"

"No, Sheriff," said Tuck. "My firearms got away from me soon as I started living on rye whiskey." He looked ashamed.

"That's what I figured." Sheriff Wright pulled a rolled-up gun belt from the drawer. The bone handle of a .45 caliber Colt stood above the well-worn holster. "It ain't loaded, but there's bullets in the drawer. I reckon you can still handle one of these without shooting your toes off, can't you?" He handed the shooting rig over to Tuck.

"I'm sure I can," said Tuck. He slipped the pistol from the holster, held it sideways, checked it, then hefted it in his hand. He spun it once and caught it in place, his thumb cocking then uncocking the hammer sleekly.

Watching him, the sheriff nodded with satisfaction. "Yeah, I can see you're familiar with the workings of a pistol. Are you any good, drawing and firing if you had to?"

"Yes, I'm a fair hand with a gun, Sheriff," said Tuck. "But to be honest, I'm going to go practice somewhere before I try to show you anything." He offered a smile. "As rusty as I am from all the drinking, I don't want to make you change your mind and take the gun back."

"There's little chance of that," said the sheriff. "I need a deputy real bad, Carlyle. Take the rest of the day off, go somewhere, and practice as much as you need to."

"What about all the dust out there on the boardwalk?" said Tuck. "Shouldn't I finish sweeping first?"

"The dust was there when I come to this town. . . .

It'll be there when I leave," said Wright. "Tell the livery man to fix you up with a horse and go do some practice shooting. You might be needing it before long."

"Much obliged, Sheriff." Tuck reached down and picked up a wooden box full of bullets. Instead of putting the gun belt on right then, he stuffed the rig up under his arm and headed for the livery barn. "I appreciate all you've done for me. . . . I won't let you down."

Sheriff Wright nodded in silence until Tuck Carlyle closed the door. Then the sheriff let out a long breath and said to himself, "I hope you won't, young man. . . . Things might get awfully dangerous around here."

At the livery barn, Tuck Carlyle told the livery man, Old John, what the sheriff had said. Old John eyed the badge on Tuck's chest, then walked out to the corral behind the barn. When he returned, he handed Tuck the reins to a big raw-boned roan. "He's uglier than mud," said Old John. "But he's the best on the place far as I'm concerned."

Tuck looked the big dapple roan up and down. The horse looked strong and full of energy.

"Take that saddle," said the old man, pointing to a battered saddle lying atop a pile of firewood.

"Much obliged, John," Tuck Carlyle said.

"Don't mention it." Old John watched him pitch a saddle blanket atop the dapple roan, then toss the saddle gently on the horse's back and shake it into place. Grinning across empty gums, the old livery man said, "A deputy, huh?"

"Like I said, it's only temporary," said Tuck. "But I'm hoping it'll turn full-time for me. I need the work." As he spoke, he adjusted the worn gun belt on his waist, getting used to it.

Old John nodded, noting the tied-down Colt. "Ain't been long since you came here wanting to

muck stalls for a place to sleep. . . . Now look at
you, wearing a badge and a bone-handled pistol."
He stepped forward and rubbed the roan's muzzle
while Tuck drew the cinch and dropped the stirrups.
"I'm pleased things have worked out well for you."

Tuck nodded. "Thanks, John. You letting me sleep
here meant a lot to me. I won't forget you for it."

"Aw, go on." Old John waved his words away.
"Get on your horse and get out of here. If you like
that big roan, I'll give you a good deal on buying
him. I picked him up from a trail crew on their way
back from Montana a month back. He knows his way
around, I reckon."

"Montana and back? I'd say he does," Tuck said,
rubbing the horse's jaw as he led it outside. "I just
might be talking to you about buying him then, if
my credit's good."

"As good as any," said Old John, stopping at the
door rather than stepping out into the sunlight. "Ride
him out first. Then let me know. We'll talk price
later." He watched Tuck step up into the saddle, col-
lect the horse, heel the animal toward the street, and
ride away. "Good luck, Deputy," Old John said
under his breath.

Tuck rode the roan three miles out across a stretch
of land dotted with piñon pine, juniper, and spruce.
He wouldn't have had to go this far to practice his
shooting. But it had been a long time since he'd been
clearheaded sober, and it felt good to just be in a
saddle again and have some time to think about
things. Losing his wife had been like suffering
through a long illness. Grief had stricken him like
some dark, terrible fever that had only recently broken, allowing some of his strength to slowly return.
All the whiskey he'd drunk hadn't helped cure him.
It had only served as a painkiller. The longer he
stayed sober, the more he realized he had to give up
the whiskey and simply learn to live with his pain.

He stepped down and hitched the roan to a piñon. He stepped off thirty-odd yards to a sun-bleached oak log and set a row of fist-sized rocks up along its surface. Back at his starting point, he held his right hand up flat in front of himself and eyed it closely. The shakes he'd been going through ever since he'd quit drinking had ceased almost entirely. Good. He raised the pistol stiffly from the holster, looked it over again, then held it out at arm's length, cocked it, and took careful aim. His first shot missed his rock target by three inches. Not good, yet not as bad as he had expected.

He holstered the pistol, shook out his right arm, and took a few deep breaths. Then he raised the pistol again, drawing it slowly, this time cocking it on the upswing. He had to relax . . . let his knowledge of shooting come back to him. *You've got all day if that's what it takes*, he told himself with resolve. The next shot left a skinned streak across the dried log less than an inch from his target. *Better*, he thought, cocking the pistol again and taking aim, *but still . . .*

Three hundred yards away, topping a low rise, Cherokee Earl Muir rode up to where Avery McRoy sat staring out at the lone gunman taking target practice. "Is that who's doing all the shooting?" asked Earl.

"Yeah," said McRoy. "Best I can make out, he's shooting at a log."

"At a log," Earl said flatly. "Wonder what that log ever did to him. Must be a kid stole his pa's pistol, out here hankering to learn how to kill somebody." He stared off with McRoy for a moment, then said, "I did the same thing when I was a youngster."

McRoy nodded. "Me too, sort of."

"Hell, that's no kid," said Earl, staring harder.

"I never said it was," said McRoy. "He's right alongside the trail. What do you want to do? Ride out wide around him?"

"Hell, no . . . we got nothing to hide." Earl jerked his horse around to face Dirty Joe as he rode up leading Ellen's horse beside him.

"Take that lead rope off her horse, Dirty," Earl demanded. He looked at Ellen. "I'm counting on you behaving yourself," he said coldly to her. "Make a run for it, the last thing you'll see is a bullet pop out of your belly. Do you understand me real clearly?"

"She won't try nothing stupid," Dirty Joe butted in.

"Oh? You do all her speaking for her now, Dirty?" Earl asked with sarcasm.

"No, Boss," Joe said quickly. "I just meant that I'll keep a close eye on her, is all."

"You've been doing that well enough, Dirty," said Earl. He dismissed Dirty Joe and looked Ellen up and down. "Fix your hair up some. Keep that horse close to Dirty till we get on down the trail to town."

"Uh, Boss?" said Dirty Joe, stepping his horse forward and untying the lead rope from the bridle of Ellen's horse.

"Yeah, what is it, Dirty?" Earl replied.

"I gave it some thought, and I just as soon you not call me Dirty anymore. My name's Joe. . . . I figure that'll be good enough from now on." He offered a faint half smile. "If it's all the same to you, that is." He coiled the loose lead rope and hooked it over his saddle horn.

Avery McRoy winced and looked away for a second, shaking his head slowly. Cherokee Earl sat staring in silence for a moment, then looked back and forth between Joe and the woman and said with a slight shrug, "What the hell do I care, Dir—I mean, Joe." He said to McRoy, "Do you have any objections to just calling him Joe?"

Avery McRoy looked down as he spoke. "I don't care. . . . Whatever suits him, I reckon." When he raised his eyes, he gave Joe a cautioning look. But Joe ignored it.

"There you are now, Joseph," said Earl with a sharp snap of emphasis. "Everything the way you like it?"

"I appreciate it, Boss," Joe said quietly, appearing a bit embarrassed. He shot McRoy a defusing glance and rode forward, Ellen Waddell keeping her horse close by his side.

When Joe and Ellen were a few feet ahead of them, Earl and Avery McRoy rode forward side by side. In a lowered voice, Earl asked McRoy, "How long has this been going on?"

"What's that, Boss?" McRoy asked in response, trying to sound unknowing of anything out of the ordinary.

"Don't play dumb with me," Earl hissed.

"Boss, I can't say one way or the other," said McRoy, begging off of the conversation. "I just came to do my job. You know that's how I am."

"Yeah, I know," said Earl, staring ahead at Joe Turley and Ellen Waddell. There was a silence as they wound down toward the main trail into Cimarron. Finally Earl said in a secretive tone, "How close are you and Dirty Joe?"

"We just ride together," said McRoy. "I never knew him before I came to ride with you. Far as I'm concerned, he's just one more gun in a world full of them."

"Good," said Earl. "Once this bank is robbed and we're in the clear, I might ask you to do me a special favor, McRoy. Think you'll be up to it?"

Avery McRoy nodded. "I can't see why not."

Tuck Carlyle was so engrossed in his shooting that he didn't notice the approaching riders less than twenty yards behind him. Only when he heard a

gruff voice call out, "Hello the camp," did he turn
and face them, his pistol still in hand but lowered to
his side.

At the sight of the tin badge on Tuck Carlyle's
chest, Ellen's heart leaped at the prospect of freedom.
She shot a quick look at the others, then almost
bolted her horse forward, ready to cry out for help
from this man.

"I've no camp here," said Tuck, "but ride on in all
the same." He gestured his free hand along the trail.
"As you can see, this is a public road."

"I saw there was no camp," said Earl, drawing
closer, having taken the lead farther back along the
trail. Earl was now being followed by Joe and Ellen,
who in turn were followed by Avery McRoy. "But
we've been hearing your shooting a long ways off.
Didn't know how close we ought to come before an-
nouncing ourselves."

Tuck raised the pistol slightly and turned it back
and forth in his hand. "Just doing some practicing,"
he said. He felt the woman's eyes burning into him.
Her expression was puzzling. What was it he read
there: fear, hope . . . a warning of some sort?

Nodding at the badge on Tuck's chest, Earl said,
"I expect that's a prudent pastime for a lawman."
He smiled flatly, his hand seeming to rest idly on
the pistol at his hip. Behind Ellen and Joe, McRoy
had drawn his rifle from its boot as he came down
the trail. It lay across his lap, his gloved hand near
the trigger.

"In my case it is," said Tuck. "I just turned deputy
today. I figure I need all the practice I can get."
Catching a quick glimpse of the woman's eyes again,
Tuck saw a change in her expression. He tried to
take a good look at the faces of the men, but their
broad hat brims along with the bright sunlight
served to obstruct his vision.

"Oh, I see," said Earl, his hand relaxing on his

pistol butt, even sliding down an inch. "Then we'll
not take up your time." He nodded along the trail.
"I take it this is the best way to Cimarron?"

"It is that," said Tuck. "Cimarron is only about three
miles farther." As he spoke, he looked the woman up
and down, wondering what had happened . . . what
had caused her to change so suddenly. But now her
expression offered no clue. Her eyes turned downward as if afraid to face him. "Have you traveled
far?" Tuck asked Earl, taking his eyes from the
woman lest he appear to be staring.

"Does Texas sound far?" said Earl. "I'm Fred Bartlett. I own a cattle operation outside Haley Springs.
Ever heard of the place?"

"So happens I have," said Tuck. "I'm a Texan myself. My name is Tuck Carlyle." He touched his hat
brim. "I've passed through Haley Springs buying cattle, making up a herd, although it has been a long
while."

Earl smiled. "Well, like as not nothing's changed
there." He tipped his hat slightly, then said, "We'll
be taking our leave now. I'm afraid we're all in sore
need of a hot bath and some food that ain't still running from us. I suppose there is a decent hotel in
Cimarron?"

"Yes, there is," said Tuck. "There's the St. James.
It's the finest hotel between here and Kansas City."

"Much obliged then," said Earl, touching his hat
brim. "That's where we'll stay."

Tuck touched his fingertips to his hat brim again
as the four riders filed past him, the woman not raising her eyes or acknowledging him again in any way.
A strange group, he thought. He stood watching them
until they rode down out of sight beneath the roll of
the land. Then he turned back to his shooting, unable
to get the woman's expression out of his mind as he
raised the pistol and cocked it. He'd have to mention
it to the sheriff tonight, he reminded himself. That

was the sort of thing a deputy was supposed to do. This time his shot was perfect, shattering the rock like glass.

Just over the rise, Ellen Waddell looked back at the sound of Tuck's shot. "You done real well back there," Earl said to her, cutting his horse to the side and stopping as she and Joe Turley rode past him. Joe took the lead rope up from around his saddle horn and uncoiled it, ready to tie it to Ellen's horse's bridle again. "Never mind, Joe," Earl said to him. "Long as she behaves, let her handle the horse herself."

"But, Boss, I've been leading her all this way." Joe looked disappointed.

"You heard him, Joe," Ellen whispered in a sharp hiss, just between the two of them. She jerked her reins away from Joe's hand before he even had time to reach out with the lead rope.

"Yeah," said Earl, with no idea what Ellen had just said to Joe Turley, "and now I'm telling you to leave her be. . . . We'll see how far we can trust her." He cut Ellen a dark stare. "Don't forget, little darling, I can still drop a bullet in you long before you get out of sight."

"I know that," said Ellen. "I'm no fool. I'll do as I'm told."

"There, Joe, you hear that?" said Earl. "This woman's not a fool. She wasn't about to say something back there to cause that poor deputy to get his eyeballs shot out. . . . The odds weren't right, were they, Mrs. Waddell?" he said with a sneer.

Ellen didn't answer. She rode on, looking down at the ground.

Avery McRoy took this time to say something he'd been wondering about for a while now. "How in the world are we going to keep her from shooting her mouth off once we get inside Cimarron?" he asked.

"We're not taking her into town with us," said Earl.

Joe Turley looked surprised. "But you just told that deputy we'd be staying at the hotel—"

"Damn it, Joe," said Earl, cutting him off. "I hope I ain't got myself in trouble, lying to a deputy of all things!" He feigned a look of fright.

"Joe, Joe, my goodness." McRoy stifled a laugh and shook his head at Turley's ignorance.

"There's a cabin I know about, four miles east of town," Earl said. "We'll hole up there until we get ready to do our raid."

"Buck and his men will be looking for us in town," said McRoy. "Want me to cut off from you and ride on in? Keep my eyes open for Buck?"

"Tomorrow," said Earl. "We'll get a night's sleep, give that deputy time to forget our faces. Then we'll take turns going to town till we hook up with Buck."

"Sounds good to me," said McRoy, heeling his horse forward. "I sure hope there is a washtub and a stove to heat some water at that cabin."

"Don't worry," said Cherokee Earl. "I think of everything." He tapped his horse up and rode beside McRoy, hearing another pistol shot resound behind them over the rise. "That's it, Deputy," Earl said to McRoy with a chuckle. "Better get good at it. You never know when it'll come in handy."

Chapter 15

The Unsled Mines, New Mexico Territory

Dave Waddell flinched at the sound of gunfire coming from inside the mining office shack, but he stuck to his job, holding the reins to Frisco Bonham's horse while Frisco performed the robbery. Since he and Frisco had joined up, it seemed that all they'd done was ride from one robbery to the next. After the stagecoach, they'd robbed a relay station north of Santa Fe, then a band of settlers headed for California. But according to Frisco, every step they took was leading Dave that much closer to finding his wife. He had to go along with things. What else could he do? he asked himself. Another shot resounded from the shack.

Dave sat watching tensely for any sign of trouble. "Damn it, hurry up, Frisco," he said to himself under his breath, seeing two miners step out of a toolshed a few yards away and look toward the office shack. Dave raised the rifle from across his lap and let the barrel loom menacingly toward them. "Get back inside, you peckerwoods! This doesn't concern you!" he shouted through the bandanna he wore as a mask.

The two miners ducked back inside the toolshed, but only for a moment. By the time Frisco came running out of the office with a canvas moneybag in one hand and a smoking Colt in the other, the miners came out again. This time there were four of them.

This time they each carried shovels or picks. One hurled a large rock that bounced off the door of the office shack just as Frisco ran for his horse. The rock came too close for comfort, and Frisco turned before stepping up into his stirrups.

"You sumbitch!" Frisco shouted. "Throw a rock at me?" He fired a shot. The bullet nailed the miner in his chest, causing him to stagger backwards, dropping the shovel he wielded above his head. The other miners caught their wounded comrade as he fell. "Let's go!" Frisco shouted at Dave Waddell as he hurled himself up into the saddle.

"Jesus! You killed him!" Dave Waddell shouted as they batted their heels to their horses' sides and sped away from the shouting, cursing miners. Frisco's only reply was a long, rowdy yell, followed by two pistol shots in the air. When they'd topped a ridge a hundred yards away, a rifle shot rang out from the direction of the mine's office. But by then it was too late. The pair of thieves rode down out of sight, onto the main trail. Then they rode at a steady clip for the next three miles.

Finally, Frisco slowed his horse a bit and laughed, pushing his hat up with a finger and jerking the bandanna down from across his face. "Now that's the way to pull a payroll robbery!" he gloated, shaking the bag of money at Dave Waddell. The both slowed their horses even more.

"It went pretty smooth," said Dave. "That's for certain."

"Smooth? Hell, yes, smooth," said Frisco. "I'm talking about right in, right out." His chest swelled with pride. "There wasn't no fooling around like some robbers do." He shook the bag again. "Davey Boy, I believe you and me could make a good team on our own! We wouldn't even need Cherokee Earl and his boys!"

"You—you really think so?" Dave Waddell shot a

nervous glance back over his shoulder, then yanked his bandanna down and ran a shaky hand across his forehead. "I don't mind telling you, I still feel pretty scared doing this."

"Like I told you, everybody gets a little spooked the first few times," said Frisco, dismissing it. "But how scared will you be running your fingers through this much money, eh?" Again he held the bag up for Dave Waddell to see. "This is the best we've done yet."

Dave Waddell studied the bulging canvas bag as their horses loped along easily. "How much you figure is in there," Dave asked, settling down some.

"Oh, four, five thousand, easy enough," said Frisco. "Maybe even more. However much there is, it's all ours!" He shook the bag again, laughing loudly.

"So maybe we better stop somewhere and split it up?" Dave asked, his greed starting to get the better of him.

"Sure, we can do that," said Frisco. He nodded along the trail ahead of them. "Or I can hang on to it till we get to Cimarron. It's only another twenty or thirty miles."

"Cimarron," said Waddell. "What's in Cimarron? A bank? Another mining payroll?"

Frisco gave him a bemused look. "Both," he said. "But that ain't all that's in Cimarron."

"What else?" Waddell asked.

"It just might be that *she's* there," said Frisco.

"She who?" Dave asked. But then he caught himself and said, "Oh, you mean Ellen, my wife?"

"Well, damn, Dave," Frisco chuckled. "Yeah, that's who I mean all right. Have you forgotten all about her?"

"Of course not," Dave responded, his face reddening. "It's just that we was talking about something else. It took me a second to catch up."

But Frisco wouldn't let him off that easy. He taunted him, saying, "You do remember your wife, Ellen, don't you?" As he spoke, he reached down into the canvas bag and pulled up a handful of dollars and gold coins and let them spill back down into the bag.

"Go to hell," Waddell said.

Frisco grinned. "I'm trying to just as fast as I can." He closed the bag and carried it on his lap. "Don't be so hard on yourself for not remembering your wife, Davey Boy. It could happen to anybody. A man gets out here, gets a taste of freedom, money, anything else he takes a hankering for . . . knows all he's got to do is reach out and take whatever he wants . . . nobody can stop him. That's a powerful pull on a man's better nature!"

Dave Waddell ignored Frisco's taunting and heeled his horse forward ahead of him. "You say Ellen might be in Cimarron?"

"Yep, she sure might be," said Frisco. "I know Cherokee has been planning a raid on the bank there. He just needed something to get him moving in that direction." He caught up to Dave Waddell and stopped his horse in front of him, turning crosswise in the trail. "What exactly have you got planned for when you catch up to Cherokee Earl, if you don't mind me asking. Are you going to shoot him down where he stands? Maybe call him out into the street, face him down gun to gun?"

Again Dave Waddell ignored him. He tried reining his horse around him, but Frisco maneuvered along with him, blocking his horse's path, forcing him to confront the situation that he'd put himself into. "Speaking of facing up to somebody, when are you going to face up to yourself? You've got no use for that woman, Dave! She's just something else you acquired along the way. Something to prove to yourself how good you were doing, some pretty trinket that you could afford at the time. You knew she was something other men would see and be envious of. Now that other men have had her, is she still going to be worth as much to you?"

"You son of a bitch! She's my wife, damn you!" Dave Waddell raged. He started to snatch the pistol from his belt. But he found himself looking down the barrel of Frisco's Colt.

"Yeah," Frisco grinned cruelly, "I'm that all right, a son of a bitch and worse. But I ain't the one having trouble choosing between my wife and stealing other people's money."

"Neither am I," said Dave Waddell. "I'm going after Ellen. If you say she's in Cimarron, that's where I'm headed. You can go or stay. I don't give a damn!" He started to spur his horse away, but then he stopped, looked at the canvas bag in Frisco's hand, and said, "I'll take my cut of the money now. I'll need it to live on in case Earl and Ellen aren't in Cimarron, and I have to go hunting them farther away."

"Hell, why not?" Frisco lowered his pistol, uncocked it, and let it hang loose in his hand. He pitched the bag to Dave Waddell. "Here, count out half of it for yourself. Leave my share in the bag."

"We both ought to count it," said Dave, wary of a trick, keeping a close eye on the Colt in Frisco's hand.

Frisco saw the apprehension in Waddell's eyes. He shoved the pistol down into his belt. "Count it yourself. I'm not worried about it. Money like that comes to me any day of the week I want to go out and get it."

Frisco watched Dave count the money onto his lap, then divvy it up and poke half of it back into the canvas bag. "There," Dave said. "It came to eighteen hundred forty-seven dollars each." He folded the bills into a thick roll and shoved the roll into his coat pocket. The loose gold coins he shoved down into his trouser pockets. "Now I'm going to Cimarron. I can't say it ain't been fun, what you and I did. But I'm no outlaw, Frisco. You was reading me wrong in that regard." He backed his horse a step away and pitched the canvas bag to Frisco. "I'd never been out here if it weren't to save my wife. I might have dealt some stolen cattle, maybe done some other little things . . . but that's the limit. I'm stopping here before I end up on a rope or dead in the street somewhere."

Frisco sat staring, his wrists crossed on his saddle horn. He nodded slightly, looking a bit bored. When Dave Waddell finished talking, Frisco said, "Well, all right then. . . . Best of luck to you. Don't tell Cherokee you've seen me. I think it's time I go out on my own: make more, keep more. Okay?"

"Sure, I won't mention you one way or the other," said Dave. He watched Frisco lift his reins and start to turn his horse. "Where are you going though?"

"That's not a good thing to ask," said Frisco.

Dave nodded. "All right." He started to turn his horse, but then he stopped and said, "You suppose when Earl gets tired of Ellen he'll just turn her loose? I mean, I hate thinking he'd hurt her real bad or maybe even kill her."

"I doubt he would do that," said Frisco. "Hell, he just saw something pretty that he wanted, so he took it. Like I said about you a while ago." Frisco shrugged. "He'll turn her loose sooner or later." He watched as Dave Waddell looked all around then stepped down from his horse and led it off the trail.

"Thought you was in a hurry to get to Cimarron?" Frisco called out, a faint smile coming to his lips.

"I am," said Dave, "but it might be better to wait till tomorrow. Let the horse rest . . . give myself time to think what I ought to do once I get there."

"That's a good idea," said Frisco, stepping down himself and leading his horse off the trail. "I might rest mine awhile too." Looking down at the trail, noting the deep wheel ruts in the soft earth, Frisco said, "I didn't mention it before, but I bet there's still a stagecoach runs through here . . . all the way up from Taos."

"Yeah?" said Dave. "Does it carry any money?"

"Oh, yes," said Frisco. "Last time me and Billy Harper robbed it we came away flush for the whole winter." He grinned and led his horse over beside Dave Waddell's, nodding down at the deep wagon ruts. "There's nothing I hate worse than passing up a nice fat stagecoach."

No sooner had Tuck Carlyle returned to Cimarron than he went straight to the St. James Hotel and rang the bell on the counter. A young man wearing sleeve garters came out from an office behind the counter. His hair was parted sharply in the middle and slicked down with hair oil. He ran a clean hand along one side of his head as if to make sure each hair was in its proper place. "Yes, may I help you?" His eyes widened a bit when he recognized Tuck and saw the deputy badge on his chest. "Oh, you're a deputy now? The last time I recall seeing you . . . well, let's just say you were doing less meaningful work." He smiled. "Congratulations, I'm sure." There was a slight haughtiness to the young man that Tuck decided to overlook.

"Thanks, Eli," said Tuck. He got right to the point. "Three men and a woman rode into town earlier, said they would be staying here. The leader was a big fellow named Bartlett . . . Fred Bartlett. Did you wait on them?"

"No, sorry," said Eli. He gave Tuck a blank stare. "Anything else I can do for you, Deputy?"

"Do you suppose Henri Lambert waited on them?" Tuck asked, referring to the hotel's owner.

"No, sorry again," Eli said crisply. "Mr. Lambert

is out of town for the week. If I didn't wait on them, they simply haven't been here."

"Are you sure, Eli?" Tuck asked. His eyes went to the guest register.

"Are you really going to ask me to check and make certain?" the young clerk asked, sounding a bit annoyed.

"No, I'm not," said Tuck, relenting. "It just seems strange they would tell me they were going to stay here, then it turns out they didn't."

"Be that as it may, they haven't been here. In fact, I haven't seen any party of four ride in off the trail all day."

"All right then, much obliged," said Tuck. Turning to leave, he saw Sheriff Wright walking along the street toward the office and carrying a pot of coffee from the restaurant, a hotpad wrapped around the metal handle. "Sheriff, wait up," Tuck called out, hurrying to catch up to him.

"Good afternoon there, Deputy," Sheriff Wright said, stopping and waiting for Tuck. "I've never seen it fail. . . . I get a fresh pot of coffee, and folks call out my name from all across town. How did the shooting practice go?" he asked as the two of them headed on to the office together.

"It started out pretty bad," said Tuck, "but I got back into the hang of it by the time I ran out of bullets." He shook his head as they walked across the street and stepped up onto the boardwalk. "I feel bad about shooting up so much ammunition."

"Don't feel bad about it, Deputy," said the sheriff. "I call it an investment in both our futures. If we should get in a tight spot, I'd like to think you capable of shooting the eyes out of a blue fly if need be."

"I can't say I'll ever get that good, Sheriff," said Tuck, "but I promise you I'll always do my best or go down trying."

"I reckon that's really all I'm looking for," said

Sheriff Wright. "Just a deputy I know I can count on." He swung open the door to the sheriff's office and walked inside, Tuck right behind him. Sitting the pot of coffee atop a small potbellied stove, he said, "I don't mind telling you, all this money arriving in town to pay for the silver is likely to draw some of the bad element. I expect to see some strange faces turning up most any time."

"That reminds me, Sheriff," Tuck said, picking up two clean cups from a shelf beside the stove. "I saw my share of strange faces today." He filled a cup for the sheriff, handed it to him, and filled one for himself. "Or I should say I *tried* to see them. I only got a good look at two of them. The sun blocked the others' faces." As they sipped the hot coffee, Tuck told him about the four riders he'd seen on the trail. Sheriff Wright listened intently, but then seemed to dismiss the matter no sooner than Tuck finished telling him. Seeing a waning interest, Tuck said, "Anyway, I thought it was peculiar, them saying they'd be staying at the St. James, then not doing it."

"I see," said the sheriff. He seemed to consider it for a moment, then said, "Do you suppose they might have just changed their mind, pushed on past town, maybe decided to make a camp?"

"Sure, they might have," said Tuck. "There was just something peculiar about them. . . . I can't really put my finger on it. Maybe I shouldn't have mentioned it."

"You did good mentioning it to me, Deputy," said the sheriff. "I'd rather hear all day about things that mean nothing than miss hearing the one thing that could get somebody killed." He offered a tired smile. "We'll both keep a lookout for them. You might even want to ride out tomorrow along the old road and see if you spot where they might have made a camp overnight. With all this silver transaction going on, it won't hurt to keep an eye on the trails in and out of town for a while."

"Sure thing, Sheriff," said Tuck, sipping his coffee, feeling like he was once again a part of the world. He noticed his hand was steadier than it had been in a long, long time.

Chapter 16

For the next four days, Tuck Carlyle rode out searching the countryside surrounding town in all directions, looking for any sign of the men and the woman. He found no trace of them. On the second day he had found a recent campsite with its ashes still warm. But upon following the tracks leading away from the clearing, he soon caught up with four independent silver miners who were headed southwest toward their holdings along the winding Rio Grande.

"We ain't seen a soul since leaving Cimarron," one of the miners told him, speaking for all four. "Of course, we left there so drunk, they could have walked over the top of us and we'd never have known it." Tuck tipped his hat and bid them a good journey.

Realizing the improbability of ever finding those four riders in the endless stretches of piñon forests and jagged bluffs, Tuck reminded himself that they weren't his only reason for being out there day after day. He made it a point to spend at least an hour a day practicing with his pistol until his hand was as steady, his draw as quick, and his aim as deadly as it had ever been. Luckily, the whiskey hadn't completely destroyed him, he thought, his hand streaking up from his holster, the pistol exploding three times just as fast as he could fire it.

Three rocks vanished in a shattered spray of dust. Tuck spun the pistol, holstered it, then drew it again and fired two more shots. Two more rocks vanished. As he walked to the log to set up more rock targets, he dropped the five spent cartridges and replaced them, having cautiously left one live round in the cylinder. When the Colt was reloaded, he spun the cylinder out of habit and twirled the pistol back into his holster. Reaching down to set up more rocks along the log, he stopped and listened to the sound of hooves moving steadily closer through a pine thicket twenty yards away.

Inside the thicket, Buck Hite raised a hand and brought Danielle and the others to a halt. They sat in silence for a moment, then Buck said, "Duggin, Eddie Ray, you two go check out that shooting, then catch back up to us."

"I'd sooner go by myself," said Danielle in her lowered voice, not wanting to risk Eddie Ray Moon trying to harm some innocent person and her having to shoot him before finding out where they would meet up with Cherokee Earl and his gang.

"I said both of yas . . . I meant both of yas," Buck said, his voice growing a bit testy.

"Yeah, so come on, Duggin," Eddie Ray said to Danielle, heeling his horse forward. Danielle nudged Sundown and caught up to him as Buck Hite, Fat Cyrus, and Clifford Reed rode on.

At the edge of the clearing, Eddie Ray stopped and looked back at Danielle right behind him. "You want to see some shooting, watch me," he said, barely above a whisper.

"Buck never said shoot anybody, Eddie Ray," said Danielle. "He just said check it out."

"I know what he said. I don't need you telling me." Eddie Ray looked her up and down scornfully. "But if the opportunity presents itself, I'll show you some shooting that'll cross your eyes."

"Hello the woods," Tuck called out, seeing the two riders just inside the tree line.

"Hello the clearing," Eddie Ray replied, his voice only vaguely concealing some sort of challenge.

Tuck! Danielle gasped, instantly recognizing Tuck Carlyle's voice. She leaned sideways to look around Eddie Ray Moon at the lone shooter standing across the clearing with the pistol hanging down at his side. *My God, it is Tuck!* Her mind raced. For a second she was caught completely off guard.

Having noted the tone of voice coming from the thicket, Tuck called out in a civil but not overfriendly voice, "Come forward and show yourselves."

"Stay behind me," Eddie Ray whispered over his shoulder.

"Like hell," Danielle hissed, coming to her senses quickly and heeling Sundown forward, forcing herself and the mare ahead of Eddie Ray and into the clearing. She made sure to tug her hat brim down. She held her reins with her left hand and made sure to keep her right hand away from her Colt. "Tuck? Tuck Carlyle?" she asked, wanting to let Eddie Ray Moon hear right away that she knew this person. "My ole trail pal from Texas?"

Tuck took a step forward, cocking his head slightly, trying to believe his eyes. "Danny Duggin?" Then he was certain. "Well, I'll be. . . . It is you!" He raised his pistol and slid it down into his holster.

Noting the badge on Tuck's chest, Danielle wished he'd kept the pistol in his hand. But it was too late to tell him that. "Yep, it's me all right, Tuck." She touched her fingertips to her hat brim, then stepped the chestnut mare forward. "Never thought I'd run into you again." She pulled the mare to one side and gave Eddie Ray Moon a look, letting him know that he'd better not start any trouble.

"Same here, Danny," said Tuck. "I've got no coffee to offer the two of you, but step down all the same. We can talk some."

"Much obliged, but not today, Tuck," said Danielle, shooting Eddie Ray a harsh glance as he started to swing down from his saddle. "We're on our way to Cimarron, on business. Just rode over from the trail to see what the shooting's about." He nodded at Eddie Ray and said, "This is Raymond Moon. I'm riding with him and some other fellows."

"Oh, I see," said Tuck, sounding a bit disappointed, looking closely at Eddie Ray. "Well, I'm deputy in Cimarron now, so I suppose we'll be running into one another. Maybe we can a have a drink at Lambert's Tavern."

Danielle nodded at the badge on his chest. "I was going to ask when you took up a tin star. I have to say I'm little surprised by it. I always figured you for a cattleman and nothing else."

A sadness seemed to come over Tuck's face. "A lot has happened since we last met, Danny. I look forward to seeing you in town and telling you all about it."

Danielle backed her mare a step. Thinking about what had happened to Tuck's old friend Stick, she said, "I have some things to tell you too, Tuck. Why don't we make it a point to meet tonight for that drink?"

"Sounds right to me," said Tuck, noting the faintest urgency in Danny Duggin's expression that he didn't think the other man noticed.

Eddie Ray Moon cut in. "Duggin, the boss ain't going to want you wandering off tonight to talk about old times with your saddle pals."

Danielle gave him a cold stare. "Go on ahead of me, Eddie. Tell the boss I ran into an old friend of mine. Tell him I'm on my way."

Eddie Ray started to protest, but seeing Danielle slip a gloved hand down near the handle of the big Colt, he only made a gruff sound under his breath and jerked his horse around toward the thicket.

As he rode off into the dense piñon forest, Tuck

said to Danielle, "Don't let me get you into trouble with your boss, Danny. We can meet tonight."

"Tuck, have you ever seen me worry about getting in trouble with a *boss*?" She didn't give Tuck time to answer. Instead, she said, lowering the range of her voice, "But listen to me. It's a stroke of luck, me running into you. I'm on the trail of some killers. These men I'm riding with are leading me to them. They're outlaws . . . they think I'm riding with them to rob a bank."

"I figured something was up," said Tuck. "I couldn't see you riding with the likes of that one. I hope your knowing me, a deputy, ain't going to hurt you any."

"It won't, Tuck," said Danielle, cutting a glance into the piñon thicket. "Meet me tonight and I'll fill you in on everything."

"You got it, Danny," said Tuck. "I'll be there for sure." He watched the big mare turn a short circle, rearing slightly on its hind legs, then come down and race away into the piñon. After a moment of reflection, Tuck turned and walked back to his horse. He had a feeling that he was about to get real busy. This was all the target practice he'd be doing for a while.

In the remote cabin tucked deep inside a woodlands alongside a wide, shallow creek, Ellen looked down at the butcher knife one of the men had left lying on a window ledge beside the woodstove. She gave a quick look at Dirty Joe Turley, who sat at the wooden kitchen table, his back turned to her. Her first impulse upon seeing the knife was to grab it and plunge it into his spine as deep as she could force it to go. But then she glanced out the window and saw that Cherokee Earl and Avery McRoy hadn't even made it out of sight yet. Their horses were still climbing the far side of the creek bank toward the trail leading to Cimarron. *Bide your time*, Ellen's inner voice told her.

On the other side of the creek, Avery McRoy looked back once toward the cabin as their horses stepped up the bank and moved out of sight. "It's none of my business, Boss," he said to Earl, "but knowing the shape Dirty Joe is in regarding that woman, is it a good idea leaving them alone like that?"

"Far as I'm concerned, Dirty Joe is a dead man soon as we get this bank robbed," said Cherokee Earl. "It's either leave him or you alone with her, and I need somebody I can trust beside me. That's why I brought you."

"Then I take it you're through with the woman?" McRoy asked.

"Yeah," Earl said sourly. "I've been through with her since Braden. She ain't much. . . . She just looks full of promise is all. Why? You want her? If you do, she's all yours soon as we get back, provided Joe ain't killed her by then."

"No, Boss, I think I'll pass," said McRoy. "It's business first with me. We get that bank money, I can buy all the women I'll ever need and be able to run them off come morning so's I don't have to hear them bellyache about anything that doesn't suit them."

Cherokee Earl grinned. "That's smart thinking on your part, McRoy. Soon as we take this bank, you kill that moon-eyed Dirty Joe—the woman too, for that matter. You and me will be equal partners from now on. How does that suit you?"

"That suits me fine, Boss," McRoy said, heeling his horse up beside Cherokee Earl's.

Inside the cabin, Ellen took one more look and, not seeing the horses now, felt her hand start to reach for the butcher knife. But just as she did, Joe Turley scooted his chair back from the wooden table, got up, and walked over to her, craning his neck to take a good look out the window toward the trail. "Good, they're gone," he said, keeping his voice lowered as if they might yet hear him. He reached hungrily for Ellen, his hands grasping her waist and pulling her to him.

"Joe, please, wait a minute!" Ellen said, stalling the inevitable.

"Wait?" Joe said, repeating her, his voice trembling. "You must be kidding! Waiting is all I've been doing. I've got to have you right now!" He forced a deep, wet kiss onto her mouth. His beard stubble assaulted her lips, her chin.

"Please, Joe!" She managed to force him away, if only for a second. "You've got to give me a moment . . . to get in the mood."

"Honey, I'm in the mood," Joe rasped. He forced her hand down the front of his trousers and pressed himself against her, clawing at the front of her dress until it came open and her breasts stood out pale and quivering. "God, I've never been more in the mood than at this minute," he whispered lustily.

"Okay, okay then," Ellen said, giving in, letting his mouth find hers again, allowing his free hand to knead and fondle her breasts. With her left hand down his trousers, she squeezed him firmly down there and heard a long moan come from his throat. Yet, as he pawed and squeezed her and held her pinned to him, Ellen's right hand went around him, reaching the window ledge, searching frantically for the knife handle until she grasped it firmly. She felt him lifting her dress above her hips, felt his belt buckle dig into her flesh. He fumbled with his gun belt buckle, loosened it, and let his Colt fall to the floor. Then he loosened his trouser belt and let his trousers fall also. "Now give it to me," he moaned.

Squeezing her eyes shut, Ellen stabbed the point

of the knife sidelong into his neck two inches below
his ear with all of her strength. She felt the knife
blade go deep, and having done such a thing sickened her. Joe lost his grip. His hands melted away
from her and shook violently for a second until real-
ization sank in. He stood staring in disbelief, his eyes
wide in terror. Then he raised his left hand, found
the handle, and grasped it tight. "I—I thought you
wanted me," he managed to say in a strained voice.

"No! Forgive me, Joe!" Ellen said shakily. For a
second, she stood transfixed by fear.

"Damn you!" Joe yanked the blade out of his
throat, and a spout of blood pumped long and hard
from his severed artery. Ellen came unstuck. She
screamed hysterically and scooted back away from
him, raising her hands to her face as if to hide the
grisly scene from her eyes. Dirty Joe staggered forward, his lifeblood leaving him quickly, his face
growing pale white. He stabbed down at her halfheartedly.

"Joe!" Ellen sobbed. "I didn't want to kill you! I
had to! God forgive me!" She jumped farther back
as he stabbed at her again. This time the knife
slipped free from his weak, blood-slick hand and
clattered to the floor at her feet. She snatched it up
as, falling forward, he lunged at her, his hand grabbing for her. With a long scream, Ellen dropped
down into a crouch, drew the knife back, and with
all her strength stabbed him again, this time burying
the blade up to its hilt in his chest, where the left
and right sides of his rib cage came together.

"*Ayieee!*" His breath left him in a rattling gust. He
stared down at the knife handle again in disbelief.
His eyes seemed to say, *My God, you've done it again!
You've stabbed me twice!* The stream of blood from
his neck splattered down onto the rough plank floor,
making a strange sound. He sank to his knees, his

mouth gaping, his tongue thick and lolling between his lips. He managed to grip the handle with both bloody hands before he fell face forward.

"God forgive me, God forgive me, God forgive me!" Ellen stood wild-eyed, her hands clasped to her ears. Around her, the small cabin appeared to have been painted with blood by the hand of a blind madman. She stood stone-still for a moment, then looked around as if to see who might be watching as she drew the open front her dress closed, hiding her blood-splattered breasts. Another deathlike moment passed before she began to tremble uncontrollably. Then she sank weeping to her knees, curled up in a ball like a small child, and lay quietly amid the carnage.

Whether she'd slept or not she didn't know. But when she stood up, it was growing dark outside and an evening chill had moved into the cabin. She took a good look at the body of Joe Turley lying in the same spot where she remembered it being. Then she looked once again around the bloody cabin, pushed her hair back out of her eyes, and busily set about preparing herself for the trail.

The first thing she did was to step over to Joe Turley's gun belt, which was lying on the floor in a drying puddle of thick black blood. She lifted his pistol, checked it, picked up a cloth from the table, wiped blood from the gun handle, and carried it with her as she lit a lantern and rummaged through the cabin for a coat and some better clothes for the trail.

When she'd gathered a pair of trousers, a wool shirt, and some long underwear, she stepped out of her dirty, bloodstained dress and, standing naked in the dim circle of light, dipped a bandanna into a water bucket and washed herself free of the many spots and smears of dried blood. Finishing, she dressed quickly, still holding the pistol as if it were her personal talisman. Stepping around Joe Turley's body, she picked up his hat, looked it over, saw that it had only a few small blood spots, and put it on her head. Her red hair flowed beneath the hat brim.

Where was she going? "Anywhere but here," she murmured aloud to herself, taking a last glance around the grisly scene in the cabin. She wasn't sure where she was going, but she knew better than to go toward Cimarron and risk running into Earl and McRoy, that much she knew for certain. She was free now . . . and she intended to stay that way. Besides, she'd seen what Cherokee Earl and his men had done to the last towns they'd ridden through. She wasn't about to pin her faith in a small-town sheriff, a deputy or two, and a handful of townsmen. Once she got onto the trail, she was heading in the opposite direction from Cherokee Earl. She'd overheard Earl and the others talk about the trail they'd been on winding downward and southwest to Taos. That was good enough for her.

Beside the door stood Joe Turley's Winchester repeating rifle. On a peg hung a bullet belt full of ammunition for the Winchester. She knew very little about rifles, but she reminded herself that she would never find a better time to learn. For one last time she looked over at Joe Turley's body and whispered, "I really am sorry I had to kill you, Joe. But it was life or death for me." Then she picked up the rifle, swung the bullet over her shoulder, and walked out the door.

Chapter 17

No sooner had Danielle and Eddie Ray Moon caught up to Buck Hite and the others than Eddie Ray began spilling his guts about Danny Duggin being friends with a lawman. When he'd finished, the men had all come to a halt and drawn their horses into a half-circle around Danielle and her mare. "Just how good of friends were you and this deputy, Danny?" asked Buck.

"We were the best of friends, Buck," Danielle replied. "But Eddie Ray has left out two important facts. First of all, it was a long time ago. . . . And second of all, Tuck Carlyle was not a lawman then. He was a drover." Danielle's eyes went across each man's face in turn. "Now, if anybody has a problem with this, we can work it out a lot of different ways right here and now." Her hand poised close to the pistol butt, making no effort to hide her meaning.

Buck Hite noted that while she'd addressed all four of them, everything about her—her voice, her shadowed face, her gun hand—appeared to be focused toward him. Buck turned his face slowly to Eddie Ray Moon. "You didn't mention all that, did you, Eddie Ray? Reckon it must've slipped your mind?" He spoke low and even, but there was a threat in his voice that caused Eddie Ray to shrink back a bit.

"All right, listen to me," Eddie Ray said, raising a hand, his voice sounding a little anxious. "I knew this fellow was new at being a lawman—he said so himself. I also figured it had been a while since they'd seen one another, the way they talked about it. But, Buck, Duggin here was talking about getting together with this man later on . . . catching up on old times, they was saying." Now Eddie Ray turned an accusing gaze on Danielle.

"Is that true, Duggin?" asked Buck Hite. "You plan on riding with us and at the same time being good friends with the law?"

"Yep, you're damn right I do," said Danielle. She paused for just a second to make sure her words sank in. "I'd make friends with every lawman in this country if I could. The more information I can learn from lawmen, the better it is for me and anybody I ride with, the way I look at it."

Staring at her intently, Buck Hite finally offered a slight smile. "Pretty damn smart, Duggin," he said. He shot Eddie Ray Moon a glance. Clifford Reed and Fat Cyrus backed their horses a cautious step away from Eddie Ray's.

"Buck, I did what I thought was best for all of us!" Eddie Ray said quickly.

"You've been on a slow burn against this man ever since he beat the shit out'n you. Now whatever you think you got to settle with him, you do it now and get it done."

"Buck, I—"

Buck cut him off. "Because we've got serious business to take care of in Cimarron. I can't have this kind of schoolkid bickering going on between grown men!" His voice grew more angry as he spoke.

"Buck, if you'll just let me explain," said Eddie Ray, growing more worried, especially now that he saw the mare take a step closer to him. Danielle had let her hand relax for a moment, but now she poised it again. "I felt like everybody here ought to know that Duggin—"

"There ain't nothing to explain, Eddie Ray," Buck shouted. He turned his stare at Danielle. "Duggin, do you think you can get close enough to that lawman tonight to find out how much silver and cash is laying in that bank?"

Danielle shrugged. "If Eddie Ray didn't put him on guard about what he tells me, yeah, I can get that close. . . . He trusts me."

A tense silence passed as Buck looked from one man to the next, then said, "See? That's called using our heads. Cherokee Earl is the one who's supposed to know how much money there is in there. But, boys, what if he's wrong? Or what if he's dead by now and ain't even showed up?" Buck raised an eyebrow, a gesture of wisdom. "It never hurts to know what a lawman's got to say." He turned back to Danielle. "Any chance this lawman could be cut in with us?"

"That's a thought," said Danielle, knowing better. "The thing is, what if I bring it up and he turns it down?"

"Yeah, good thinking," said Buck. He nodded toward a clearing ahead alongside the trail. "Let's camp out up there. We'll ride into town tonight. While Clifford and Fat Cyrus and me look for Earl and his boys, you keep Eddie Ray with you, find out what you can from the deputy. Does that sound all right to you, Duggin?"

"That sounds fine to me, Buck," Danielle said.

From beneath the shelter of her broad hat brim, she saw a faint smile of satisfaction come to Eddie Ray Moon's face. Danielle understood why. Even though Danny Duggin had just gained some important respect from Buck Hite, it was still clear to her that Buck didn't trust Danny Duggin completely. He was leaving Duggin and Eddie Ray Moon together, knowing that Moon still had enough of a grudge to keep a close eye on every move Duggin made. *So be it*, Danielle said to herself. Once in Cimarron she'd just have to find a way to shake loose from Eddie Ray.

All of this had happened earlier in the day. Now, after thinking about it for a few moments, Danielle stood up from lying back against her saddle in the thin shade of a cottonwood tree and dusted the seat of her trousers. After spending the afternoon resting the horses and themselves, Buck Hite and his gang were ready to ride the rest of the way to town. Eddie Ray seemed to have forgotten the near altercation between himself and Danny Duggin as they stood side by side, saddling their mounts and making ready for the trail. When the men gathered at the edge of the clearing, Buck Hite sat chewing a mouthful of tobacco. He spat and ran a hand across his lips.

"Boys, when we get into Cimarron, remember why you're there. We want to find Cherokee Earl and his men, nothing else. If you need to wet your whistles a little, that's fine by me. But remember this well." He raised a gloved finger for emphasis. "You're not there to chase whores, play poker, or get blind staggering drunk. If you do, just expect that I'm going to put a bullet in you once we're out of town. We're there on business." He spat another stream, then turned his horse to the trail, the others falling in behind him single file. "Don't nobody make me say it again."

The men all nodded silently among themselves.

The last few miles into Cimarron went quickly, but by the time their horses gathered on the edge of town, darkness had fallen across a starlit sky. The sound of a tinny piano danced along the street from the direction of Lambert's Tavern, a building attached to the right side of the St. James Hotel. The tavern's front doors were wide open, lantern light spilling out onto a dozen or more horses standing at hitchrails and hitchposts out front. A woman's shrill laugh resounded playfully along the street.

"I'm glad you said it was all right to wet our whistles, Buck," said Fat Cyrus. He licked his lips. "But suppose if I went out back with a whore only wasn't gone for longer than say . . . three or four minutes? Would that be okay?"

"Good God, Cyrus," said Clifford Reed, shaking his head. "You ought not admit something like that."

"Like what?" Fat Cyrus looked confused. "I'm quick at most everything. A man ought to be proud how fast he can—"

"Shut up, Cyrus!" Buck Hite barked, cutting him off. He turned his gaze to Clifford Reed. "Clifford, keep his mind on what he's here for, or so help me . . ."

"I'll try, Buck," said Clifford. "That's all I can do."

"Duggin," said Buck, turning to Danielle, "since you're going to meet this deputy at the tavern, you and Eddie Ray get on over there. Clifford, you and Cyrus start making some rounds—restaurants, billiard halls, faro tables, wherever you might run into Earl and his boys. I'll be laying back out of sight, keeping an eye on things."

Danielle and Eddie Ray Moon broke off from the others and rode their horses to Lambert's Tavern. They stepped down from their saddles and tied their horses to one of the crowded hitchrails. At the open front doors of the tavern, they both stopped dead still when two pistol shots exploded from the long, crowded bar inside.

"Don't turn your back on me, Mr. Deputy, you cowardly polecat!" shouted a raging young man with his pistol smoking in his hand. Danielle stood transfixed, seeing drinkers clear away from the bar, leaving only Tuck Carlyle facing the young gunman, who had three more gunmen standing behind him. The three spread out slowly, taking a fighting position.

"Oops!" Eddie Ray chuckled beside Danielle. "Well, Duggin, looks like your lawdog friend is about to become your ex-lawdog friend."

Without answering, Danielle took a step inside the open doors and spread her duster back behind her pistol butt. The piano had fallen abruptly silent; the tavern customers stood tense and expectant. "Hope I'm not interrupting anything, Deputy Carlyle," Danielle said, using her strongest man's voice.

Behind her, Eddie Ray Moon whispered, "If you'll just excuse me, Duggin. He's your friend, not mine."

Danielle heard Moon's boots hurry away. At the bar, Tuck Carlyle said, without taking his eyes off the gunmen facing him, "Not at all, Danny. In fact, I was just wishing you'd pop by here, spread a little laughter my way." His voice was dead serious in spite of his dark irony.

"That's what I do best," said Danielle. She stepped farther into the tavern, then stopped fifteen feet from the gunmen and plated her boots shoulder-width apart, her hat low across her forehead, hiding her face.

"This ain't your concern," said the young gunman, his hand seeming to get a little nervous now that someone had tipped the odds a little. The three men behind him looked at Danielle. They too seemed suddenly put off by having the deputy in front of them and now a lone gunman taking off his right glove slowly, one finger at a time, behind them. They noted how the big tied-down Colt on the lone gunman's hip glinted in the light of the many lanterns flickering around the tavern.

"Now that makes me feel unwelcome," said Danielle.

"You ain't welcome!" the young gunman raged.

"Now get out, or die here!" He half-turned to face
Danielle, something that even his friends behind him
knew was a bad mistake: standing that close to a
man he'd just challenged and then turning to face
another gun halfway across the floor.

"I won't be doing either tonight," said Danielle,
her voice strong, as if tempered by iron. She saw the
slightest move among the three gunmen. Two of
them reached for their guns at once. At the same
time, she saw the gunman in front of Tuck start to
cock his smoking pistol. But she paid him no mind.
Instead, when her pistol streaked up from her holster, she threw her shots at the other two. Her shots
fired almost as one, the first snapping the gun from
the man's hand in a spray of blood and broken metal.
Her second shot nailed the other man in his right
shoulder and slammed him back against the bar.

"Jesus!" The third man bolted across the floor
and burst through the rear door, his boots pounding loudly until they faded into the night. On the
floor at Tuck Carlyle's feet, the first gunman lay in
a crumpled heap, his hat gone from the top of his
head, replaced by a bloody knot the size of a duck
egg. Tuck stood over the man with his pistol in his
hand, having knocked the young man cold with
the barrel.

Danielle walked to the bar with her pistol still
cocked and ready. She looked at the other two gunmen as she spoke to Tuck Carlyle. "What about these
two? Do you want them in jail or out of town?"

"Out of town will have to do," said Tuck. "The
sheriff's gone for a few days. I haven't jailed anybody
yet, and I'm not sure what to do." He gave Danielle
a bemused look. "Sounds foolish, don't it?"

"Yep, a little," said Danielle. "But I suppose everybody has a first time for everything." She and Tuck
looked at the two men.

"Get Rance up from here and get him out of

town," said Tuck. "If I see any of you again tonight, you'll all go to jail."

"What about my shot hand?" The gunman held up his wounded hand, blood running down between his thumb and finger, dripping onto the floor.

"What about it?" Danielle said coldly.

His eyes were wide with fear, anger, and pain. "I need a doctor or something! Damn! You can't just shoot a man and run him out of town with no medical attention! I could bleed to death!"

As he spoke, Danielle reached out, untied his bandanna, and yanked it from around his neck, stirring up dust. She flicked it once to get the rest of the dust off, then laid it across his wounded hand. "Wrap it tight until the bleeding stops."

"That ain't no way to treat a wound!" the young man bellowed.

"Keep running your mouth, and I'll see to it that you do bleed to death," Danielle said. She turned to the other gunman, who stood with his back against the bar for support, a hand pressed to his bleeding shoulder. His face was stark white.

"What about you?" Danielle asked. "Are you able to ride, or are you going to need a doctor too?"

"I'm able to ride," he said defiantly. "Just let me out of here. I don't want your help."

"Good," said Danielle. "You can help get this one out of here." She and Tuck lifted the knocked-out gunman, who was now reviving, from the floor and stood him between his two wounded friends. He wobbled back and forth on spindly legs, looking unsure of himself, of who he was or where he'd been.

"If you come back here threatening me, boy," said Tuck, "I'm going to forget how stupid you are and go ahead and put a bullet in you." He looked closely at the young man, then gave up, realizing it was useless talking to him right then. "Get him out of here," Tuck said to the other two.

As the wounded, crestfallen gunman was dragged out through the front doors, Tuck turned to Danielle and said, "Much obliged, Danny. If you hadn't showed up when you did, I'd have sure had my hands full."

"Glad I could help, Tuck," said Danielle. Looking around to make sure Eddie Ray or none of the others were present, Danielle added in a lowered voice, "Let me tell you while I can. These men I'm riding with are here to rob the bank." Seeing Tuck's expression turn concerned, Danielle went on. "Just listen for now while they're not around. The men I'm hunting are Cherokee Earl Muir and his gang. They have a hostage, a woman they took from her home near Haley Springs. Her name is Ellen Waddell—"

"Does she have red hair?" Tuck asked.

"Yes, she does," said Danielle. "Have you seen her?"

"I believe so," said Tuck. "She's traveling with a man who calls himself Fred Bartlett. There's two men riding with them, but I didn't get a good look at their faces."

"Fred Bartlett, my eye," said Danielle. "I bet that's Cherokee Earl. Do you know where they went?"

"No," said Tuck. "I even went searching for them, but I never came up with a trace of them. It seems like they've dropped off the face of the earth."

"They'll be back, Tuck—you can count on it. They've been leaving towns in ruins from here to Haley Springs . . . and they mean to rob the bank here. They know there's a big silver exchange going on."

"Then we've got to stop them," said Tuck.

"Yes, but we've also got to save Ellen Waddell," said Danielle. "If we jump too soon and tip our hands to the men I'm riding with, that poor woman will likely end up dead."

"All right, Danny, I'm backing you," said Tuck. "You call the play."

"We wait until the day they come in here all together. Then we take them all down at once. Meanwhile, I'll keep an eye on things, find out where the woman is so we can free her once they're all taken care of."

"Then that's how we'll do it, Danny," said Tuck. "I'll wait for your call."

"Thanks, Tuck, I knew I could count on you." Danielle hesitated, then said in a gentler tone, "And, Tuck . . . I hate telling you this, but two of these men killed our old friend Stick."

"Oh, no, Danny, not Stick," Tuck said, his grief showing instantly. "That man was like a daddy to me, Danny."

"I know he was, Tuck." Danielle hung her head for a moment. "Stick was on the trail with me, searching for these men after they stole the Waddell woman. But he and I started off looking for you. He told me what happened to your wife—I'm sorry, Tuck—and he told me you were somewhere drinking your brains out. We were coming to get you, see to it you straightened out. I'm glad to see that you've apparently already taken care of that."

Tuck looked pained and ashamed. "Yes, I've gotten over drinking my brains out. . . . But the other part, losing my wife, is something I doubt I'll ever get over. It hurts just as bad today as it did the day I lost her." He struggled silently for a second to keep from breaking down. "Something's missing inside me, Danny. I'm managing to get by without the whiskey, but that's just pure stubborn pride that keeps me going. I couldn't stand thinking that whiskey was going to kill me. So I'm fighting hard." He took on a determined expression and let out a tight breath. "But listen to me going on about my misfortune . . . while some poor woman is being held by outlaws."

"Don't worry, Tuck. We'll get her freed," said Danielle. "And once all this is over, you and I are going to have a long talk."

"About what, Danny?" Tuck asked.

"About me," said Danielle, aching to throw off her hat, shake out her hair, and tell him everything. "There's something I've needed to tell you for the longest time .. just seems like there's always something else going on to prevent it."

"Danny? Are you all right?" Tuck asked.

"Yeah, Tuck, I'm all right. Now that I'm here, I'm fine. The rest will have to wait till later." Danielle had caught herself and settled her mind to the task at hand. "We'll be talking about it real soon, I promise."

Chapter 18

Out of consideration for Tuck Carlyle and his battle with the bottle, Danielle did not drink any whiskey or beer. Instead, she drank the same thing Tuck drank: a cup of coffee from a fresh pot the bartender kept behind the bar. No sooner had the tinny piano started again and the smoke from Danielle's Colt drifted away than Eddie Ray Moon came through the front door of the tavern, a sheepish look on his face. "I heard the shooting," he said, sidling up to her. "Thought I better come see how things turned out."

"As you can see," said Danielle, "we managed to get by without you." Tuck Carlyle had stepped out the rear door to relieve himself. Offering a wry smile, and to show there were no hard feelings, Danielle asked, "Can I buy you a drink, Eddie Ray?"

Eddie Ray rubbed his lips, looking at the long row of bottles standing against the wall behind the bar. "I could sure enough stand one."

Danielle gestured the bartender to pour Eddie Ray a shot of whiskey. As they stood watching the glass being filled, Eddie Ray looked at Danielle's coffee cup. "I see you ain't drinking nothing yourself."

"That's right," said Danielle, not wanting to even try to explain why to the likes of Eddie Ray Moon. "While you were gone, did you see Cherokee Earl or any of his men?"

"Not a hair," said Eddie Ray. He raised the shot

glass to his lips and drained it in a single gulp. He released a deep whiskey hiss. "But they'll show, if they ain't been killed or caught."

The bartender had left the bottle of rye standing in front of them. Danielle picked it up and poured Eddie Ray another drink.

Eddie Ray grinned. "I think I might have been wrong about you, Duggin."

"Really?" Danielle looked surprised to hear him admit such a thing.

He looked repentant, and shrugged. "Yeah . . . we just got off to a bad start. I never should have come to the hotel acting so pushy that day. I reckon I'm trying to apologize for it. See if we can't go ahead and become friends."

"You saw the whole shooting through the window a while ago, didn't you?" Danielle asked matter-of-factly.

Eddie Ray's face reddened. "Yeah, I might have," said Eddie Ray. "But still, I'm offering my hand in friendship. We're riding together, so we ought to try to get along, don't you think?" He extended his rough right hand timidly.

"Yep, why not?" said Danielle, shaking his hand, then turning it loose as soon as she could lest she bring to his mind how small her hand was in his. "From now on we'll try to get along," she said, repeating his words.

Tuck Carlyle came back to the bar and, seeing that one of the outlaws they'd been discussing had joined them, remained friendly enough to his ole pal Danny Duggin yet a little standoffish toward Eddie Ray Moon. Raising his cup to this lips, finishing the coffee off, and setting the cup empty back on the bar top, Tuck took on an aura of authority. "Well, it's time I got back to making my rounds. It's been good to see you again, Duggin. And I appreciate your help a while ago. But remember what I told you. It makes no difference what you and I done together in the past. Now that I'm wearing a badge, upholding the law comes first." His eyes drifted from Danielle to Eddie Ray. "I hope you and your friends understand that."

"Yeah, I understand that, Carlyle," said Danielle, sounding less than enthusiastic. "Good to see you too." She touched her fingers to her broad hat brim.

"Evenin' then," said Tuck, tipping his hat and stepping away from the bar. Danielle and Eddie Ray both turned and leaned back against the bar, watching the deputy leave. "Well, there you have it," said Danielle, a sound of regret in her best man's voice. "Never stay friends with a lawman. That little piece of tin must have a way of changing a man through and through."

"I've always said that very same thing," said Eddie Ray. He chuckled and tossed back his rye whiskey. "And I'll drink to it every time."

Turning around to face the bar again, Danielle pushed the coffee cup away from her and, feigning anger, said, "To think I stood here drinking coffee like some sort of dandy." She gestured the bartender to her and said, "Clear these cups away and give me a shot glass. I've got some catching up drinking to do."

"Now you're talking my language," said Eddie Ray.

As the two stood at the bar, Eddie Ray not seeming to notice that he was the one doing all the drinking, Avery McRoy, who had been watching them from a far corner, slipped in beside them. "Mind if I join you fellows?" he asked.

Danielle, who had noticed him watching them for the past few minutes, looked him up and down, then said, "That all depends, mister. What's on your mind?"

McRoy looked back and forth between them, then said, "I was hoping you could help me out some.

See, I'm supposed to meet a fellow here on business. . . . His name is Hite. Either of you ever hear of him?" He gestured to the bartender for a glass, then filled it form the bottle on the bar.

"Yeah," said Eddie Ray, his voice starting to take on a whiskey slur, "we're riding with—"

"That all depends too," said Danielle, keeping Eddie Ray from blurting anything out.

"A lot of things depend with you, don't they, mister?" said Avery McRoy in a testy tone of voice.

Danielle turned to face him, a hand on her tied-down Colt. "You came to us, mister, not the other way around. If you've got something to say, spit it out. If not, swallow it." She stared at him coldly until he was forced to look away.

"All right," said Avery McRoy, raising his hands chest high in a show of submission. "Maybe I shouldn't have approached you two this way. No harm done, I hope." His voice lowered almost to a whisper. "I'm looking for Buck Hite and his boys. Cherokee Earl sent me."

Danielle offered a half-friendly smile. "See, that wasn't so hard, was it?" She nodded. "Yeah, that would be us all right. Where's Earl?"

"Easy now," said McRoy. "I've never seen either one of you before. Earl sent me to find you boys and make sure everything is on the up and up, the way we've planned it. I need to see Buck Hite so I'll know everybody here is who they say they are."

"Makes sense to me," said Danielle. "I'm Danny Duggin. This is Eddie Ray. Come on, we'll take you to see Buck Hite right now."

"Real good," said McRoy, raising the drink to his lips. He downed his whiskey, then looked closer at the shadowed face beneath the broad hat brim. "Duggin, you look familiar. Have you and I run across one another before somewhere?"

"Maybe." Danielle shrugged. "Who knows?" She

stepped back from the bar and thumbed toward the door while the music from the piano filled the tavern. "Want to stand here all night talking about it, or go find Buck and see what we've got to do to make some money in this wide spot in the road?"

"Mister, are you always this unobliging?" said McRoy, turning away from the bar.

"My pal Duggin here has no play in him at all," Eddie Ray chuckled. "I found that out the hard way."

Leaving Lambert's Tavern, the three walked along the darkened street until they spotted Buck Hite's horse hitched out front of a run-down saloon where a scraggly row of chickens sat perched along a wooden bench out front. As the three approached, the chickens protested in a raised cackling and a flurry of batting wings.

"What the hell kind of place is this?" Eddie Ray Moon asked no one in particular, fanning small feathers from the air.

A fat black man stepped out of the dark shadows and said in a deep, flat voice, "This is Chicken Mama Loo's place. Like the sign done said." He pointed a large, long finger up at a sun-bleached wooden sign hanging by one corner chain.

Eddie Ray Moon stopped fanning his hand and looked up in the darkness. "Jesus," he said in disgust. "That sign ain't said nothing since Napoleon wore Josephine's bloomers."

Upon hearing Eddie Ray's words, all cordiality left the big black man's face. "What you men want here? You come for some of the hot pipe?"

"I never use it," said Eddie Ray. "What about you, Duggin? Care for some tar opium?"

"I pass," said Danielle, stepping closer to the door. Avery McRoy and Eddie Ray followed.

"Where you think you're going?" the black man asked.

"We're here to see the man who's riding that horse," said Danielle.

"He a friend of yours?" the man asked.

"If he wasn't a friend, we wouldn't be standing here asking—we'd already have shot him and you both."

The black man nodded, then looked at Buck Hite's horse and said, "Yeah, okay, he's in there." He stepped to one side, turned down a thick metal door handle, and shoved the door open. "I 'posed to ask for your guns, but I don't expect you'd give them to me, would you?"

"It ain't very likely," said Danielle, stepping inside the dark opium-clouded saloon.

The big black man laughed under his breath. "That's the same thing your friend told me. Yes, sir, he did."

A thick cloud of gray-brown smoke loomed heavily inside the small dirty saloon. Many of the drinkers stood slumped on the bar top. Others lay sprawled on tabletops, where candles stood in tin holders for the purpose of lighting the bowls of smudged opium pipes. Danielle spotted Buck Hite lounging at one of the tables in the back corner, and she walked straight to him. "Wake up, Buck," she said, kicking the leg of his chair. "We've met up with one of Cherokee Earl's men."

"Hunh?" Startled, Buck Hite fumbled with his chair, trying to scoot it back from the table. "I ain't asleep," he said as if denying an accusation. "I was just watching these boys, seeing what all the fuss is about." He looked back and forth among the three figures standing over him in the swirling drift of smoke. "I never smoke this stuff myself." His eyes were shiny and red-streaked. His voice sounded thick.

"Good," said Danielle. "Then you won't mind us pulling you away long enough to talk business." She grabbed his chair and tipped him out of it. He staggered to his feet. "Come on," she said firmly. "Let's go outside and get some air."

Buck looked at Avery McRoy and asked in an almost belligerent tone, "Where the hell is Cherokee Earl? We're supposed to meet with him, not one of his flunkies."

McRoy bristled at Buck Hite's words, but he managed to keep himself in check. "Earl sent me because I can be trusted. There's only three of us, and the third man is busy taking care of something."

They'd started for the door, but Buck Hite halted and looked at him pointedly. "There's only three of you? I thought this was going to be a big operation! Why am I throwing in with a three-man gang? I can get better than that on my own."

Avery McRoy walked on to the door as he spoke, causing Buck Hite to follow reluctantly. "We've got a couple of men still coming to join us. They stayed back along the trail to take care of some business." He stopped out front of the run-down saloon amid fleeing chickens and batting wings.

Buck Hite closed the saloon door behind them. "Still, this gang of Earl's ain't sounding as strong to me now as it did back when we talked about joining forces."

Avery McRoy started to speak, but from the darkness came Cherokee Earl's voice as he walked forward, kicking a chicken out of his path. "I'm going to pretend like what I'm hearing is just your dope talking, Buck. Otherwise you and me would be shooting holes in one another right here and now. I hate belligerence of any sort."

The sight of Cherokee Earl with his thumb hooked in his belt near his tied-down Colt had a sobering effect on Buck Hite. "Hell, Earl, you can't blame a man for asking questions . . . looking out for his own interest, can you?"

Cherokee Earl didn't bother answering him. Instead, he looked across the shadowed faces standing before him. "Like McRoy said, we're waiting for Harper and Frisco to join us. Unless something bad has befallen them, they'll be along most any time." Nodding at Danielle, he said, "You picked up a new man?"

"Yeah," said Buck, trying hard to clear the opium stupor from his head. "This is Danny Duggin—a good gunman. He's riding with us now."

"Duggin," said Cherokee Earl, touching his fingers to his hat brim. Then he said to Buck Hite, "What about the two men you sent back to check for those troublemakers?"

"They're dead," Buck said bluntly.

"Who killed them?" asked Earl.

"Duggin killed them," said Buck. "They jumped him on the trail, and he took them both down. That's why I hired him. If he can handle Daryl and Lon Trabough, that's good enough for me."

Cherokee Earl took a step closer, suspiciously eying her up and down. "Duggin, huh?"

"Yep, Duggin," she repeated, standing her ground.

"So, Duggin, just what was you doing on the trail at that time?" Earl asked.

Here stood the man responsible for Stick's death and all the other trouble she'd gone through. Danielle felt herself bristle slightly at his question. But she kept her anger in check and said coolly, "I felt a powerful urge drawing me in this direction . . . must've been so's I could get up here and answer a bunch of damn fool questions—why else?"

A tense dead silence fell over the group for a moment. Then Cherokee Earl let out a short laugh, saying, "I guess that's about as straight an answer as I'll ever get out of you."

"Just about," said Danielle flatly. "Anything else I say would just be me looking for the kind of answer I think you want to hear." She shrugged one shoulder. "Either you pards need me working for you or you don't." She looked back and forth between Buck and Cherokee Earl. "It's your call."

Cherokee Earl nodded, understanding that if this Danny Duggin had anything to hide, he sure wasn't worried about it. "Down to business then," said Earl. "They've been moving lots of silver through this bank, but mostly in small lots from the independent mining companies. What we're waiting for is a large shipment that'll be here in two days. As soon as I get the word, you'll hear about it from me or McRoy here. Meanwhile, we sit tight, keep a man in town at all times so we'll know when to draw our men together."

Thinking about the Waddell woman and how to get to her to save her, Danielle asked, "Shouldn't we be camped together now? It looks like that would make it easier for everybody concerned."

"You're right, Duggin. It would," said Earl, again eying him as if wondering what his interest might be. "But I make it a practice to keep a large body of men spread out a little before a raid. It's a practice that has served the James Younger gang and others well over the years. I'm sticking with it." He grinned, looking from one to the other of the men. "Besides, I'm what you might call *honeymooning* right now. I need a little privacy, if you understand what I mean." He winked.

"Sure, no problem," said Buck Hite, still sounding a bit groggy from the opium. "So long as you drop her ankles and pull your pants on quick once you hear about that silver load."

The men chuckled, Earl included. "Don't worry, Buck," he said. "I've been with this woman long enough that I'm losing interest. Far as I'm concerned, you can have her once we take care of business here."

"Much obliged, but none for me," said Buck. "I know better than to take a woman offered to me for free. There's a catch to it somewhere."

"You might be right," said Earl. "If she was all that much, I wouldn't be getting rid of her. You saw right through that, Buck. Looks like you and me might be riding together for a nice long time." His grin widened as a ripple of laughter stirred across the men. Danielle just listened, wondering how she would go about getting Ellen Waddell out of this alive.

Chapter 19

Ellen Waddell made good time starting out, riding down the steep, winding trail toward Taos. Yet once darkness had completely enveloped the land and she began to realize she had put some distance between herself and her captors, she slowed the horse to a walk and let the animal lead the way. Coming down out of a stretch of low hills onto some grasslands, Ellen caught sight of a campfire glowing in the distance. Using caution, she approached the fire as quietly as possible, the rifle lying across her lap.

When she'd reached what she judged to be a distance of a hundred yards, Ellen stepped down from the horse and led it through low brush and over loose rocky ground. She almost held her breath with each slight sound of the horse's hooves. Reaching a stand of scrub cedars, she stopped the horse and knelt in the darkness, listening until she heard the sound of two men's voices drift across the night. After a moment she stood up silently and whispered in the horse's ear as if it understood her words. "You'll have to wait here," she said, tying the reins to a low scrub cedar.

She moved quietly, measuring and testing every step before setting her foot down firmly on the ground. She had no idea how long it had taken her to move the few remaining yards, but when she stopped again and sank down in the cover of wild grass, she could make out the fire clearly and see the two men huddled near it, their faces obscured by their wide hat brims. The smell of hot coffee and beans made her empty stomach moan softly. She knew she had to make a decision pretty soon whether or not to announce herself or move on. Looking down at the rifle in her hands as she smelled the food and coffee, she made up her mind. Taking a deep breath, she stood up and called out, "Hello the camp," hearing the shallow sound of her voice in the broad, empty land.

"What the hell?" Frisco Bonham's coffee cup fell from his hand at the suddenness of a shrill voice reaching out of the darkness. His right hand clasped his pistol butt, but then stopped before drawing the gun from his holster. "That's a woman's voice!" he said, lowering his voice to Dave Waddell.

"Yes, it is," Dave replied, already recognizing his wife's voice but not yet daring to believe his ears. He stood up in the firelight, looking toward the voice. "Ellen? Ellen Waddell? Is that you? It's me, Dave!"

Frisco gave Dave Waddell a bemused look, thinking he'd just lost his mind. "Hey there, partner, you better try to get a grip on yourself—"

"Shhh," Dave said quickly, hushing him up. "That's my wife! I know it is!"

Hearing her name called out, Ellen's first instinct was to turn and run, fearing these men were a part of Cherokee Earl's gang and that somehow Earl had informed them that she was missing. But seeing the man stand up in the glow of the fire, hearing his voice, and watching as he looked back and forth trying to locate her, Ellen gasped, "Oh my God, Dave?" Then, realizing that it really was him, she called out loudly as she began to run toward him. "Dave! Dave! Yes, it's me!"

Dave jerked his hat from his head as if to better

identify himself. "Ellen! My God, Ellen!" He ran to
her as she came into the firelight.

Frisco Bonham stood watching, stunned, as the
two met and sank to their knees sobbing, embracing.
His eyes searched the surrounding darkness. If this
woman was here, it was pretty good odds that Cherokee Earl and the boys were too. He eyed the rifle
that Ellen Waddell had dropped to the ground. *Dirty
Joe's rifle,* Frisco said to himself.

When Ellen could speak, she said to her husband,
"I—I thought you were dead, Dave. I had no
idea . . ."

"That I would be searching for you?" Dave said,
finishing her words for her as he wiped his eyes.
"Ellen, I've nearly gone crazy looking for you!" He
nodded quickly toward Frisco, then said, "This is
Frisco Bonham, one of Cherokee Earl's men. He's
been leading me to Earl . . . so I could come get
you."

Ellen tensed in her husband's arms, having heard
Frisco's name spoken by Dirty Joe and others of
Earl's men. She looked up at Frisco just as he bent
down and picked up the rifle she'd dropped.

"Evening, ma'am," Frisco said, nodding with a
slight grin. He held the rifle up, looking it over. "This
belongs to Dirty Joe Turley. . . . Ain't no way he
would have given it up. So I figure you got it some
way and snuck off with it."

Ellen gave her husband a terrified look. The two
rose from the ground. Dave drew the pistol from his
waist on their way up. He held it pointed at Frisco
as he drew Ellen tight against his side.

"It makes no difference how she got the rifle. She's
here now, and that's all that—"

"Hey, hey, take it easy," said Frisco, grinning, raising his hands chest high and waving them back and
froth. "I'm with you, pard, remember? I'm the one

brought you two happy young lovebirds back together!"

Dave Waddell eased his grip on the pistol and on his wife. "He's right, Ellen," Dave said. "If it hadn't been for Frisco, I wouldn't have been here tonight."

"Ma'am," said Frisco, "I might be an outlaw . . . but your husband will have to admit I've been a man of my word. I told him to stick with me, that I'd bring him to you. And so I did." In a grand gesture, Frisco swept off his hat and took a short bow.

"The most important thing is we're back together now," said Dave to Ellen.

"Yes, we're together," Ellen said, still standing against her husband's side, "but we might not be for long if we don't clear out of here before Earl finds out I'm missing."

"If you don't mind me asking," said Frisco, "how did you manage to get away?" He studied Dirty Joe's rifle in his hands as he asked.

Ellen looked into her husband's eyes for support, then turned to Frisco and said bluntly, "Earl left Dirty Joe to watch me. I killed Dirty, took his rifle, and made my getaway."

"Killed him how?" asked Frisco with a wry smile. "Dirty Joe Turley was no easy piece of work as I recall."

"All right," she said, tilting her head up as if telling herself and the world that she was not ashamed of what she'd done. "I gained Joe's confidence. . . . Then, while he wasn't expecting it, I stabbed him to death with a butcher knife."

"Ouch!" said Frisco, still grinning. "I bet ole Dirty didn't care for that one bit."

Ellen turned her gaze back to her husband. "But like you said, the important thing is that we're together. Now we need to get out of here quick."

There was a questioning expression on Dave Waddell's face as he asked her pointedly, "Gained his confidence how?"

Ellen just stared at him for a second. Then, before she could respond, Frisco cut in, saying, "I don't mean to throw cold water on whatever high opinion you might have of yourself, ma'am, but if Cherokee Earl's in Cimarron, you won't have to worry about him looking for you. He's got plans for a big robbery there . . . big enough that he won't let losing a woman interfere with it."

In spite of Frisco's reassurance, Ellen looked skeptical. "I think we better get moving, Dave."

"Sure thing," said Dave, holding her close with his arm wrapped around her shoulders, his free hand stroking her hair. "God, I've missed you so much!" Then he snapped a glance back to Frisco and asked, "Just how big is this robbery you're talking about?"

Frisco shook his head back and forth slowly as if in awe at the thought of such an amount of wealth. "It's big enough that even once it's split a bunch of ways, nobody involved will ever have to pick up another branding iron for as long as he lives . . . unless he does it to light his cigar, that is."

"Dave?" said Ellen Waddell. "What does that matter? We're leaving right now . . . aren't we?"

Dave seemed not to hear her until she shook his coat sleeve. "Aren't we?" she repeated.

"Uh, yeah," Dave said finally, snapping out of a deep train of thought. "We're both heading out of here. We're not taking a chance on Earl showing up, robbery or no robbery."

"All right, pard," Frisco said reluctantly. "But I've got to say, it's a damn shame, you missing out on this big job after coming all this way."

"What is he talking about, Dave?" Ellen asked. "Why does he keep calling you pard?"

"It's a long story, Ellen," said Dave Waddell. Dismissing her question, he turned to Frisco. "My wife's right, Frisco. She's the reason I came this far. Now that I've got her, all I want to do is return home and live in peace." He drew Ellen even closer. "For my wife and me, this nightmare is over."

"In that case," said Frisco, pitching Dirty Joe's rifle to Dave Waddell, "I'll take my leave and go on to Cimarron."

"You're not going to tell Cherokee Earl where we are, are you?"

"Of course he will," Ellen cut in.

"No, ma'am, you're wrong there," said Frisco. "I won't mention you two if you don't want me to. But believe me, it ain't as important as you think it is. Sure, Earl did a wrong, stealing you the way he did. But if he wasn't through with you, he wouldn't have left you in Dirty Joe's care in the first place. The fact is, if Dave showed up with me, Earl would cut him right in on this robbery and let bygones be bygones." He shrugged. "That's just how he is . . . all us outlaws, for that matter."

"Don't take me for a fool, Frisco," said Dave. "You mean he would still let me ride on this big job after all that's happened?"

"I'm saying he would," said Frisco. "He'd forget the past if you would. And sure he'd let you ride with us after all the thievery you and me's done together. . . . You're an old hand at it now."

Ellen looked on in disbelief. "Dave, what is he talking about, all the *thievery* you've done together?"

"Like I told you, Ellen, it's a long story," said Dave.

"I have time to listen," said Ellen, pulling away from his encircling arm.

Over the next few minutes, while Ellen Waddell sipped coffee from Dave's battered tin cup, she listened to her husband tell her about everything that had happened since she'd last seen him lying in the dirt out front of their home. Dave told her how their neighbor, Danielle Strange, and the old man Stick had ridden by searching for Cherokee Earl. He told her how the two had found him there and brought him along to search for her. Then he went on to tell Ellen about Billy Boy Harper shooting Danielle Strange and about Frisco shooting Stick. Ellen sat amazed, a tear falling from her eye as Dave told her about the robberies he'd committed with Frisco in order to raise money and supplies to keep on her trail. When he'd finished telling her the whole story, he let out a long breath and sat slumped for a moment.

"Ellen," he said at length, "I'm ashamed of these things I've done . . . but I had no choice." Now a tear ran down his cheek as well. "I had to find you. I couldn't give up the hunt until I knew you were all right."

"But, Dave, those people . . . they were innocent, hardworking folks for all you know. How can you justify robbing them? You have to do something to make all of this right."

"Uh, well, it's something I'll sure do some serious thinking about," he said to Ellen, shooting Frisco a knowing glance as he spoke. In telling Ellen his story, Dave had failed to mention that there had been murder committed, and that, although he hadn't been the one to do the killing, he was still in it up to his neck. Legally, he would hang alongside Frisco if the law ever found them.

"You'll *think* about it?" said Ellen, surprised by her husband's attitude. "You'll simply have to go to the law and tell them what happened. You'll explain why you did what you did and that you'll pay back every dollar you took."

Dave Waddell wiped his eye, gave Frisco another glance, then said, "Ellen, believe me, sometimes it's better to just let things lie. In the long run everybody will be better off."

Listening closely, Frisco shook his head and cut in long enough to say, "If you two will excuse me, I'll just get my stuff, get saddled up, and move right along."

"In the middle of the night?" Dave asked.

"Yeah, I think so," said Frisco. "I know when I'm the third wheel."

"But you can wait till morning," said Dave, half rising from the ground beside the fire. Ellen stared at him curiously.

"Thanks but no, thanks," said Frisco. As he walked away toward the horses, he paused for a second, looked around at Dave Waddell, and said, "Not saying that you will of course, Dave . . . but if you should change your mind for any reason and want to join me, I'll be riding the Cimarron trail all the way to town."

Dave only glanced at Frisco long enough to see the knowing smile on his face. Then Dave hung his head and said, "No, Frisco, I reckon I'll be riding on back home now . . . my wife and I."

Ellen still only stared at him, not sure how she should take his words. Was there a sound of defeat in her husband's voice? The two sat in silence until Frisco stepped up into his stirrups and rode off into the darkness. "Well, that's that," said Dave Waddell, standing up beside the fire, shoving his hands down into his trouser pockets. "It would probably be best if we moved our camp away from here."

"Yes, I believe it would be wise," said Ellen. She stood up beside her husband, studied his face in the fire glow, and said quietly, "You want to ride into Cimarron with him, don't you?"

"What? No . . . Hell, no," said Dave Waddell. But the look in his eyes told her he was lying, and he knew it. He relented a bit and said in a softer tone of voice, "Well, let's face it, he's talking about a lot of money. It would sure make up for what-all we've lost these past days.

"So you do want to ride with Cherokee Earl?" Ellen asked.

"Well . . ." Dave let his words trail. Then he said, "But even if I did, what about you? We need to get you home, let you put all of this behind you."

Ellen caught herself again staring at her husband, wondering how she could have lived with a man so long and never realized until now just how little she knew him. "You would ride with the men who kidnapped your wife," she said flatly.

"No," said Dave, "because, as you can see, I'm still right here, ain't I?" He spread his hands to take in the campsite. "Right here where I should be. By your side."

Ellen detected a faint sourness in his voice, but she let it pass without commenting on it. After a lengthy, awkward silence, she said, "A lot has happened to us, Dave. We'll need to take some time to let things heal."

"I know," he said. "And we'll take all the time we need." After another pause, he said, "I—I don't dare ask how you were treated, or what he and the others did to you."

"Thanks, Dave, for understanding," Ellen said softly. "It's something I can't talk about. . . . Not now, perhaps never."

Facing away from her and staring down into the fire, Dave said, "I'm sure you did whatever you had to to stay alive, so I'll never question your judgment . . . or blame you for any of it."

Blame me . . . ? She stared at him. "Dave, no matter what I did or didn't do, I was kidnapped . . . taken against my will, forced against my will to do whatever that dog—" She stopped, then said aloud to herself, "What am I doing? Defending *my* actions?"

"No, don't, please," said Dave. "We don't need to go over the details."

"Good," Ellen said sharply, "because for a moment there I was afraid you might not approve of the way I allowed myself to be pawed and violated by that sweaty, greasy pig."

"Please don't!" said Dave. "I know it wasn't your fault, none of it. I just have to find a way from now on to accept the fact that another man has—" He stopped himself, then said, "Well . . . you know."

"Oh, well, thanks," said Ellen sarcastically. "I feel much better now."

"I didn't mean it like that, Ellen," he said, reaching with both arms to hold her.

"I'm sure you didn't," she replied, backing away.

"I'm sorry," said Dave. "That's all I can say. Think of me here, of what I've been through . . . knowing what was happening, being powerless to stop it. I've been through hell!"

"Yes," she said, "what time you weren't robbing people with your pard, Frisco Bonham!" She looked him up and down. "Frankly, Dave, you don't look all that hurt to me."

"Yeah? Well, neither do you, if I might say so," Dave hissed, his temper rising.

"What is that supposed to mean?" Ellen asked heatedly.

"You're a woman of the world now," said Dave. "You figure it out."

"A woman of the world?" Ellen repeated his words, feeling rage begin to boil inside her. "Because I'm not standing here with my face beaten in, my bones broken! Because of that, I have somehow let you down? I turned loose of my virtue too quickly, too easily? Is that what you mean?"

"Did you even put up a fight?" Dave asked, holding nothing back now.

"No!" Ellen shouted. "I did not put up a fight! I

let him do whatever he wanted to do to me. I made no effort to stop him! I lay there like a sack of feed while he grunted and slobbered and bored himself inside me!"

"Stop, that's enough!" Dave shouted, unable to abide the terrible scene her words evoked in his mind. "I don't want to hear any more!"

"You're a liar, Dave." Her voice dropped low, like the harsh purr of a mountain cat. "You want to hear more. . . . You want to hear every sick detail. But you want to hear it on your terms. You want me to clean it up, tell it to you in a way that will allow you to forgive me for it." Her voice rose suddenly. "You son of a bitch! You want to know if I enjoyed it! You stupid bastard! No, I hated it! If I hadn't managed to play Joe Turley along, make him promises of giving myself to him, let me tell you what I would have done."

"No, stop!" said Dave.

But she ignored him and continued. "I would have given myself to Earl on the ground, buck naked, while the whole gang watched!"

"I mean it, Ellen—stop it!" Dave threatened.

She didn't seem to hear him. "If I would have had to, I would have groaned and moaned and screamed in delight! And while I did so, I would have been slipping my hand along his thigh until I could close it around his pistol!"

"Damn you! Shut up!" Dave slapped her. She reeled but refused to stop.

"Then I would have blown my brains out!" Her hands covered her face. She wept violently.

Dave stood helplessly by, unable to approach her, unable to console her. When her crying subsided and she wiped her eyes and stared into the fire, she said in a calm voice, "Dave, there is something about me you should know." She hesitated, then went on. "Before I met you? Remember I told you I was away in a ladies' business college? Well, that wasn't true. I lived on my own, Dave, in Washington, D.C., less than three miles from the White House. I made a living entertaining men in private.''

"What? My god!" said Dave. "I had no idea!"

"I know," said Ellen. "I kept it a secret from you." She sniffled and wiped her nose on her coat sleeve. "When I met you in Colorado, I knew I could make you a good wife. After all, I know how to please. . . . I should, I've done it often enough."

"I'm not going to listen to any of this," said Dave. "I think you're making it up. I think you're talking out of your head. We shouldn't have ever let this conversation get started. Let's stop it right now."

Her face still stung from where he'd slapped her. "There's no stopping now, Dave. It's all coming out into the open. I don't want to hide who I am or what I've done. It's all that's kept me alive throughout this ordeal." She paused and considered things, then said, "Funny, isn't it? I left that life because I felt like public property to any man who would pay me. Now, all these years later, I used the skills I learned in that life in order to keep myself alive—protect your personal property, so to speak. Now it appears that my having done such a good job of staying alive is being called into question." She sighed long and deep, then murmured, "Men. . . . What the hell do you fellows want?"

"I don't know," said Dave, his whole demeanor suddenly rigid and unyielding, "but after this conversation, I don't think it's you." He refused to face her as he spoke. "I think when we get somewhere where there's a stagecoach, it would be best to put you on it. I often thought there were things I didn't know about you. You've deceived me all along. I will never be able to get over that."

"I understand," said Ellen. "I suppose I wouldn't expect you to."

As Dave stared into the fire, Ellen walked away for a moment.

"I know I ain't perfect," said Dave. "Maybe I've dealt a little dirt in business deals. I've put my hands on stolen cattle. But up until this thing happened, I've never robbed anybody, brought harm to anybody. I've only done what a man does. All I ever wanted was a good, decent, honest wife," Dave said down to the licking flames. "I thought that was what I had. Now it turns out I was wrong."

"I've let you down something terrible, haven't I?" said Ellen.

"Let me down? Ha! To say the least, you've let me down." He turned his eyes to hers as she returned to the campfire. "I wish to God we'd never met," he said bitterly.

"So do I," said Ellen. Dirty Joe's rifle bucked once in her hand, the explosion causing something above them in the scrub cedars to take flight, letting out a short screech and a windy sound of powerful beating wings. Dave Waddell hit the ground stone dead, one arm flinging over into the licking flames of the campfire.

Ellen reached out with the toe of her scuffed and ragged shoe and flipped his arm from the flames just as the skin on his hand began to sizzle and blacken, peeling back in layer after layer. She looked around the small campsite, then back down at the body of her husband lying dead on the ground. "Earl, you son of a bitch," she hissed as if Cherokee Earl was standing there. "I've got one more stop to make. . . . Then I'm going home."

Chapter 20

Frisco Bonham had heard the gunshot as he rode toward Cimarron. While the echo of the explosion still rolled across the land, he'd smiled to himself and said to his horse and the surrounding darkness, "Looks like they just settled their differences the hard way." Laughing aloud at his little joke, he batted his boots against his horse's sides and rode on toward Cimarron. Less than a mile from town, as his horse rounded a turn in the road, Frisco came upon Cherokee Earl and Avery McRoy as they made their way back to the shack hideout.

"Damn, Frisco," said McRoy, settling his startled gelding, "don't spook the horses!"

"I didn't come looking for you just to spook the horses," Frisco replied, his horse turning a complete circle before coming to a nervous halt. He studied their shadowed faces in the thin moonlight. "What's the odds of me running in to you two?"

Both Cherokee Earl and Avery McRoy looked equally surprised to come upon Frisco so suddenly in the dark of night. "Pretty damn good, I'd say," Earl chuckled. He leaned slightly and looked along the trail behind Frisco. "Where's Billy Boy?"

"Billy Boy's dead, I reckon," said Frisco, his voice taking on a sad edge.

"You *reckon* he's dead?" said Cherokee Earl, sounding a bit testy about Frisco's answer. "You mean you don't know for sure?"

"Boss, Billy Boy shot that woman you sent us back to ambush. He shot her with that hideaway gun he carried. But then she nailed him with a Colt .45. So, yep, I'd say for sure poor Billy Boy's dead."

"All right," said Earl. "At least he managed to kill the woman for me." He eyed Frisco. "What about the old man riding with her? Is he dead?"

"He is," said Frisco. "I shot him myself, left him dead on the trail."

"Good enough," said Earl. "Things are starting to come together for us. We didn't need those two dogging us."

"Hold on to your boots, Boss," said Frisco. "I got some strange news for you."

"Yeah? What's that?" asked Earl.

"I fell in with Dave Waddell on the way up here. He was with the old man and the woman when we ambushed them."

"I thought I left him in the dirt," said Earl.

"I know," said Frisco. "That's what he told me. Evidently, the woman and old man showed up and saved him."

"Then why didn't you kill him when you had a chance?" Earl demanded.

"Kill him hell," said Frisco. "He saved me from those two. Besides, he helped me rob a stagecoach and some settlers on the way here."

"That figures," said Earl. "I always knew he was an outlaw at heart."

"Yeah, well, he said you stole that pretty red-headed wife of his." Frisco spat, wiped his mouth, and chuckled. "The damned fool said he aimed to take her back from you."

"He's welcome to try," said Cherokee Earl. "The fact is, I wore out on her awfully quick . . . but I promised her off once I was through with her. I'll just have to explain all that to Dave if he shows up." He grinned. "I hope he understands."

"I don't think that matters now, Boss," said Frisco. "It's a fifty-fifty possibility he's dead by now. Him or that redheaded woman."

Earl and McRoy stared at him in the darkness. "What are you getting at, Frisco?" asked Earl.

"Boss, me and Dave ran into his wife on the trail. She told us you left Dirty Joe watching her, and she stabbed him to death with a butcher knife."

"Damn it to hell!" Earl cursed. "Here I am needing men to rob a bank and that damned Dirty Joe goes and gets himself killed!"

"I know, Boss, it's a shame," said Frisco. "I hate being the bearer of bad news, but I thought you'd want to know before you ride on to the hideout and find Dirty Joe bled out all over the floor."

"This leaves me stuck with Buck Hite, who's a dope smoker, and his three men, a bunch of idiots, all of them together too damn dumb to prime a dry pump." Earl shook his head slowly in disgust and dismay. "It's getting harder every day to hold a good gang together. Sometimes I wonder why I even try."

"For the money, that's why," said Avery McRoy, hoping to cheer Earl up. He looked at Frisco. "Why do you figure it's a fifty-fifty chance one of the Waddells is dead?"

"I left because I saw a big fight coming," said Frisco. "They were all lovey-dovey when they first got back together. But it didn't take over five minutes until she was on the verge of riding him out about helping me rob the stage."

"That's a woman for you," said McRoy.

"Yeah," said Frisco, "but I could also see that it wouldn't be long before Dave was going to start asking her some questions himself." Frisco nodded solemnly. "You could tell Dave is a greedy, jealous man. I left before the sparks started to fly. Then I heard a rifle shot before I'd gone a mile."

"That don't mean one of them killed the other,"

said McRoy as if looking for a brighter outcome to the story.

"Let's put it this way," said Frisco. "They was both armed and ready for some serious marital discussion." He gave each of them a look of dread. "And it was too dark out to be shooting at rattlesnakes."

"Then I suppose you're right," Earl said to Frisco. "One of them's dead, and the other is long gone, would be my guess."

"Say the word, Boss," said Avery McRoy. "Me and Frisco will find out what's gone on."

"No," said Earl. "It's no big concern to me. We've got business to take care of. Besides, I'm sorry I ever wasted my time on that woman. Far as I care, they can kill each other." He let out a sigh. "They always struck me as one of those couples who just weren't meant to stay together." He heeled his horse forward at an easy walk. McRoy and Frisco rode along, flanking him on either side.

"Is losing Dirty Joe going to leave us short-handed?" asked Frisco.

"It would have," said Earl. "But lucky for us, Buck Hite took on a new man . . . a young gunman called Danny Duggin. ever heard of him?"

"No," said Frisco. "Can't say that I have."

"Me neither," said Avery McRoy. "And believe me, I know every foulmouthed, low-down, back-shooting, murdering, crazy sumbitch in this territory."

"So do I," said Cherokee Earl. "That's what worries me about him."

"You seemed to trust him all right back in town, Earl, from all outer appearance," said McRoy.

"Get this straight, McRoy," said Earl, turning in his saddle to face him. "From all outer appearance you would think I trust my own mother . . . but you'd be awfully wrong thinking it. I'm going to stay one step ahead of Mr. Danny Duggin. You can count on that."

"Stay one step ahead of him how?" McRoy asked.

Cherokee Earl gave them both a smug, crafty smile. "For starters, did either of you know there's a shortcut runs from behind our hideout all the way back to Cimarron?"

The two looked at each other. "No," said McRoy. "We had no idea."

"Well, there is," said Earl, "and we're fixin' to check it out. Don't' get too comfortable tonight, boys. Things are going to be happening fast and furious."

McRoy and Frisco grinned at each other. "We can hardly wait," said Frisco.

McRoy said, "You mean there's something you know about when the money's arriving that you ain't told nobody yet?"

"You saw the shape Buck Hite and his boys are in," said Cherokee Earl. "Would you trust telling them fools anything?"

When neither man answered, Earl said, "Boys, I know when the money is coming. . . . I've got inside information on it. We're going to use Buck Hite and his boys in case things don't go the way we want them to. But I wasn't about to tell them anything until it's time to make our play. We'll round them up on our way to town."

"See?" McRoy said to Frisco. "I knew the boss had this all taken care of."

They rode farther along on the main trail until they came to a fork, where they turned toward the secluded hideout.

Had Earl, McRoy, and Frisco lingered a few moments longer at the fork in the trail, they would have heard the hooves of Ellen Waddell's horse and met her as she rode through the night, headed for Cimarron. For a cautious second, Ellen stopped the horse in the trail and stared upward along the dark path toward the shack. She was struck by the sudden urge to ride up there tonight, stick the rifle barrel through

a crack in the wall, and blow Cherokee Earl to kingdom come. But she fought the urge, reminding herself how it would be for her should something go
wrong and land her right back into captivity. "I'll
wait," she whispered to herself. "And I'll be there
when the time is right."

In the gray hours of morning, Eddie Ray Moon, Clifford Reed, and Fat Cyrus Kerr lay snoring in their
blankets. Buck Hite sat slumped beside the fire in a
glaze-eyed opium stupor, a long wooden pipe lying
across his lap. Lying with her head on her saddle,
her hat pulled low across her face, Danielle's eyes
darted back and forth beneath her lowered hat brim.
Satisfied that no one would be awake for at least
another couple of hours, she stood up and walked
quietly to the horses, carrying her saddle with her.
Checking again over her shoulder, she took Sundown's saddle blanket from the bought of a tree,
smoothed it onto the mare's back, then pitched the
saddle upon the mare and cinched it.

When she'd finished preparing the mare for the
trail, she walked the animal away from the campsite
to a place alongside the road where the night before
she'd arranged for Deputy Tuck Carlyle to meet her.
As soon as she stepped out upon the trail, she saw
him riding out from Cimarron. A half mile behind
him, the town's roof line loomed in a silvery mist.

As Tuck rode up, he glanced off the trail toward
the high curl of smoke from the spot where Buck
Hite and his gang lay drunk and unconscious around
the low fire. "Think things will be okay here,
Danny?" Tuck asked.

Danielle stepped up into her saddle, making sure
to turn up her coat collar and lower her hat brim.
"Yes, these boys will keep until we're finished with
Cherokee Earl. The main thing is we've got to get
Ellen Waddell safely away from Earl before all hell

breaks loose. We'll take care of the Buck Hite gang
on our way back to town." She looked off toward
the snoring campsite with a wry smile. "Provided
they're sober enough to stand up by then."

"Are you the one who's supposed to be in town
keeping an eye out for the big silver load?" asked
Tuck.

"Yes," said Danielle. "I'm the man in town today.
That gives me a reason for not being here when they
wake up."

"Good thinking," said Tuck.

They turned their horses and rode off along the
main trail. But before they'd gone three miles, they
sighted a riderless horse grazing along the edge of
the trail, it reins dangling freely in the dirt. "Whoa,
Sundown," said Danielle, reining the chestnut mare
down far enough back not to spook the grazing
horse. Tuck reined down beside her.

"What do you think, Danny?" asked Tuck, slipping his pistol from his holster. "Think it might be
a trick of some kind?"

"I don't know," Danielle said in a soft tone.
"Cover me from back here. I'll go check it out." She
stepped down from the mare and handed Tuck her
reins. Then she walked the few yards separating her
and the riderless horse with her hands out to her
sides in a show of peace. "Easy there," she whispered, getting closer. The animal nickered low but
didn't spook and bolt away. When she got close
enough, she took a hold of the dangling reins and
ran a gloved hand down the horse's muzzle, calming
it. She looked all around and started to lead the horse
back to where Tuck sat keeping her covered.

But Danielle stopped abruptly when she heard a
moan coming from a patch of waist-high wild grass.
Upon looking closer toward the sound, she saw a
woman's red hair glisten through the tall swaying
grass. "Tuck, over here," she said, gauging her tone

of voice, keeping it loud enough for Tuck to hear but not loud enough to carry much farther. Leading the horse, she hurried to where the woman sprawled face down. Recognizing Ellen Waddell, Danielle knelt quickly and turned her over, laying Ellen's head on her lap. "Take it easy, Mrs. Waddell," Danielle said, feeling Ellen try to resist even in her weakened condition. "We're not going to hurt you. You're safe here."

Catching a glimpse of Danielle's face before Danielle lowered her hat brim between them, Ellen squinted her eyes and said, "Who are you? I've . . . seen you before somewhere."

"No, ma'am," said Danielle. "You don't know me, Mrs. Waddell. But I know you. I've been hunting you ever since you left your place near Haley Springs."

"You're not . . . one of them?" Ellen asked, her eyes beginning to well with tears.

"Them? You mean one of Cherokee Earl's gunmen? No, ma'am. I'm Danny Duggin. I started out hunting them for what they did in Haley Springs . . . but then I began hunting them to get you away from them."

Tuck stepped in, carrying a canteen of water. "And I'm Deputy Tuck Carlyle. You're under our protection now. Don't worry about a thing." He twisted the cap of the canteen free and passed it to Danielle, who in turn helped Ellen raise it to her lips. She took a long sip, then closed her eyes for a moment as if trying to accept that this was real, that she was finally free. When she opened her eyes again, tears ran down her cheeks.

"I didn't know anybody was trying to save me," she said. "I thought I was all alone."

"No, ma'am," said Danielle. "I was there, right behind you all along. Now you take it easy for a minute or two, make sure you've got your head clear." Danielle gently touched the large bump on

Ellen's head. Luckily, it was only going to leave a large bruise. The skin was not broken.

"I fell off the horse last night in the dark," Ellen said. "I must've hit my head pretty hard."

"Yes, ma'am, you did," said Danielle. "But you're going to be fine, I can tell."

"Thank you, Mr. Duggin," Ellen said in a weak voice. She tried to reach a hand to the rifle lying nearby. Danielle reached over, picked it up, and laid it across Ellen's lap.

"There you are, ma'am, if holding it makes you feel better. As soon as you feel like getting up on the horse, we're going to take you to Cimarron and get you looked at by a doctor."

"Deputy," aid Ellen, trying hard to focus on Tuck Carlyle, "I think you need to know that Cherokee Earl and his men are intending to rob your town's bank." She paused, then said, "That's why I was headed to town: to warn you about it." She wasn't sure how to present what had happened between her and her husband.

"Much obliged for the information, ma'am," said Tuck. "But thanks to Danny here, I already know about it. I'm ready for them any time they feel like taking me on."

"The fact is," Danielle said to Ellen, "we were on our way to try to find you this morning and see if we could sneak you away from Earl and his men. We weren't about to hit the gang nose to nose until we knew you were safely out of our line of fire." Danielle looked at Tuck and nodded, then looked back at Ellen. "Now that we know you're all right, ma'am, there's nothing to keep us from hitting them as hard and as fast as we can."

"Now you're talking, Danny," said Tuck. Together they reached down and helped Ellen to her feet, holding her between them.

"I don't want to hold you up from getting to

them," Ellen said. "Help me up onto the horse. I'll go with you."

"No, ma'am," said Danielle. "That's out of the question. Tuck and I both have more experience at this sort of thing. Let us handle it."

"Why, Mr. Duggin?" Ellen asked. "Because I'm a woman?"

"No, ma'am, that's not it at all," said Danielle, thinking how ironic it was that Ellen Waddell should think such a thing. *If you only knew*, Danielle thought. But all she could say was, "Ma'am, it's not because you're a woman that we can't take you with us. Tuck and I just know about how one another works is all."

"Mr. Duggin, I want you to realize what this animal has done to me," said Ellen. "To be honest with you, now that I know how to fire this rifle . . . I want to kill him. I know that doesn't sound very ladylike, but it's—"

"Ma'am," Danielle said, interrupting her, "you've taken a hard lick on the head. We can't afford to take you out there and find out you're hurt worse than we thought. I hope you understand that."

Ellen relented and said with a trace of regret, "All right, Mr. Duggin, you win. I'll go to town and see the doctor."

Chapter 21

Cimarron, New Mexico Territory

Danielle and Tuck escorted Ellen Waddell immediately to the doctor's office and waited in an adjoining room while the young doctor examined her. While they waited, Tuck walked to the front window, pulled back a curtain, and looked out along the main street. "There was a lot of townsfolk watching us ride in. They'll be having questions about who she is and what happened to her. Do you suppose I ought to let a few of them know what we're expecting here?"

Danielle walked over and looked out with him. "Now that the woman is safe and we know where to look for Earl and his men, go ahead and tell them before we leave town. It was important to keep this a secret before. But now it's better that these people be prepared in case Earl manages to get around us and hit the town while we're not here."

Tuck nodded in agreement, then said, "Before leaving town, we might just as well round up Buck Hite and his boys. Once we throw them in the slammer, we'll have that much less to deal with."

Staring out along the street to the north, Danielle saw the large green and red express wagon come lumbering into town, flanked on either side by a horseman riding guard, each carrying a rifle across his lap. "Uh-oh," she said. "I think the silver exchange money is arriving right now!"

Now Tuck Carlyle saw the wagon. "That's it, all right. I wish Sheriff Wright was back. We're going to get spread awfully thin here if we ain't careful."

"This changes our plans," said Danielle. "We can't run the risk of going after Cherokee Earl and leaving the money or this town unguarded." They watched the wagon stop out front of the bank. The two guards and the wagon driver stepped down and began opening a steel security box that stood bolted to the floor of the wagon.

"Right," said Tuck. "The first thing I better do now is let the townsmen know we've got trouble coming."

"You do that," said Danielle. "I'll go tell the wagon guards and driver the same thing." As Danielle and Tuck turned from the window and headed for the door, she said, "There's three more guns on our side." They stepped out onto the boardwalk outside of the doctor's office, and Tuck closed the door behind them.

In the other room of the doctor's office, Ellen Waddell heard the front door close. She sat halfway up, seeming startled, and said, "Doctor, was that Mr. Duggin and the deputy leaving? Where are they going?" Her eyes went to the rifle she'd clung to throughout her ordeal. "Hand me that, please," she said, struggling to raise herself the rest of the way up from the cot. "I've got to get up from here and get busy."

Out front, Tuck said to Danielle, "I'll hurry, Danny. As soon as I tell them there's outlaws coming, I'll—"

"Save yourself the trouble, Tuck," Danielle said, nodding toward Avery McRoy, who stood in his long riding duster and leaned against the front of a building. "The outlaws are here already."

"How in the world . . . ?" Tuck's voice trailed as the two of them sidestepped along the boardwalk, then down into the shelter of a narrow alley.

"Cherokee Earl and his men must have doubled back along a side trail in the night," said Danielle, scanning the street now for any other familiar outlaw faces. There's Eddie Ray Moon," she added, gesturing toward a stack of nail kegs out front of the town mercantile store across the street from where Avery McRoy stood with his head bowed, trying to go unnoticed. "Earl and his men must've gotten them up right after we left this morning."

"He's gotten ahead of us on knowing the money was arriving today," said Tuck. "But how?"

"I don't know," said Danielle. "But any minute now this street is going to turn into a battlefield." As she spoke, they both saw Fat Cyrus and Clifford Reed stepping down from their horses at the edge of an alley that ran between the mercantile store and the barbershop. "Why didn't they hit the wagon while it was on its way here?" Danielle asked.

"Because they're greedy," said Tuck. "This way they hit the bank and get the money plus the silver."

Danielle nodded. "Then it will be their greed that causes their downfall."

"Let's hope so," Tuck said. He looked back and forth quickly, taking in the street. Then he said, "You stay here. I'll circle around behind the buildings, get to the guards and let them know what's about to happen."

"Go ahead," said Danielle. "I'll keep watch from here. As soon as I can get to my saddle without tipping our hand, I'll get my rifle and keep this end of town covered."

"Be careful here, Danny," Tuck said. Danielle only nodded as he turned and hurried away along the alley.

"You too, Tuck," Danielle whispered under her

breath, scanning the street like a hawk. "I don't want to lose you again."

Running in a crouch, keeping close to the side of the building, Tuck hurried to the long alley running behind the town. As soon as he knew there was little chance of being stopped from the street, he came out of the crouch and ran faster, his Colt in his hand. At the rear door of the bank, he pounded hard until he heard the voice of the bank manager say, "Who goes there?"

"Mr. Scally! It's me, Deputy Tuck Carlyle! Open the door, quick!"

"Now see here, Deputy," said the manager's gruff voice. "I never open this door unless it is an extreme emergency!"

"This is an extreme emergency!" Tuck said, trying to keep from shouting. "There's a robbery about to take place!"

"A robbery?" The manager's voice sounded suddenly hushed and anxious. "One second, sir!" He shakily turned a key in the lock, then threw back a heavy steel door latch and swung the door open a few inches. "Now what are you talking about?" He stood blocking the door with his square, portly chest.

"I'm coming in, Mr. Scally." Tuck shoved the man back out of his way and stepped inside. On the other side of the room, the two guards stood holding their rifles at port arms. Upon seeing Tuck shove his way inside, they both leveled their rifles at him. "Easy, fellows, I'm on your side," Tuck said, raising his hands chest high and at the same time nodding at the badge on his chest.

"What's going on, Deputy?" the bank manager asked.

"There's a gang in town, Mr. Scally," said Tuck. "Don't ask me how, but they knew the money was arriving today." He looked at the two guards. "They'll be coming any minute. I've got a man covering the other end of the street. He'll move this way once the shooting starts."

"The shooting? Oh, my!" said the bank manager as if the possibility of getting shot had just crossed his mind. "What on earth shall I do?"

"Get a gun," Tuck said flatly.

"I have no stomach for this sort of thing, Deputy," said the manager. He placed a hand to his sweat-beaded forehead in anguish and terror.

"Then take cover and stay out of our way," Tuck said. "These guards and me will have our hands full."

"That's right, mister," said one of the guards, a tall raw-boned man with a sandy-red mustache. "We won't have time to wet-nurse you." As he spoke, he stepped over beside Tuck and looked out through the empty bank lobby to where the wagon driver stood staring out the front window. "Fred? How do things look out there?" the guard asked.

"So far, so good," said the wagon driver, a grizzled old teamster with a tobacco-stained beard.

"All right then," said the guard. He gave Tuck a smile of confidence and nodded. "Everything is under control." But as he turned to step back over beside the other guard, his free hand snatched Tuck's Colt from his holster. Before Tuck could react, the guard swung a hard blow with the pistol barrel and cracked Tuck across the side of his head, sending him to the floor.

"Damn, Roy!" the other guard shouted. "What the hell are you doing?" As he asked, he swung his rifle barrel and pointed it at him. His thumb went across the hammer, ready to cock it.

"Sorry, Smitty," said guard Roy Sadler to the man who had been his partner for the past year. "You just got put out of work." The rifle bucked in his hand. Smitty slammed backward against the door of the big vault, then slid down to the floor.

"My God! Help!" the bank manager shrieked, throwing his hands up and cowering back against the vault door. His plea was directed at the wagon driver in the other room. "We're being robbed!"

"Is that the truth?" the old wagon driver called out, a slight chuckle to his voice.

"Yep. It's the truth, so help me," Sadler replied, smoke curling up from his rifle barrel.

The wagon driver called out. "What the hell happened back there? You wasn't supposed to do any shooting until everybody got in here."

"I know it," said Sadler, "but Smitty here had more guts than I thought. He was all set to cock and fire on me. I had to kill the idiot."

"Damn it, that rushes everything up too much," said the wagon driver. "You could have slugged him. Why did you have to pull that damn trigger?"

"It couldn't be helped," said Sadler. "I don't like slugging a person. It's bad on a gun barrel. Now wave Earl and the others in here, Fred. . . . Let's get this damn thing done and clear out of town." He turned to the terrified bank manager. "Old buddy, you better get that safe open like your life depends on it. Because it *does*." He jammed the tip of his rifle into Scally's big belly.

"Oh dear, oh dear!" said the frightened bank manager, his trouser legs shaking along with his trembling knees. "My mind has gone blank on me. I'm too scared to remember the combination!"

"Then you better take a few deep breaths, count to ten, and start remembering. Otherwise, I can't think of any reason not to kill you right now." He cocked the rifle. "I'll even count to ten with you." He pointed the rifle into Scally's round belly. "One . . . two . . . three . . ."

"Wait! Please! Just give me a moment!" Scally pleaded. "It's coming to me. . . . Yes, I think I remember now." He turned to the vault and began quickly turning the combination dial. His fingers shook violently. Then he stopped twisting the dial, turned the steel door lever, and swung the big door open with both hands.

Sadler grinned, looking inside the vault at stacks of silver bars in the middle of the floor and stacks of cash on shelves reaching almost to the ceiling. "I find that looking down a rifle barrel always jogs the memory." He shoved the manager inside the large vault and into an empty corner. "Now, you sit your scared-to-death ass down and don't open your mouth, *comprende*?"

"Yes, sir," the bank manager said shakily, covering his face with his forearms.

At the far end of the street, when Danielle had heard the rifle shot, she immediately ran to her saddle and snatched her rifle from its boot. Now, as she turned toward the bank, she saw Avery McRoy and Frisco Bonham hurrying through the door. "Tuck!" she said aloud to herself, the rifle shot having conjured up all sorts of dark possibilities. Down the street she saw Buck Hite, Cherokee Earl, Fat Cyrus, and Clifford Reed, all four mounted, wearing long dusters, converging on the bank with their pistols blazing in every direction.

Townsfolk scattered and sought shelter where they could from the barrage of gunfire. At the wagon, Eddie Ray leaped forward and grabbed the reins to the team of horses to keep them from spooking and bolting away. Instead of dismounting, the men rode their horses right inside the bank building, leaving Eddie Ray Moon standing outside as a lookout. Danielle saw Eddie Ray pull a double-barreled shotgun from under his duster. In a flash it came to Danielle that the key to breaking up this raid and saving Tuck Carlyle—if he was still alive—was to take control of the wagon. Without the wagon, the silver ingots weren't going anywhere. Turning, Danielle swung up atop Sundown and heeled the mare straight toward Eddie Ray Moon.

"It's Danny Duggin!" said Eddie Ray, seeing the horse and rider pound toward him. He raised his hands and waved the shotgun back and forth above his head. "Hurry up, Danny! The raid's already commenced!" he shouted. "Get on in there—you're missing everything!"

Before he realized what was happening, Danielle swept past him on the big mare, jerked her boot from the stirrup, and kicked Eddie Ray solidly in the jaw, sending him sprawling. While Eddie Ray rolled on the ground, still grasping the shotgun, Danielle slid the mare down to a halt and leaped from the saddle into the wagon seat. She grabbed the discarded traces and slapped the horses' backs. "Yieee!" she shouted, sending the horses lunging forward into a run down the middle of the street.

Feeling the wagon slide a bit sideways turning the corner around the livery barn, Danielle caught sight of several townsmen encircling the bank with their rifles and shotguns in hand. When she'd hitched the wagon and jumped down with her own rifle, she heard Cherokee Earl's gruff voice shout from the boardwalk out front of the bank, "Where the hell is the wagon?" Then rifles, shotguns, and pistols began to explode all at once.

Danielle made it to the front corner of the livery barn in time to look across the street and see Eddie Ray Moon hurrying to the door of the bank on all fours, his shotgun still in hand. Rifle shots from a rooftop across the street followed him in a jagged row, ripping up splinters from the boardwalk.

"Boys, that damn Danny Duggin stole our wagon!" Eddie Ray shouted loudly.

"What?" said Cherokee Earl, who'd just stepped out the door and been met by whistling bullets slicing past his head. He had been carrying two bags, one full of silver bars and the other full of money. But he dropped the silver bars and backed inside the shelter of the bank, his big Colt blazing in his hand, returning fire.

In the back room of the bank, Tuck Carlyle had regained consciousness enough to realize what was happening. He'd managed to inch his way closer to the rear door when the shooting began out front. Sadler the guard saw Tuck reaching out for the partly opened door. "Where do you think you're going, lawdog!" he growled, raising a boot and slamming the door shut. He pointed his cocked rifle down at Tuck's face.

"Don't shoot him," Cherokee Earl commanded. "He's our free ride out of here."

Sadler stared at Earl, along with the others, while bullets pounded the front of the building. "They've got our wagon, damn it!" Earl shouted above the roar of gunfire. "We'll have to trade him for it if we're going to take everything here with us."

"Forget taking everything, Earl," said Buck Hite. "Let's grab whatever we can carry! They've got us pinned down here like ducks in a shooting gallery. Let's load these horses down and get the hell out of here!"

"Like hell," said Earl. "I planned this job to be big, and by God it's going to be big!" He glared at Buck Hite. "Show some guts here, Buck. We don't have to settle for less. Let's be bold as brass! Any objections?"

"No, sir," Buck Hite said, looking down at the smoking Colt in Earl's hand. "None at all."

"Good!" Earl said sarcastically. He looked back at Sadler and said, "Bring the deputy up here and stick him in the door where the town can see him."

Sadler dragged Tuck through the bank, then pulled him to his feet with Earl's help. Earl held Tuck by his lapels and said close to his face, "Your friend Danny Duggin took our wagon, lawdog. Now we're going to give you a chance to see just how good a friend he is."

"I'm not telling Danny to deal with you, Earl, if that's what you're thinking," Tuck said defiantly. Blood ran down his cheek from the short gash the pistol barrel had left on the side of his head.

Cherokee Earl grinned. "I knew you'd say that. You lawdogs are all alike . . . always looking for a way to be some kind of half-assed hero!" He looked at Eddie Ray Moon, held out his hand, and said, "Eddie Ray, give me your belt and shotgun."

"My gun belt? My shotgun?" Eddie asked, looking worried, afraid he'd be blamed for letting the wagon get away from him. "Why, Earl?"

"No, not your gun belt, idiot!" said Earl, snatching the shotgun from his hands. "Give me your trouser belt. Come on, hurry up!" He snapped his fingers impatiently.

"All right," said Eddie Ray, reluctantly unbuckling his belt and pulling it loose. He looked to Buck Hite for support, seeing none. "But now my britches are going to fall down." He clasped his trousers at the waist to keep them up. Bullets continued to whistle in from across the street and pound the front of the building. At the broken front window, Clifford Reed and Avery McRoy returned fire. Behind them their horses stamped back and forth in fright on the bank's polished floor.

"They've surrounded us now, Earl," shouted Fred from the back room. Three bullets pounded the back door like someone knocking with an angry fist.

"Somebody get these horses in the back room," Earl demanded. He turned Tuck around and drew Eddie Ray's belt snug around his neck. He striped the length of the belt back along the shotgun barrel until he held it gripped in place, his finger across the triggers. The tip of the barrel pressed securely against the back of Tuck's head at collar level. "Now, let's see what this town really thinks of you, Deputy! Get over here in the door!"

"Go to hell!" Tuck said, standing firm.

But it did him no good to resist. "Not without you, I won't!" said Cherokee Earl. He yanked hard on the belt around Tuck's neck and pulled him fully into the open doorway, into plain sight from all directions. "Here's your deputy, folks!" Earl shouted, standing directly behind Tuck. Firing stopped immediately. Cherokee Earl gave his men an I-told-you-so look, then grinned and shouted out to the street, "That's it, gentlemen. Hold that fire! If I hear one more shot out there, I'll make a dead lawdog out of this boy. I swear I will."

There was a tense silence for a second. Then Danielle said in her best man's voice, "All right, Earl, what is it you want?"

"Why, Danny Duggin!" said Cherokee Earl in feigned surprise. "Is that you out there?"

"You know it's me, Earl," Danielle said flatly. "Now what's your deal?"

Cherokee Earl wasn't ready to make a deal just yet. "What are you doing, siding with the townsfolk? I thought you were in with us on this raid."

"I changed my mind," said Danielle, her firm tone of voice unchanged. "Now what's your deal?"

"Imagine my sore disappointment," said Earl, still putting off any serious discussion about Tuck Carlyle, "looking out there and seeing you on the side of law and order. It nearly shook my faith to the foundation." He cackled aloud behind Tuck Carlyle.

Danielle shot a glance along the boardwalk where townsmen looked at her with uncertainty. "Don't worry," she said. Lowering her voice to the men huddled with their rifles and shotguns behind wooden shipping crates and rain barrels, she added, "He's looking for any opening he can find."

"Who are you, mister?" asked Angus O'Dell, the owner of the town's mercantile store.

"My name's Duggin, just like he said. "I'm a friend of Tuck Carlyle." Danielle nodded toward Cherokee Earl standing hidden behind Tuck Carlyle. "If I was riding with these outlaws, would I have taken off with their getaway wagon?"

"He's got a point there, Angus," said John Dash, the town barber. Along the boardwalk heads nodded in agreement.

Angus O'Dell asked Danielle, "What about the wagon then, Mr. Duggin? Are you going to give it back to them?"

Danielle didn't answer right away. Finally she said, "We'll see." Then she turned away from the townsmen and called out to Cherokee Earl, "The town knows whose side I'm on, Earl. Now what's your deal?"

"You know I need that wagon, don't you, Danny? That is why you took it, right?"

"Yep, that's why," said Danielle without mentioning the fact that her greater reason for taking the wagon had been to either trade it for Tuck Carlyle or at least to slow things down long enough to find a way to free him. Now that the time was at hand, she waited, saying no more about it. It was Cherokee Earl's move.

"The deal is this, Duggin," said Cherokee Earl. "I get the wagon and a free ride out of town with my money and silver. You folks get this deputy back with his head still sitting up on his shoulders. You can't ask for better than that, can you?" As Earl spoke, he motioned Buck Hite forward. "Take over for me, Buck: I need somebody I can trust," he whispered.

Buck stepped in, taking the offered shotgun from Cherokee Earl's hand as Earl stepped back and let Buck take his place.

"Good man," Earl whispered, patting Buck Hite on his shoulder before stepping farther back. From her position across the street, Danielle saw some movement behind Tuck Carlyle, but she didn't manage to see the exchange take place.

"No deal," Danielle called out to Earl, hoping her concern for Tuck's well-being didn't show in her voice. "I'll give up the wagon for the deputy, but from there we go back to where we started. You've got to get out of this town the best way you can."

Danielle had been checking her rifle while she spoke. She took out a cartridge, checked it for perfect roundness, checked the casing, then put it up into the chamber. She licked her thumb, rubbed the tip of the front sight, and did the same to the rear sight. Then she took a firm grip on the front corner edge of the building protecting her, making a shooting brace, and laid the rifle into the V of her thumb and index finger. "God help me, Tuck, this better work," she whispered to herself.

"Get out of here the best way we can?" Earl called out from a few feet behind Buck Hite. "Hell, Danny, that's no kind of deal at all!" Earl and Frisco began busily tossing bags of money and silver back across the floor to McRoy and Clifford Reed, who had moved from the front window to the back room. They caught the bags and loosely piled them near the rear door, where the horses stood nervously, ready to bolt and run should the opportunity present itself.

"That's the best deal you're going to get from me today, Earl," Danielle said. "Take it or leave it."

"I'll leave it, Duggin," Earl called out from the back room of the bank while he and the others stuffed the bags of money and silver into their saddlebags and readied the horses.

Holding the shotgun to the back of Tuck's head, Buck Hite looked over his shoulder and saw what

Earl and the men were doing. His face turned pale. "Hey, am I missing something here? You're not leaving me holding the bag, are you?"

"Hell no, Buck," said Cherokee Earl. "Whatever gave you that idea?" As he spoke, Earl tied more bags of money to his saddle horn.

"What gave me that idea is that you're doing it!" Buck stared, wide-eyed.

"Buck, listen to me," said Earl, slowing for a moment to explain things. "Somebody has to hold things down here while the rest of us get away. This time it's you. . . . Next time, who knows, it might be me. But it's always somebody's turn, ain't it?"

"So I'm staying here to face this whole town?" Buck couldn't seem to grasp what was happening to him.

"You heard Duggin," said Earl. "He ain't going to make a deal that suits us. And like you said yourself, it looks like this is all we're going to get."

"So you're just leaving me here alone?" Buck Hite had begun to sweat profusely.

"Why do you keep asking me that, Buck?" said Earl. "You're my right-hand man. If I don't leave you in charge, who'll keep this whole thing from falling apart?"

"By God, I don't know," said Buck, "but it for damn sure ain't going to be—"

"What about the rest of us—Eddie Ray, Fat Cyrus, and me?" asked Clifford Reed, cutting in. "Are we supposed to just stand here too, get shot to pieces while you and your men ride away with the money?"

"Well, no," said Cherokee Earl, sounding put out with the man for asking. "When we throw this back door open, you do whatever you need to do to get away. Now have you got any more stupid questions?"

Clifford Reed looked stunned. He turned to Buck Hite. "Damn it, this ain't right, Buck. I might not know much, but I know that this ain't right!"

While turning his attention to the back room, where Cherokee Earl and his men prepared for their getaway, Buck Hite had not kept Tuck Carlyle directly in front of him in the open doorway. Tuck knew it, and he had inched as far to one side as he could. He looked toward the corner of the building where Danielle knelt, holding the big rifle poised for a precision shot. Unable to nod or give any kind of a signal, Tuck hoped his friend Danny Duggin could read the expression on his face and take action.

"Don't move on me, Tuck," Danielle whispered, her sights already fixed, her finger already beginning to squeeze the trigger. "Whatever you do, please don't move."

Chapter 22

"Get ready to open the door when I tell you to," Cherokee Earl barked at Fat Cyrus and Eddie Ray Moon. The two bewildered outlaws looked helplessly at their leader, Buck Hite, for some sort of guidance. But they turned their attention back to Earl when he swung up into his saddle, cocked his pistol in their direction, and said, "You better do like you're told, then grab yourself a horse and make tracks out of here."

"Damn it to hell, Earl!" Buck Hite shrieked. "I ain't going to forget this, I swear to God I ain't!" As he raved at Cherokee Earl, he let himself take a half step farther out from behind the shield of Tuck Carlyle. "No matter where you go, no matter how long it takes—" His words stopped abruptly as Danielle sent a bullet spinning through his brain.

"Lord God almighty!" Clifford Reed shouted, seeing Buck Hite's wide-brimmed hat sail off his head in a long, spraying mist of blood. The shot resounded from across the street. The impact flung Buck Hite's body forward like a bundle of loose rags. The shotgun flew from his hands; so did the belt around Tuck Carlyle's neck. Tuck didn't hesitate. As soon as Danielle made the shot, he hurled himself forward, through the front doors, off the boardwalk, and into the street, coming up into a full run.

"See," said Cherokee Earl, gesturing down at Buck Hite's body, "he's forgot it already." Earl swung his cocked pistol at Fat Cyrus. "Now open this damn door, or you'll be laying there with him!"

"Hell, I'll open the door," said Sadler, reaching down from atop his horse and grabbing the door handle. "Everybody ready?" He looked around at Fred, riding double behind him, then at Earl, McRoy, and Frisco.

"Hell, yes! Let her rip!" said Cherokee Earl.

Out front, taking Danielle's shot as a signal, and seeing their deputy freed and rushing to safety, the townsmen opened fire once again. Bullets zipped through the bank building like hornets. As the men bolted their horses out into the back alley, where more gunfire awaited them, the bank manager, still cowering in the vault, eased forward across the floor, reached up with both hands, and began easing the vault door closed. Seeing what the man was doing, Fat Cyrus flung himself inside the vault, out of the hail of gunfire. "Please don't shoot me!" shouted the bank manager.

"Shut the hell up! Scoot over!" Fat Cyrus screamed above the deafening roar of gunfire, shoving the manager back into the corner. "I'm worried about getting shot myself!"

Clifford Reed and Eddie Ray Moon made their way out of the bank building and onto the dirt street before the townsmen's bullets began slicing through them. Clifford Reed fell first, managing to crawl a few feet before additional rifle fire tried to pound him into the ground.

"You dirty sumbitches!" Eddie Ray Moon screamed as bullets nipped at him, taking off chunks of flesh and leaving bloody rosettes in their wake. "I dare any one of yas to come face me one-on-one. You damn cowards! Guess you're too damn scared to do that, ain't you?"

The firing stopped short. Eddie Ray Moon looked around, stunned to think that his words could have had such a powerful effect on these people. "Well, now! That's more like it," he said, a slight smile of satisfaction coming to his bloody face. "Let's do this thing face-to-face. Give a man a fighting chance!" He lowered his bloody pistol into his holster and spread his wobbly feet shoulder-width apart, preparing himself for a showdown. "Now, send one of yas on out here," he said.

"Ready . . ." a voice said along the boardwalk.

Eddie Ray Moon's smile melted at the sound of the voice followed by the sound of many rifles and shotguns cocking at once. "Now wait a damn minute!" he screamed.

"Aim . . ." said the voice as if not having heard Eddie Ray's command.

"Well, shit," said Eddie Ray. "I mighta known. There ain't a real gunfighter in the bunch of yas."

"Fire . . . !" said the voice.

Danielle hadn't stuck around to see Eddie Ray Moon and Clifford Reed die in the street. As soon as Tuck Carlyle ran out of the bank building, the belt around his neck trailing in the air behind him, Danielle met him in the street, her rifle in one hand and her Colt in the other. Already figuring out that the rest of the men would be making a break out the rear of the building, Danielle pitched her Colt to Tuck Carlyle, saying, "Come on, Tuck, they're getting away!" Together they ran toward the alley. Yet even as the two hurried to catch Cherokee Earl and his men behind the bank, Earl, leading the others, had to rein his horse down hard as a rifle shot hissed past his cheek.

"What the hell is this!" Earl shouted, the men and horses bunching up behind him in the narrow alley. At the far end of the alley stood Ellen Waddell, looking like some wild-eyed ghost straight out of a nightmare. Bareheaded, her red hair stood out sidelong on a passing wind. Having shed her riding clothes and hat, she wore nothing except the thin cotton nightgown the doctor had provided her. The wind pressed the flimsy cotton against her body, revealing her every curve and feature as if she were nude.

"You weren't leaving without me, were you, Earl?" she called out in a strange maniacal voice. "Me? The woman you had to have? The woman you couldn't seem to live without?" A shot blossomed and exploded from her rifle, slicing through the air close to Cherokee Earl's thigh. "Come take me with you, Earl! I'm free now. My husband is dead. Come take me, Earl."

"You crazy bitch!" Earl fired his pistol twice, but was too far out of range. The shots kicked up dirt four feet in front of Ellen Waddell. Oblivious to the danger, she stalked slowly forward, levering another round into the rifle, her tender bare feet not noticing the sharp, stony ground. Earl slapped a hand to his rifle boot but found it empty. "Damn it! Somebody shoot her!" he shouted over his shoulder, where both horses and riders were waiting impatiently. The horses stomped back and forth, crowding and butting one another.

"I've got her, Boss!" said Avery McRoy, raising a rifle and taking aim, his restless horse keeping him from getting a good bead on her.

Ellen fired again. This shot grazed Cherokee Earl's horse and sent it rearing upward in a frenzy, twisting and turning in the air. Earl lost his reins and fell backward, coming out of his saddle but getting one boot stuck in a stirrup. "Help me! Damn it!" he yelled after hitting the ground. But with his big horse turning on the other riders who were jammed together in the tight alleyway, it was all the men could do to keep from falling themselves.

"That's all of you!" Avery McRoy shouted at Ellen Waddell. He fired, and he didn't miss. His shot hit Ellen squarely in her left shoulder, sending her spinning backward until she crumbled to the ground, the rifle still grasped tightly in her hand.

Coming around the corner of the alley, Danielle and Tuck Carlyle saw what had happened. Danielle's rifle came up to her shoulder and she fired into the tangle of men and horses. Avery McRoy flew from his saddle with a bullet through his heart. The others tried to turn their horses and make a run for it in the other direction, but Tuck and Danielle gave them no opportunity. They fired on Sadler and Fred, sending both men from the horse they were sharing. Fred hit the ground dead, but Sadler came up onto his knees with a rifle and bean screaming as he fired.

Frisco Bonham, seeing Sadler make a dying stand, turned his horse and heeled it hard in the other direction. He turned the corner of the alley toward the street just as Cherokee Earl's boot came loose from his foot and left him sliding to a halt in a cloud of dust. "Hot damn! What a ride," said Earl, reaching up for Frisco as Frisco slowed his horse enough to reach down and grab his stranded leader. "I hope one of you killed that crazy redheaded woman!" he shouted, swinging up behind Frisco.

"McRoy shot her," said Frisco. "I don't know if he killed her or not."

"I hope to hell he killed her," said Earl. "She's been nothing but troublesome ever since I laid eyes on her." He drew a pistol from his waist and checked it quickly as Frisco heeled the horse toward the street. "Get us past these townsmen. Then stop at the first horse you see unattended." He looked around Frisco at the bags of money tied to his saddle horn, then stared back and forth along the street as Frisco turned the horse onto it and spurred the animal hard. Shots fired in their direction. Frisco leaned low on the horse, spurring it harder and harder, sending it out of town.

Cherokee Earl fired back at the townsmen until his

pistol was empty. Then he snatched Frisco Bonham's
pistol from its holster and continued firing. "Give me
that rifle, quick!" he demanded of Frisco.

"It's not loaded," said Frisco, still spurring the
horse for greater speed.

"Stop up there!" said Cherokee Earl, pointing at a
barn fifty yards ahead, where he saw a corral fence.
Shots whistled past them from the direction of the
boardwalk across from the bank. "Maybe we'll find
a horse there!"

"Good thinking!" said Frisco Bonham. He spurred
the horse to the barn, then slid it to a halt. Looking
all around the corral, he said, "Damn, you're out of
luck, Earl. There ain't a horse in sight."

"Hellfire!" Earl cursed and looked back toward the
street through the center of town. "They'll be coming
any minute! Are you sure that rifle ain't loaded?"

"Yes, I'm sure," said Frisco. "I fired it out back in
the bank. I've got bullets in my saddlebags, but I
ain't had time to reload it."

"I see," said Cherokee Earl. He poked the pistol
barrel against Frisco's head. "Get down, I'm taking
the horse!"

"Do what?" said Frisco, not believing what he
heard.

"I said, get the hell down from this saddle, or I'll
blow your stupid head off! I'm taking the horse.
You'll have to find you another one."

"but where? How?" Frisco looked all around, then
said, "What about my money? You're not taking it,
are you?"

"You tell me," said Cherokee Earl. He poked the
pistol barrel harder.

Frisco slid down from the saddle and looked up
at him. "If it hadn't been for me, you'd be laying
back there in the alley, waiting for the town to come
string you up."

"I know," said Earl, "and don't think I ain't grate-

ful for it. It's just time we split up and go our sepa-
rate ways. . . . You need to stand on your own."

"Like hell," said Frisco. "I know when I've been
double-crossed. I'll find me a horse all right, and
when I do, I'll—"

"Then you better get to looking quick," said Earl,
cutting him off. He gestured his pistol barrel back
toward town. "They'll be getting here any minute."
He swung the horse around and spurred it out back
onto the open trail. *"Adios!"* he called out over his
shoulder in a grandiose manner, raising a hand in
the air.

Frisco Bonham just stared in bewilderment as his
horse and money rode farther and farther away.

"Ellen, are you all right?" Danielle asked, once again
holding Ellen Waddell's head in her lap. Ellen looked
up at her, struggling to remain conscious, the impact
of the bullet through her shoulder having nearly
knocked her cold.

"Did . . . I get him?" Ellen asked. Danielle looked
at Tuck, then back down at Ellen.

"Yes, ma'am, you got him. You got him good.
Now I'm going to go find him and finish him off for
you, all right?" The sound of gunfire from the street
told Danielle there were still outlaws there, making
their getaway.

Ellen smiled weakly but with much satisfaction.
"That son of a bitch. . . . He'll never do another
woman . . . that way."

"He sure won't, ma'am," said Danielle, handing
Ellen over to Tuck. "Take her back to the doctor's,
Tuck," she told him. "I'll see what's left to do out
there."

"Wait, I'll go with you, Danny," said Tuck.

"No," said Danielle. "This is your town—stay and
take care of it. I'll be back soon."

"You better, Danny," said Tuck. "You told me we

needed to have a long talk. I'm curious to find out what about."

"And we will have that talk, I promise you," said Danielle, turning to leave as scattered gunfire from the street continued.

"Be careful, Danny," said Tuck, standing with Ellen Waddell in his arms. "We've both been lucky so far. . . . Let's keep it that way."

Danielle nodded in agreement. She ran to where Sundown stood at the hitchrail out front of the doctor's office. In a moment, Danielle was racing the big chestnut mare down the middle of the street in the direction the townsmen stood pointing. Now that someone was on the outlaws' trail, the townsmen all lowered their rifles and began shaking hands and slapping one another on the back for a job well done. A few of them ran to their own horses, mounted up, and heeled out in the same direction Danielle had taken, although knowing it would be difficult to catch up with the big mare.

Tuck Carlyle carried Ellen Waddell to the doctor's office and laid her back on the cot where she'd been lying earlier. The doctor hurriedly rolled up his sleeves and leaned down, examining her shoulder wound. "I'm sorry I've been such . . . a bother, Doctor," she murmured.

"Nonsense, no bother at all," said the doctor, "although you will owe me extra for a new cotton gown, having gotten a hole shot in this one."

Tuck Carlyle smiled and watched the doctor cut the bloody gown with a pair of scissors in order to get to the wound. Outside, the street had grown quieter, but as Tuck began to relax a bit, a shot resounded from the direction of the bank building. Even before Tuck could get through the door to the street, a small boy came running in out of breath, crying, "Deputy! Deputy! Come quick! There are still outlaws robbing the bank!"

Tuck ran quickly ahead of the boy, drawing the pistol Danielle had given him from his belt. "Stay back, young man," he said. "This might be dangerous." The boy lagged back a little, but wasn't about to stay too far away and miss all the action.

"The shot came from the bank, Deputy!" shouted a townsman as Tuck ran past the crowd in the street and on toward the bank building. "Mr. Scally is still inside. We heard him holler like somebody was killing him!"

"All right, stay back behind me," said Tuck, the gun in his hand cocked and ready. Tuck slipped inside the open front doors to the bank with his pistol ready to fire. Gathered behind him, the townsmen stood with their rifles ready. But once inside the building, Tuck froze at the sight of the bank manager being held from behind with a gun barrel to the side of his head. "Easy, fellow," Tuck said to the frightened face looking at him over the bank manager's plump shoulder. "Nobody has to die here."

"The hell they don't," said Fat Cyrus Kerr, his voice trembling in fear. "Either way it goes, I'm done for. I'll either hang or get shot down in the street. I've already reconciled myself to it, unless I can get me a fast horse and a clear run out of town!"

Tuck kept his pistol steadily poised, but he tried to appear at ease. "If that's all it takes, we'll get you a horse. We'll even back away and give you a clear run out of here, provided you do Mr. Scally no harm."

"Then quit talking and get moving!" said Cyrus. "I want out of this place bad!"

"All right, take it easy," said Tuck. Without taking his eyes off Fat Cyrus, he called out to the townsmen gathered outside the doors. "Somebody get this man a horse . . . no tricks, either. We don't want to get Mr. Scally hurt, do we?"

The townsmen grumbled quietly among themselves. Then one of them said, "All right, Deputy, we'll get him a horse. He can ride out of here. But he gets no promise that some of us won't be on his trail by dark."

"Is that fair enough, mister?" Tuck asked. "You can't expect them to let you get away without trying to catch you, can you?"

Cyrus considered it for a second, then said, "I'm taking this man with me!"

Tuck shook his head slowly and called out to be the townsmen. "Never mind getting him that horse. . . . He's not going anywhere after all."

"Wait!" said Cyrus. "I ain't taking him with me. Go on, get me a horse. The bank manager stays here."

"You heard him," Tuck said to the townsmen. "Get him a horse after all." He looked squarely at Fat Cyrus Kerr and said, "Now how are you going to turn him loose?"

Fat Cyrus looked perplexed, having not thought things through that far.

"Mister," said Tuck, "I've only been a deputy a short time, so I don't know how this kind of thing usually goes. But I give you my word nobody here is going to try to stop you. Is that good enough for you?"

"Your word?" said Cyrus in disbelief. "Hell, no, that's not good enough! What good is your word to me? I'm the one who'll have every gun in this town pointed at him! There ain't a sumbitch out there who wouldn't love to put a bullet in me!"

"That might be true," said Tuck. "But if I give you my word nobody is going to try to harm you, that's a fact."

"Words, facts—this is all moving too damn fast to suit me!" Cyrus raged.

Tuck could see the man was getting confused and

anxious. He tried to calm him. "All right then . . . you tell me what you want to do. I'll go along with—"

"Shut the hell up!" Cyrus screamed. He panicked, shoved Scally forward, and began backing quickly to the vault room, where the open back door beckoned him. Screaming, firing the pistol as he went, Cyrus left Tuck no choice but to return fire. As the fourth shot exploded from Cyrus's pistol, Tuck put two shots into the big outlaw's chest, slamming him against the back wall. Once again Earnest Scally found himself huddled on the floor with his arms wrapped around his head. Behind Tuck, the townsmen rushed in through the front doors. "Get that bastard!" one of them yelled.

They hurried past Tuck and into the next room. There they stopped, seeing the dead outlaw on the floor slumped against the wall, a smear of blood down the wall from the exit holes in his back. "Whoo-ee!" said one of the townsmen. "Good shooting, Deputy! Damn good shooting!"

When Tuck didn't answer, the men turned as one and saw him standing slumped against the edge of a desk, leaning on one hand, his other hand pressed against the bloody bullet hole in his lower left side. The pistol had fallen from his hand and lay on the floor at his feet amid widening drops of blood. "Oh, Lord, no, Deputy," said the same townsman. "You've been gut-shot something awful."

"I know," said Tuck in a strained, breathless voice, his face pale and bloodless. "Tell Danny I did the best I could. . . ." Then he fell to the polished floor.

Chapter 23

At the barn outside of Cimarron, dust from the outlaws' horse still hung in the air when Danielle slid the chestnut mare to a halt and slipped quickly down from the saddle. Hearing a commotion from inside the barn, she slapped Sundown on the rump and shooed her out of harm's way. Seeing dust hover above the trail leading off to the lone rider in the distance, it only took a second for Danielle to put together what had taken place between the two outlaws. With her Colt drawn, Danielle hurried quietly to the front of the barn and stood with her back pressed to the weathered boards, listening intently to Frisco Bonham cursing a donkey and the donkey braying as if in reply.

Inside the barn, Frisco grumbled, "I don't like this a damn bit more than you do, you stiff-tailed little peckerwood! Now stand still!" He tried to toss a saddle upon the animal's thin, knobby back, but the donkey would have none of it. The animal brayed loudly, spinning and kicking at Frisco.

"Damn you!" Frisco raged. "If I didn't need a ride, I'd put a bullet in you . . . if I *had* a bullet!" There was a brief pause, then Frisco said despondently, "What the hell am I talking about, *a bullet*? I don't even have a damn *gun*."

Danielle heard him clearly, yet she wasn't taking any chances on him being unarmed. She looked back toward Cimarron at the fresh dust rising up behind the townsmen who had grabbed their horses and followed her. She wasn't going to waste time here and let Cherokee Earl get away. Just as she was about to grab the barn door and swing it open, she saw the door come swinging open from the inside.

"All right, you stubborn, good-for-nothing dog bait!" Frisco shouted, dragging the donkey forward an inch at a time by a six-foot length of lead rope. The donkey brayed and resisted strongly.

Danielle stood back with her Colt drawn, watching. Frisco was so engrossed in his struggle with the stubborn animal that he didn't notice her standing only a few feet away.

"I swear to God!" Frisco said to the donkey. "If I get away from here, I'll roast you over a fire and eat you quicker than a wolf will eat a jackrabbit!"

He tried twice to swing a leg over the donkey's back, but each time the nimble little animal stepped out of the way. His second try landed him face down in the dirt. As he tried to stand up, Danielle planted a boot on the back of his neck and pinned him down. "It's the end of the line for you, Frisco," she said, making sure he heard her cock the Colt only inches from his head.

"Damn it!" said Frisco in a release of breath. "I have never been so put upon in my life! Cherokee Earl abandoned me. I guess you know!"

"Yep, that's what I figured when I got here and saw somebody out there making tracks for the high country," said Danielle. "How is he armed?"

"Oh, he's armed fine, the rotten turd!" said Frisco. "He's got my pistol and my rifle!"

"You're rifle too, huh?" said Danielle, gaining information that might come in handy real soon.

"Yes . . . and I hope you kill the sucker! If you kill him, tell him I said good riddance! Will you do that?"

Danielle didn't answer. Instead, she stared down,

watching him prepare for his next move. Even as he spoke, she saw his right hand reaching down toward his boot well. As he bent his leg to bring his boot up into reach, Danielle saw the top of the knife handle sticking up.

"For two cents I'd let you go ahead and pull that pigsticker, Frisco," she said. "After what you did to my friend Stick, there's nothing I'd like more than to empty this Colt into you."

"Oh," said Frisco. His hand stopped reaching; his leg straightened. He turned his head enough to look up at the face above him, squinting in the afternoon sun's glare. With Danielle's face hidden by the darkness beneath her wide hat brim, Frisco saw nothing. "Do I know you?" he asked, turning his gaze up the open bore of the cocked pistol.

"Not if you thought you could pull that knife on me," Danielle said flatly.

"You said your friend Stick," Frisco said. "Do you mean the old man I shot and killed a while back?"

"Yes, that's who I mean," said Danielle. Thinking about it caused her hand to tighten on the pistol butt.

"You're not . . . ? You're not that blasted woman, are you? The one what gave me and Billy Boy Harper such a hard time?"

"What do you think?" Danielle asked.

Frisco considered it for a moment, then slumped onto the dirt. "Naw . . . hell, no. She was a tough little filly. But no woman could have stuck with it, stayed on our trail all the way up to this Cimarron country. That's too crazy to imagine!"

"Yeah, I suppose you're right, Frisco," said Danielle, not wanting him to know who she really was since she would be sending him back to Tuck with the townsmen. Telling Tuck who she was would be something for her and her alone to do. "A woman tracking you, Cherokee Earl, and that bunch? That would be too crazy to imagine."

Danielle reached down and pulled the knife from Frisco's boot. She cut the lead rope from the donkey and tied Frisco's hands behind his back. Then she helped him to his feet, walked him to the corral fence, and with the remaining length of the rope, tied him to a post. The donkey followed her like a pup and watched with great interest. "This ought to hold you until those fellows get here," she said, nodding in the direction of the approaching horsemen from town.

"They're just going to hang me," said Frisco with certainty, bowing his head at the thought of it. "You'd do me a favor if you'd just put a bullet in my head and go on."

"I don't owe you no favors," said Danielle. She walked to the mare, stepped into the saddle, and began riding away. Before she'd gone thirty feet, she heard the donkey braying loudly again. She looked back and saw Frisco spitting and cursing.

"Get out of here, you sumbitch!" Frisco screamed. "Now you want to be pals! Get the hell away from here!" But the donkey stepped forward and stuck its wet muzzle to his face as Frisco screamed and spat at it.

"Stick," Danielle said under her breath, "that's the best I can do for you right now." She heeled the mare up into a run and rode toward the lone rider in the distance.

A mile ahead, Cherokee Earl looked back as he pushed the tired horse up off of a stretch of flatland into some low hills. The horse faltered, slowed, and finally came to a staggering halt, having started out at a full run carrying two men and the bags of silver and cash. Now, although one man was gone, the poor horse had spent itself. Going from the flatland onto an uphill trail was more than the animal could take.

"This can't be happening to me!" Earl ranted,

jumping down from the saddle and trying to pull the horse up the steep trail by its reins. "You ain't giving out on me now, you ornery bastard!"

But the horse not only couldn't take another step, it dropped down onto its knees and lay there, its breath pounding like a broken bellows. White froth swung from its mouth and streaked its sides. Earl dropped the reins and looked back at the lone rider gaining ground. Beyond that rider came other riders, but it looked as if they would never catch up. "All right," Cherokee Earl said to the front rider as if he could actually be heard. "You've got a good, fast horse. . . . I can see that." He grinned. "Real proud of that horse, are you? I bet you are."

Stooping down, still watching the approaching rider, Earl took some rifle cartridges from the saddlebags and slipped the rifle from its boot. The winded horse started to struggle upward onto all fours, but Earl pressed a hand on its neck. "Naw, you lay still, you lazy hunk of hide. . . . You're fixing to be replaced by a big, fast ground stormer." He loaded the rifle and leaned it against his side. While he waited for the rider to draw closer, he loosened the bags of money and silver bars from the saddle horn and stacked them neatly at his feet.

Looking back again in anticipation, he said, "Bring that horse on up here. I ain't got all day." Then he cackled aloud to himself. "Damn it, Earl boy," he said to himself. "You never cease to amaze me!"

Drawing nearer, Danielle caught a glimpse of Cherokee Earl ducking behind a rock a few yards farther up the trail from the downed horse. Knowing he had a rifle, Danielle stopped the mare a long way out, taking as much advantage of the sun glare as she could get. To the left of the flat trail, a mazelike string of rocky ground reached upward for the hills. She pulled the mare over into cover and studied the hillside carefully, keeping herself out of sight.

Seeing how the rider had stopped far back on the flatlands, Cherokee Earl slumped and shook his head. "Thank you all to hell, Frisco, you big-mouthed sumbitch!" said Earl as if talking to Frisco Bonham in person. "I shoulda known you'd spill your guts the first chance you got . . . tell him I've got a rifle! I hope you're laying back there right now with crows plucking your lousy eyeballs out!"

After a silent pause, Earl stood up halfway behind his rock cover and looked down in the direction where he'd seen the rider lead the horse off the trail. A watery veil covered everything Earl looked at out in the harsh sunlight. "Danny Duggin? Is that you?" He waited, squinting beneath the shelter of his hat brim.

Danielle could hear his voice only with the assistance of its echo off the rocky hills. She didn't answer.

"If you can hear me, Duggin," Earl screamed out, "I've got a proposition for you."

Danielle still didn't answer.

"Damn it, man," Earl bellowed, looking back along the trail, searching for the other riders but not finding them. "Talk to me, here. We can work something out! I've got money—silver! By God, don't tell me you can't use some silver!"

Danielle ignored the outlaw's rolling, jumbled echo and sat with her back against the rock. While Earl went on, shouting his enticements, she raised the long-range sight on the rifle, rubbed it clean with her fingertips, raised it to the five-hundred-yard mark, and tightened it into place. Satisfied, she turned around, laying the rifle barrel up over the top of the rock.

"Duggin, listen to me," Earl called out. "This ain't no small amount of money! You can go anywhere in the world with this kind of money!"

Danielle half closed her eyes for a few seconds,

looking down within the circling shadow of her hat brim on the rock, keeping her eyes relaxed, avoiding any strain from the sun glare. Even when she opened her eyes and adjusted the rifle into the pocket of her shoulder, she didn't look down the sights just yet. *Save it for the shot,* she told herself.

"Duggin, are you listening to me?" Cherokee Earl shrieked. Then he said in a lowered tone to himself, "All right, by God, you want to play this way? I can play this way. You want a shoot-out, boy, you're going to get a shoot-out!" He snatched the rifle up and stared down through the harsh sun glare. "I wanted to do this different . . . get you off guard, kill you unexpecting like and take that horse. But no," he said, making a face, "you won't do it that way. All right, suit yourself. . . . I can do it this way. Makes me no difference!

"Duggin!" Cherokee Earl bellowed, even louder than before, looking out and seeing the riders now. They were tiny black dots in the wavering heat, yet with every passing second Earl knew they were drawing closer. "Duggin! Damn it to hell! Will you answer me?" He raised up above the rock, exposing himself from the waist up. With one gloved hand cupped to his mouth, he screamed even louder. "We've got to get this settled! Before they get here!"

I've got you, Danielle thought to herself, looking down the long-range rifle sight at the third button on Cherokee Earl's dusty shirt. She had to make her move quick, before the sun glare got to her, or before Earl dropped back down out of sight. She took a breath, let it out, then cut it off. The rifle settled dead still in her hands. She began to squeeze the trigger, but at the last second moved the sight up his chest and a bit to the left. Through the recoil of the rifle, she could see the puff of dust as the bullet nailed through his shoulder. There was a spray of blood that seemed to hang in the air after Earl had already flown backward and down out of sight. His hat, too, seemed suspended in the air for a second. Then it fell zigzagging to the ground.

Danielle stood up and dusted her knees, her seat, and leveled her hat down onto her forehead. She looked back toward the oncoming riders, then walked to the mare, took up the reins, mounted, and rode to where Cherokee Earl lay bleeding into the dirt. When she reached the spot where the downed horse lay breathing heavily in the thin trail, she stepped down and coaxed the winded animal up onto all fours. The horse stood wobbling for a moment while Danielle slipped off its saddle and bridle. A bit more rested now, and carrying only its own weight, the horse shook itself out and walked away, down to the flatlands.

Danielle left Sundown on the trail and stepped up among the rocks where she'd seen Cherokee Earl fall. She knew she'd hit him good and hard, yet she used caution until she stood up on a rock, saw the smear of blood, and looked down to where he lay on the rocky ground. His rifle lay a few feet away, but looking up at her, he made no move for it. That told her something. She waited for a second then leaped down easily and stood over him, her rifle in hand. "That was . . . nothing but a lucky shot, Duggin," Earl rasped. "You'd never do it again. No man shoots that good."

"You might be right, Earl," said Danielle. "But then, I'm not a man."

"Hunh?" Earl stared in stunned silence as Danielle reached up, pulled off her hat, and shook out her long, flowing hair. "You're not a man? You're not Danny Duggin?" he asked, appearing completely dumbfounded.

"That's right, Earl. I'm not a man. I'm not Danny Duggin," Danielle said.

"Then who or what the hell are you?" Earl asked, his weakened voice growing stronger all of a sudden.

Danielle saw his right hand crawl beneath his back, but she glanced away as if not seeing his move. "I'm just a woman, Earl, a woman no different than Ellen Waddell or any other woman you've mistreated your whole worthless life. This is for Ellen," she said. She cocked the big Colt with her thumb.

"Hold on now! I never mistreated that woman— that's just a damn lie! All I've ever done to any woman is what she wanted done to her. I'm a man. . . . Don't blame me for doing what any man does. I never forced myself on Ellen Waddell. . . . Well, not that much anyway," he said. "There was no harm done! I never hit her! She's got nothing to complain about."

"You stupid bastard. You really believe that, don't you?"

"Damn right I do!" said Earl. "Anyway, look at me now. What chance have I got to defend myself? You women are all alike: you only listen to what you want to hear! What chance has a man got? I reckon I'm at your mercy. . . ." His words trailed off hopelessly. But Danielle saw that his hand under his back had found something there. She saw his arm tighten as he grasped the hidden pistol butt.

But before drawing the pistol from behind his back, Earl saw the look in Danielle's eyes and stopped short. "Huh-uh," he said. "I'm giving myself up. I see what you're waiting for—I see what you want."

"Do it, Earl," Danielle whispered, stepping in close and standing astraddle of him, her feet spread apart. She looked down at him, her hand holding the big Colt. "Pull it out, Earl," she whispered, her voice sounding almost seductive. "Pull it out and show me what you can do." Without her hat on, the wind swept her long hair across her face like a veil.

Staring up at her, Earl imagined her smiling at him

behind that veil. Smiling? No: laughing! Laughing at him.

"Why, you man-teasing, no-account little bitch!" he shouted. His gun hand came out quickly from under his back. But not quickly enough. He saw her eyes, cold, haunting, and without mercy, like the reflection of his own eyes in the face of every woman he'd ever seen this close and under these circumstances. "No!" he said. "No, please! *Please!*"

Danielle didn't seem to hear him.

"My God!" said Angus O'Dell. "What's going on up there?" As one, the townsmen reined their horses to a halt and stared at the hills lying ahead of them in the afternoon heat. They listened as the big Colt fired steadily, one shot after another until, after the sixth shot, it fell silent.

"Whoo-ee!" said another of the townsmen. "I'd hate to have been on the wrong end of that gun battle!"

"I hope Mr. Duggin is all right," said O'Dell, heeling his horse forward again now that the shooting had stopped. He looked back at one of the townsmen leading the donkey. Over the donkey's back lay Frisco's body, flopping up and down with each bouncing step, his blue-veined hands still tied behind his back, a black, gaping bullet hole glistening on his forehead. "Hundley," said O'Dell, "You can't hurry that little donkey. We're going to ride on ahead in case Duggin needs our help. You catch up as you can."

"Yeah, why not?" said Hundley, the town auditor. "Go on ahead. I'm in no hurry to get shot at anyway." He watched the others gallop ahead while behind him the little donkey took its time carrying Frisco Bonham's body. After a while, Hundley grew impatient and jerked hard on the lead rope. "Come on, you little varmint! I'll see to it you get up some speed!" But the donkey went wild, kicking and braying until it jerked the lead rope loose from its bridle and took off out across the open wilderness, the body of Frisco Bonham appearing to stare back at the bewildered auditor. "Well, I'll be," said Hundley to himself. "Now what do I do?" He stared after the donkey for a moment, then shrugged, heeled his horse forward, and rode hard to catch up with the other townsmen.

By the time O'Dell led the townsmen to the spot along the upper trail where the chestnut mare stood pulling at a mouthful of tall wild grass, Danielle had tucked her hair back up under her hat and stood replacing the six spent cartridges in her Colt.

"We heard a bunch of shooting up here, Duggin," said O'Dell. "Are you all right?"

Danielle only nodded. "I thought I heard a shot back there a while ago," she said. "Did you find that outlaw tied to a fence pole where I left him for you?"

The townsmen looked at one another, avoiding Danielle's eyes. Finally, Angus O'Dell said, "Aye, we found him. But the belligerent arse that he was, he tried to put up a fight. One of us had to shoot him."

"*One* of you had to shot him?" asked Danielle. "You know who?"

"As long as we can't remember who," said O'Dell, "we won't have to worry about getting anyone in trouble, now, will we?"

"I don't know," said Danielle. "In this case, I don't expect the law will press too hard."

"Just dandy then." O'Dell grinned. "And what about the one you chased here? I presume he is dead?"

"Deader than he ever hoped to be," said Danielle.

"What happened with him—more of that same outlaw belligerence, I take it?" asked O'Dell.

"Yeah, you might say so," said Danielle. "He went

for a gun. I wasn't in the mood for it." She nodded upward toward the rocks where she'd left him. "I was just getting ready to go drop a loop on his ankle and drag him down here."

"Nonsense, Mr. Duggin," said O'Dell. "You take yourself a breather. We'll take over from here."

"Much obliged then," said Danielle. "I've got somebody I need to have a long talk with back in town." She smiled, touching her fingertips to her hat brim, then walked to the chestnut mare, stepped up into the saddle, and rode back toward Cimarron. On the way, she passed Hundley on the trail. When he excitedly told her what had happened to Frisco's body, Danielle shook her head and looked all around the vast, empty land.

"I don't know what I should do," said Hundley. "I don't want to get out there and get lost. This can be dangerous country, especially at night." The two looked around, noting how their shadows had grown long on the ground.

"Wait here for the others and don't worry about it," said Danielle. "That donkey has probably kicked itself free of the body by now. If not, it will soon enough."

"Goodness, I hope so," said Hundley. "There are settlers scattered out through there. What a terrible surprise that would be, finding something like that in their front yard."

Danielle thought about it for a moment, then shook her head to clear it of such a thought. "Let's hope for the best," she said. "I'm going back to town." She nudged the mare forward and didn't look back.

Epilogue

Danielle was not prepared for what she met upon her return to Cimarron. The first person she saw was Ellen Waddell, who came running to her as soon as Danielle had guided Sundown to a hitchrail. "Mr. Duggin, something terrible has happened," Ellen said.

"What is it, ma'am?" Danielle asked, swinging down from the saddle and spinning Sundown's reins around the rail. She didn't like the tragic look in Ellen's eyes.

"It's your friend, the deputy. He's at the doctor's. I'm afraid he's been badly shot!"

"Oh, no," said Danielle. Without another word, she rushed to the doctor's office, barely aware of Ellen Waddell beside her, still talking.

"Did you find Cherokee Earl?" Ellen asked, running out of breath in keeping up with Danielle.

"Yes," said Danielle absently. "Earl's dead. He won't be bothering you anymore." Then, without missing a beat, Danielle asked, "Who shot Tuck?"

"It was one of those outlaws. He stayed behind and hid in the bank vault. The deputy killed him, but not before getting shot himself. Are you sure Cherokee Earl is dead?"

"Without a doubt," said Danielle, still hurrying.

"Thank God," said Ellen, and with that, she stopped in the street and just stood there as Danielle continued on to the doctor's office. Once inside the office, she walked right on into the back room, where Tuck lay unconscious.

"Mr. Duggin! Sir!" said the doctor. "You shouldn't be in here right now! I've given your friend the deputy something to make him sleep. He'll need plenty of rest."

"How bad is he, Doctor?" Danielle asked, going straight to Tuck's side and easing down into a chair close to the bed.

"Well, he's lucky," said the doctor. "The bullet went through him, so I haven't had to do any cutting. What bleeding he's done has been good and red, so it looks as if nothing vital has been damaged."

"Thank God!" said Danielle. "Then he's going to be all right?"

"Unless he takes some unforeseeable bad turn, yes, I believe he'll pull through just fine. He'll need rest and healing."

"I'll see to it he gets plenty of both," said Danielle. She reached a hand over and placed it gently on Tuck's forehead. The doctor gave her a peculiar look.

"Mr. Duggin, is there something about you and the deputy you'd like to tell me?" he asked carefully.

"No, Doctor," said Danielle. "It's just that I love him so much . . . and I was afraid I was going to lose him again."

"Oh, I see. . . ." The doctor stood dumbfounded, not knowing quite how to respond.

At the touch of Danielle's hand on his forehead, Tuck Carlyle stirred, opening his eyes slightly. "Is that you, Danny?" he asked, barely above a whisper.

"Yes, Tuck, it's me," said Danielle, moving from the chair over onto the edge of the small bed. The doctor's eyes widened in astonishment. Danielle clasped Tuck's hand.

"Am I—am I going to be all right?" Tuck asked, his voice weak and groggy from medication.

"Yes, Tuck, you're going to be all right," Danielle

said, feeling the tears spill down her cheeks. "You're going to be fine! Just fine! I'm going to take really good care of you from now on."

Even in his semiconscious state, Tuck seemed surprised at his friend's words and manner. "Danny?" he asked. "Are you . . . crying?"

"Yes, Tuck," Danielle said, offering a tight smile through her tears. "I am crying. So what?"

Tuck closed his eyes and shook his head back and forth slowly. "My, my. I never thought I'd see you crying, Danny. This certainly has been a day full of surprises. . . ."

"Surprises?" Danielle sniffled and wiped her eyes. She could see that he had drifted back off to sleep, yet she continued speaking to him all the same. With her free hand, she reached up, pulled off her hat, and sailed it across the room. She shook out her long hair, hearing the doctor gasp then sigh in relief behind her. "Just you wait, Tuck Carlyle," she said. "You haven't seen *surprises* yet."

JUDSON GRAY

RANSOM RIDERS   20418-2

When Penn and McCutcheon are ambushed on their way to rescue a millionaire's kidnapped niece, they start to fear that the kidnapping was an inside job.

CAYWOOD VALLEY FEUD   20656-8

Penn and McCutcheon are back! This third novel of the American frontier takes readers to the Ozarks, where a mysterious gunman has been terrorizing an Ozark family called Caywood—picking them off one by one. The gunman's description matches McCutcheon's good friend Jake Penn. And now, he must find Penn and prove him innocent before more blood is spilled.

JASON MANNING

Mountain Honor   0-451-20480-8

When trouble arises between the U.S. Army and the
Cheyenne Nation, Gordon Hawkes agrees to play peace-
maker-until he realizes that his Indian friends are being
led to the slaughter...

Mountain Renegade   0-451-20583-9

As the aggression in hostile Cheyenne country escalates,
Gordon Hawkes must choose his side once and for all-and
fight for the one thing he has left...his family.

The Long Hunters.   0-451-20723-8

1814: When Andrew Jackson and the U.S. army launch a
brutal campaign against the Creek Indians, Lt. Timothy
Barlow is forced to chose between his country and his
conscience.

To Order Call: 1-800-788-6262